Andy Bray was born in Nuneaton in 1979. He was raised and educated in Leicestershire before going to Essex University to study Psycholinguistics. Andy is now an English teacher in his former college in Hinckley. **'Dark Globe'** is Andy Bray's first book.

DARK GLOBE

A n d y   B r a y

Dark Globe

Vanguard Press

A CIP catalogue record for this title is
available from the British Library

ISBN 1 84386 216 6

Vanguard Press is an imprint of
Pegasus Elliot MacKenzie Publishers Ltd.
www.pegasuspublishers.com

First Published in 2005

Vanguard Press
Sheraton House Castle Park
Cambridge England

Printed & Bound in Great Britain

ACKNOWLEDGEMENT

Special thanks to Dave Prosser
for the cover illustration

Chapter 1

Joey Carlton

Here lies the town of the past. Come for a walk.

Once upon a routine, along unchanging streets, we might have heard the uneasy whine of the old wives gossiping or the seamless clatter of the old men laughing from inside the pub. Where now the stones are slumped, scarred and slanted there was once a face that beamed, glowered, spoke.

Now they lie still; rotting side by side in the unchanging underground. Some of them never got to tell that last sensational slice of local scandal, some never got to repeat that final side-splitting joke. I remember when such people filled the Red Lion pub with an endearing racket that you thought could never end, then I remember the shudder of disbelief that came whenever the pub lights were dimmed and the noise disappeared for the night. It was a temporary still, a brief, expectant silence that merely filled the vacant hours until the pub reopened. Here, though, the vacant hours have an extended license.

In this perpetual lull it is hard to sense the hustle and bustle that all of these bones once made as beloved sons or old grouches. All you can see here are timeless yews, unremitting grass and gravestones: those artless indicators of a single, special life.

Each grey slab is easy to ignore; it could be an ugly marker of handsome times or a convenient shield to fatal torments. Think of the fear with which these cadavers vied as they fell towards their final curtain. Imagine how it might sound if the agonised shrills of each body were ever to be heard all at once, reliving their last tortured breaths together. Stop yourself before you call this a place of peace - gravestones are a fine alternative to that other anguished soundtrack.

Yet this story is not about death. I move along the road past Henry the jolly butcher and Carl the singing plasterer, then I come to the Whiplash Women, hunched together at the end of the street.

It seems unfittingly serene here. These people and I bore passive witness to a mutating planet, side by side for many years until the tabloid papers tracked me down. It was then that they turned.

I had endured a shameful childhood; one plagued with immorality and misadventure. As a result I was rehabilitated and dropped into university with a new past to my new name. The Press, appalled by my offence, had often tried but always failed to hunt me down. Nobody had an idea who I was or what I had done and I had started to think that nobody could care less anymore.

By the most extreme perversity of fate I became a teacher at the local eleven to eighteen school, loosely spraying literary jargon about the classroom, bouncing Shakespeare and Coleridge around like directionless ping-pongs against hollow teenage heads. The education system had become one devouring leviathan to me; masticating young minds, chewing them into a more orderly and unwanting state. It seemed horrendously efficient.

And then there is Agatha. I had no idea how I ever fell into her unloving arms - she was far more dull and harmless than the only other woman I had thought to seduce: The chipper Miss Moriarty from Home Economics was enticingly dry and risible but surely too well-seasoned for a love victim like me.

I would spend most of my days reflecting on how disillusioned I was with my work, love life and rapidly receding personality. I had long abandoned the shame of my regrettable childhood; my terrible crime had left my everyday thoughts and was now, it seemed, safely settled in my brain's darker recesses... and yet the Devil found a way of making me remember. I was hammered to death and kicked from Hell to Heaven.

So this is a tale of reinvention, of how a man traversed the mountainous mud-tracks of anger, confusion, fear and disillusion... then scaled the lofty reaches of rejuvenation. More than anything though, it is about learning from our own misdeeds and how, then, even the vilest of evils can lead to true redemption.

Chapter 2

The Beginning

The first of the telephone calls came on a Thursday afternoon after school. It was also General Election day, although I cared little for that.

It was a strange day. Spring's first, fresh heat was in the air like an airborne plague; inescapable. The seasons were changing and the people had taken to the streets as if their anthill had just been tapped. There was an assuring warm breeze climbing, swooping, singing and drifting through the new blue sky; it nagged at my back like a hirsute beast fussing behind me.

At the time of the call I was considering whether or not to investigate a brothel which I had overheard several sixth formers raving over. I had never been to a prostitute before and truly doubted that I would ever have the nerve. Nonetheless, it was a thought more enticing than the loveless body heat of Agatha's pale, perspiring bedtime form.

The phone rang twice. I picked up before the answer machine cut in and I murmured my welcome, "Hell-o. Joey Carlton speaking."

"Yes hello Mr. Carlton," answered a quick, high, gasping male voice, "can we ask you some questions?"

"Well, I'm afraid I'm a bit short of time." I never had the heart to routinely dismiss salesmen.

"This isn't market research or anything like that," replied the slippery little voice. Then there was a pause.

"How can I help you then?" I asked him, while gargling a mouthful of cold tea.

"I want to ask some questions."

"I gather that." I was beginning to feel irritated.

"Questions about you."

In retrospect, the grave danger should have been clear before I even put the telephone down. I should have dialed immediately for help, but I did not. It occurred to me for a mere second that somebody could be hankering after the distasteful past, but that moment was forgotten and I quickly returned to thoughts of prostitutes, finally deciding, in the absence of a better plan, to investigate.

In order to reach this flat of ill-repute I had to take a short-cut through a small industrial estate. It was past six o'clock and although the spring evening was mild and clear the light had already started to dim. A few plumes of low factory smoke spiralled easily up around the tall, anonymous concrete blocks all around. In reply the sky offered a few thin sympathetic rafts of cloud, spirited in from some measureless beyond. As the blue sky dipped to purple, the industrial chimneys blackened to silhouettes. I thought they looked a little like skeletal fingers pointing ambitiously to the heavens - and they felt so understanding and near. I began to wonder why I had ever wasted my evenings inside, but that thought soon went away.

When I reached the flats I proceeded quickly to the one that I believed - based on loosely assembled knowledge - to be the brothel. I was fairly convinced straight away that this was the real thing although, having never been to a whore house before, I had to rely on a definition relayed to me by more worldly-wise friends. I stood a yard back from the double-glazed glass door and listened in as best I could, constantly reminding myself that this was the stupidest thing that I had ever done. After thirty or forty seconds the door suddenly swung over. "Come inside love," said the woman while I blushed outside.

It seemed somewhat odd that while bedspring croaks of love-humping sounded about the abode, I was offered nothing more than a cup of tea by the four women that I saw. They were guarded, polite and surprisingly conversational, asking for little more than sketchy details on my political inclinations. In response I recalled a few apt socialist views from my university years and claimed (falsely) to have stumbled across their flat on the way back from the polling station. They rewarded my active democracy with a couple of malted milk biscuits.

I felt sure at first that this could not be a whore-house; I had anticipated blonde, shapeless thirty-somethings strutting about readily and full of enticing small-talk. I had imagined sleazy fifty-something men with comb-over hair, all waiting in line.

Instead there was little more than the eager promise of discussion. I could hear occasional jolts of intercourse from somewhere within the flat but had no idea as to how I could come to indulge in that fine act. The only point at which any of the women referred to sex was when I mindlessly asked what one of the ladies did for a 'day job'. "I'm a twenty-four hour whiplash woman," she replied, with a wry smile.

After fifteen or twenty awkward minutes I decided that a sexless night next to Agatha might not be so bad. One of the women - a forty-something named Gwyn - insisted on taking my mobile phone number. I was wary about this; I hate mobile phones as much as I hate giving my number to strangers, but for some reason it seemed wrong to pretend that I did not own one. Besides, I had already told too many lies that night. So Gwyn took my number and I took hers.

Afterwards I took a long and ponderous walk home. I began to wonder what my subject manager would think of what I had just done, then I agonised over how to relay the evening's events to my friends. I concluded that I had probably been to the right place for sex but followed the wrong procedure for attaining it. Perhaps Gwyn had identified my ambivalence, or, perhaps these Whiplash Women were not prostitutes at all; perhaps they were free love's last liberal campaigners. Perhaps while half of the flat were making revolutionary conversation the other half were making sweet love. Not having sex, but making love. Perhaps that was the deal.

By the time I came to the Red Lion pub on my way home I had persuaded myself that an offensive, beery breath would be a better excuse for my late return home than any excursion to the polling booth. I was hoping that one of my friends, perhaps Kemi, Marc or Harry, had grown bored with election television and made some unannounced journey to the pub. I told myself that if none of them were at the bar then I would make a quick unnoticed getaway, but as soon as I walked in the landlord fixed me with a welcome glance.

About four gulps into my first beer and already resigned to

a maddening rant from Agatha; I decided to prove wrong any slurring local that might have thought me to be a social outcast. I ambled up to the payphone to call Kemi, but not before having to squeeze past a melee of ragamuffins huddled aside the pool table. I had never seen them here before. I was given a few forewarning glares and, after passing, I caught the half-chuckled exchange of belittling remarks. For a few seconds I felt dejected and small, but then suddenly became indignant at the thought that these bleach blond, ear ringed clones had taken offence at my unfamiliar face. Were they proud of spending their lives between the pub and the hosiery? Was it necessary for them to confront me so territorially?

I wanted to address them on these issues, but instinctive placidity prevented me.

I felt much more secure once Kemi had arrived. Kemi was a cool-headed, ever-unruffled child of twenty-eight years, burdened by nothing more than a nettlesome knack of seducing more women in a night than certain others could manage in a lifetime. I had met him in my first year of university, but he dropped out during the summer and the next thing I knew he had been locked up for bedding one precocious thirteen-year-old girl. Although mortified by his crime Kemi would happily recount the events in private conversation; "She didn't have a birth certificate on her at the time," he would recall. I think he well understood at the time that the girl was not yet sixteen, but the alcohol had possessed him. Whatever the circumstances and however appalled he was by his actions it all made Kemi a paedophile, technically.

Beyond his name there was little on the surface to give away the eastern roots. His short untidy hair and half-open eyes were a deep dark brown, but his skin was light and the accent unmistakably London (in my opinion, he was too smart to be called a cockney. That implies something of an insular geezer mentality). He was trim, healthy and casually unconcerned; a side burned hero but also an accomplished Vodka drinker... which made him a perfect companion on that troubled night. He was also prone to regular bouts of over-enthusiasm and amateur philosophy, but I suppose nobody is perfect.

I always envied Kemi; he was a product of abject poverty and horrendous abuse. Yet he was street-wise and fortunate enough to stumble across a fine, caring foster family. I, on the other hand, came from a wretchedly aseptic upper working class background. My father was, from what little I recall, far too harmless to ever be interesting. If I ever chose to speak - or even think - of my family, then I would probably send myself to sleep. Or so I believed. On the other hand Kemi could be sure of a captive audience whenever he recounted his fascinating formative years.

When Kemi and I staggered from the Red Lion at about 11.40pm we decided to dodge the election tattle by heading for the park. Kemi had a bottle of whiskey in his overcoat pocket and wanted to sit down for a drink and maybe even a reefer. As we approached the green there were a couple of lads kicking a ball about in the car park, so we joined in for an hour. Kemi was a cool, gifted footballer with some deft, party trick touches up his sleeve. I, on the other hand, was a bit of an embarrassment and had long-since become bored with strenuous physical activity.

At one point I remember one of the locals strolling across the park with a trio of Alsatians, telling us that we should either move on or be moved on. One of the youngsters argued with him but I found the whole matter comical: I deduced that the presence of the Alsatians was designed to terrify us and that the purpose of this well-respected man's stroll through the park nightlife was to apprehend what he guessed to be a motley crew of villains. Without question he would recount this fine act of upstanding citizenship tomorrow, over the garden fence to Mrs. Mickletit next door. It had not occurred to him that our hushed and playful kick-about was far less harmful to others than his dogs' scattered, abandoned faeces. Neither had it crossed his mind that if we were indeed villains at work - pedaling heroin or buying sex (God forbid) - then we would be unlikely to advertise the issue with a roadside game of football.

Nonetheless it was a fine, therapeutic night out for me. My head was spinning from a combination of beer and weed, a snapshot reminder of what it had felt like to be young. When I finally pulled open the door to my house I sighed with relief at the empty blackness which told me that Agatha was in bed. Without a sound I kicked off my trainers and sprawled across the ragged skeletal sofa. I did not even think to watch for the election result. It was not that I had no interest in politics - I most certainly did - it was just that these things were usually inevitable and unchangeable.

There was something on the television, though, and I watched with the sound turned low. It was a dire British film from the late 1990s depicting Ibiza's club culture; a shallow 'laddish' sludge full of indistinctive, thudding beats and equally dull cliché-puppets prancing about to the noise. The male holiday reps and tourists were invariably young, beery fools on a mission to test their fledgling manhood on as many female sex tools as they could. They took the same stimulants, bore the same reddish tan, drank the same watery lager and were often distinguished by no more than the designer label on their sunglasses.

Most of the cast sported obscene Cockney accents and stumbled through the graceless script as if they were a bunch of eight-year-olds imitating substance abuse. Far more offensive though, was the one whisper of a plot that existed; a single black youth was abstaining from the perpetual sex festival because he was "looking for something deeper in a woman". It followed, then, that the film's defining moment was when an anonymous young girl rekindled the youngster's passions by telling him that she quite liked to read. This was enough to prompt a slow-motion sequence of the two 'individuals' splashing about together on the beach to even more indistinctive, thudding beats.

Such 'free' spirits were the fashion-mongers of a generation, although I could not help but believe that these B-movie bit-players had hoped for something better than this. Those young souls were perhaps already more weary than their audience might choose to believe, but I was still somewhat saddened at the thought that anybody could possibly admire them. This was the type of sterile spectacle that profoundly reduced my faith in the human race. At some point in the proceedings I fell asleep, feeling wearily uncomfortable.

Chapter 3

School

The extreme right-wing opposition had seized power - thanks to a pitiful twenty-five per cent election turn out - but this could so easily have been just any other day. The country had changed but the classroom remained the same, a simmering collection of remittent young minds, each either dormant or waiting for its chance to upstage Teacher.

As for Teacher - well, he had lost the urge to impress on them and had long since started to dream in teaching terminology; curriculum goals...attainment targets...'could do better'...level…six...F+...core…subjects...group…effort...specifi cations...life choices... detention...suspension... 'cooling off' periods...conduct logs…specific measurable targets…

Aaron was my funniest and most intriguing pupil. Beneath the fresh-faced smirk and unminted tobacco perfume there was something that I looked forward to each lesson. More than his peers Aaron seemed completely without tension, complaint or vitriol - he was a free soul. What made this all the more interesting was the unshakeable truth that, a few fun years down the line, Aaron would be a dull, desolate soul bereft of spirit and vision - much like the rest of us. I probably cherished his teenage liberty more than he did - for I could guess how temporary it might be, while Aaron himself had never dreamt that he would be slouched behind an office desk, or brushing leaves, or pushing a pram in but a few years.

For some time now I had felt pathetically sentimental about a number of my students. I was unsure whether this had been because I longed to revisit adolescence in all its brief burning simplicity, or because my ageing soul clock - the same one that tells every man when in life they should start work, marry or take up golf - was starting to ring time for fatherhood. At thirty I knew deep down that I should be taking toddlers off to Disneyland or Butlins. I should be telling them stories about Black Annis or The Pied Piper of Hamlin. As for my woman, Agatha, she should surely be putting her career on hold in favour of making babies. That is how it should be. In reality of course I knew when I first dated Agatha that she could never have children. It was a major attraction back then.

Inside the classroom there was a damp, unkind air. The walls were a chilly pale blue while the protruding pipes and far up ceiling were messily daubed a lifeless lime green for the sake of variety. There was the occasional poster, tacked up years ago by some unknown art fanatic teacher or even a precocious pupil from the past. Below, the carpet looked like tightly knitted brown wire wool. Above, the tube light's flicker went unnoticed because of the morning's harsh white light flooding through huge uncurtained windows. The classroom smell was a venomous curry of unclean armpits, tobacco breath and untreated mould. Nobody could question for one second why many students were short on inspiration. In fact one of the only things that this room had ever inspired was violence - which from time to time offered a vaguely entertaining sideshow to the lesson.

All of which made kids like Aaron seem all the more intriguing:

"Mr. Carlton."

"Yes, Aaron?"

"...I'm thinking of becoming a teacher."

"Really?"

"Yeah, I like the idea of twelve weeks holiday a year."

"It's not that easy..."

"Was it your ambition to be a teacher?"

"Erm, no it wasn't actually Aaron."

"What was your ambition?"

"Ambition," I rejoined, "is a wild beast. If you have control over ambitions then they're usually worthless, and if you don't then they're usually unattainable." I felt pleased with this epigram and repeated it to myself in a whisper. Aaron rolled his eyes.

"Whatever, Mr. Carlton. So, how much do you earn?"

"Ah..."

"Because I heard that teachers get the same pay as postmen nowadays, but whereas teachers get an extra hour or two in bed and have the chance to ruin people's lives, nobody really cares if their gas bill doesn't get delivered by the postie. I think, all things being equal, that I'd rather make a difference... "

It was this kind of discourse between Aaron and I that frequently stirred desperate self-analysis. Why couldn't I just give it all up? Is life long enough to spend my active years on the mundane quest for finance and security? When was I going to abandon it all to rediscover my lust for living?

I perpetually delayed my second coming; I would rest assured that twelve or twenty-four months down the line I would quit teaching, buy a motorbike and leave Agatha behind in my tracks. Occasionally I heard her choking on the sandy, gravely dust kicked up by the bike's back wheel. Then... gone forever.

Back in school the world was still unchanged. I was tucked tightly under the bulky wooden desk trying, as much as I could, to avoid lecturing the incurious ragamuffins before me. This same seating position was a traditional favourite with aroused male teachers in the early morning.

As for now, the kids knew what they were supposed to be doing (which was more than enough) and besides, I was as bored as they were. Morning break was fast approaching when the mobile shuddered into action in my right trouser pocket, tirelessly bleeping its mindless rendition of the Italian Job theme music.

"Excuse me," I told the class. I could feel my cheeks flashing red and my eyes blinking awkwardly, because teachers were supposed to detest all things garish or loud. In reality the class could not have cared less; the room was often a jangling fifteen or sixteen piece orchestra of beeping gadgets; watches, phones, pocket games, anything that made a high-pitched, unavoidable noise.

I prodded randomly at the phone until I thought I had turned it off. I felt sure that it must have been Agatha calling with a stern reprimand for my late last night. It could wait until the morning break at ten o 'clock.

"HELLO?" somebody screamed through the phone as I tried to bury it in my suit jackets inside pocket. Finally I addressed the caller. It was indeed Agatha.

"Yes?" I whispered impatiently.

"Joseph," replied the formidable female voice.

"Uh?" I suddenly recalled the whore house of political discussion from the night before, where moans of pleasure were muffled by debate and where I did not find the effortless sex that I had wanted at first. I sensed a pending reproof. "Agatha, are you angry with me about something?"

"I've had two men here this morning, Joseph."

"Okay. And...?"

"Two men snooping around the back garden, going through our rubbish bins. Is there something you should tell me?"

I paused for a few seconds. What on earth did she think I was up to? "I have no idea what you're on about," I replied truthfully.

"Does this have something to do with Kemi?" She was always suspicious of Kemi.

"I don't know!" I hushed, "Listen I'm in class. Don't call me in class to tell me that somebody's taken a look in the dustbin. Call me if they burn the house down or kill the cat, but don't ring me to say somebody's been sifting through our old newspapers and used teabags!"

"If they come back then I'll call the police," Agatha snapped, as if somehow threatening me, "and I suggest you turn your mobile off when you're at work." With that the telephone was dead and the poisonous witch was gone. I poked the button that I supposed would turn the thing off and then laughed out loud. It was the first time I had laughed in a classroom for a long while.

Outside the classroom on morning break duty I had to patrol all of the usual cigarette smoking haunts. Should teachers have genuinely wanted to stop the kids from smoking then they would probably choose to take their tuna mayonnaise sandwiches and coffee straight to the side of the tennis courts, the back of the tuck shop, or to the wall of trees that sloped down from the sports fields - all the usual smoking haunts. Of course it was far easier for us to meander lazily around the football and rugby pitches. At this time of year, in the spring, the mornings were invariably mild with a fresh but prickling wind and, usually, an open white sky. The grass was deep green, overgrown, unsoiled.

On this particular morning I decided to follow Aaron and company out of the classroom. He walked towards the tennis courts with his friends, Sharon, Damon and his 'other half' Gemma. Completely oblivious to my presence they sparked alive their ready cigarettes and huddled next to the eight foot wire fence of the tennis courts. I stood aside them, longing secretly to be a part of their inner circle, but knowing that those days were inextricably bound to another - long gone - time.

In the meantime I stared down at the ground below; at the copper coins, chocolate wrappers and roached cigarette ends stamped into the earth. When I looked up I could see that the empty tennis courts were surrounded by groups of smokers, like ball boys and girls at a football match that was yet to start, each group ignoring the next and keeping a safe distance. I gazed up into the sky and saw that this circuit had created the most monumental of smoke rings - a group effort smoke ring. It was almost worthy of applause.

I began to imagine that there was a bomb in the school; that the place could erupt into a human fireball at any moment; that a hundred brick walls worth of lime green and icy blue paint could melt away around the flaking, peeling, dissolving faces of every teacher and pupil. I could imagine the half-scrambled amusement on faces of blazer-clad students as they watched from afar. Most of them would be glad to have the afternoon off.

After these thoughts I had to compose myself in one of the graffiti-laced toilet cubicles that the teachers shared with the sixth-formers, then I lazily set about my third class of the day. I gave the pupils a Ted Hughes poem to analyse and spent the lesson scratching away at the flaking varnish on my much-scarred wooden desk, attempting to ignore the tumult of classroom murmurs. In turn, they diligently discovered origami with their poem worksheets.

It was a miserable day after a fine night out. After school I returned home and went up to my study; my own private sanctuary first shaped - and later disordered - to my very own taste. Agatha was out, thank Heaven. On the inside of my wardrobe the calendar was stuck to May 2005 where the year's finest lesbian figurine never required overturning. The picture held little interest any more, but it had been undisturbed for so long that I lacked the will to remove it.

At times like this I truly understood how vapid my existence had become. It was time for a holiday.

Chapter 4

Respite

At the time I had no concept of how much danger I was in. It never struck me that those well-concealed and truly forgotten past evils could return quite so venomously. Yet even as I planned my summer retreat the worms were already writhing.

Ten days had passed from the ridiculous 'dustbin episode' when Agatha, after a torrent of unrelated incidents, suddenly left for another "more interesting" man. It seemed fantastically convenient; I was almost liberated.

I had grown irreconcilably bored with England; from the clogged, overhanging bleakness of its skies, to its lugubrious citizens with their unhappy, well-defined routines, right down to the crumbling concrete and clay beneath its streets. I devised an upbeat mantra, *I can do better than this... I deserve better than this...*

I needed a holiday and, with the summer break fast approaching, there was no better time. Most of all I understood that I had to revitalise myself, I had to rediscover my function in life. I knew that it was possible for the sickest, wildest criminal to be reinvented as an obedient citizen, so I was hopeful that a long escape could remedy my niggling disillusionment.

I decided that I would take a ferry to France and travel through Europe by train; down into Germany, Austria and Italy. I wanted to bathe in the cultures of Munich, Innsbruck, Salzburg, Sienna and Florence. I had no misgivings about travelling alone but mentioned the idea to Kemi and he instantly hijacked the whole excursion. It was immediately decided that Harry, he and I would descend through Europe with a tent and, making as few stops as physically possible, hit the beaches and tavernas of Corfu or Kefalonia. I felt sudden deflation, but to Kemi this was the perfect compromise between his vacation-ideals and mine.

We left for Dover in mid-July. The night before our departure we all stayed at Kemi's place. Harry, a hopelessly sardonic 25-year-old Physics graduate with a freckled face and vomit-blond hair, spent most of the night playing Chess with himself downstairs. Harry had a vexingly beautiful long-term girlfriend but tended to enjoy his own company. I had never grasped why it was people had so much more time for him and his dismal outlook than they had for me. It was easy to foresee a clash between his moods and my own.

Kemi and Harry were supposed to be sharing the double bed for the night. I was left out of this pre- departure bonding session and got assigned the attic's dusty, mite-packed sofa-bed instead.

Kemi's house was old and the loft ceiling was low, which suggested that its architects were from a shorter age than our own. It was decorated with a maze of confused cobwebs; a network of spider design laid out over twenty or thirty years. Enmeshed somewhere between was a beam and a lightbulb made visible by a narrow window's full-moonlight. I had never liked spiders, so I darted into the downstairs bathroom for a couple of large, unclean bathroom towels into which I wrapped myself.

That was the night of my first nightmare: I dreamt that I was being led into an immaculately clean, plain beige room with no windows. I was made to sit down on a chair and then I was left alone. After a few moments I became aware of the voices; deep, fractured cackles - some loud, some whispered - and they were commanding me to do something, although I could not remember what exactly. Then, abruptly, I became aware of a smartly dressed man opposite me, seated behind a desk that had appeared from nowhere. Now the walls were an icy blue like those in my classroom at school. His face was oddly familiar and he was politely, formally asking questions but I could not hear them for the looming voices... When I awoke everything seemed terribly real and tangibly demonic. I had to leave the attic, fearful of a dark and troubled spiritual presence, but it made no difference.

The oddest aspect of the nightmare was that I only ever

usually remembered the most bizarre and abstract of my dreams; for instance one about a golden retriever falling from scaffold and turning into a red, pulsing tomato when it hit the bottom. Then there was another one about Kemi skiing down the alleyway opposite my bedroom window and exploding when he reached the bottom. These dreams were all of randomly assembled, meaningless and impossible events. Oddly, that night's mare seemed both likely and forewarning.

The next morning we took the expensive bus to Dover, that strangest of English towns where the whole country is just cut off in mid-air, left to plummet down the cliff-face and into the foul sea below. I always enjoyed ferry crossings and was disappointed that the crossing to Calais was so brief. Ferries are like towns stacked compactly on the water; with everything from discos, bars and restaurants to bed chambers, pools and convenience stores. As a child I had imagined how it might feel to be a wanted man confined to the ferry at sea; being pursued by a maniac through myriad rooms, stairways and compartments but always finding some dark, enshrouded recess just in time.

We spent the next ten days proceeding along railways. Our progress was slow, almost imperceptible at times. Despite having taken a tent with us we stayed mainly at hostels. We passed through France, Belgium, Germany, Austria and then on into Italy where we stayed for two nights in a hostel on the hills overlooking Florence. Every morning I would watch the bland, grey smog rise from the ground, each time unveiling a cluster of sunny foreign suburbia.

It was in Florence that I finally, inevitably, turned on Harry. Kemi had made it clear that he wanted to leave the city in favour of a few days on the nearby beach at Rimini. I, on the other hand, was firmly contented in Florence. Harry had the casting vote and predictably sided with Kemi.

The unspoken hostility that I felt for our misanthropic colleague suddenly erupted.

As soon as that episode had passed I felt much more comfortable with Harry even though he continued to say very little to me; I had unleashed a little pent up vitriol and felt much-improved for it. I knew that everything would be forgotten within a couple of days and, even though I was forced to leave Florence, the air felt far clearer.

I made a point of being bored for our two days in Rimini; trying as subtly as I could to ruin the stop-off for Kemi and Harry. I wasted much of my time on the hostel veranda, by day I watched the winged ants conspiring and the dragonflies buzzing blissfully about their pleasantly pointless lives. By night I spied on the clumsy, clueless moths. I had never spent so much money on fly-spray in my life; I would corner a wasp, coat it in foam and watch as it squirmed its last, always wondering whether the little creatures had any feelings - perhaps of terminal panic or despair. I almost wished that they did, because I could see little purpose in God creating such pernicious pests unless they did have feelings. I attained a truly nefarious satisfaction from these moments.

From Rimini we journeyed down to Brindisi where we caught a ferry to Corfu. We toured the Ionian islands; from Levkās to Ithaca, from there to Kefalonia and then on to Zante. I felt revitalised. This was far, far away from the cold pre-school dawn walks that I would often take after restless nights; past crawling milk floats or early workers on their way... Each one a solitary soul, trudging routinely with plaster-coated shirt and lunch-box in hand, glowing beneath the still-orange streetlights and slowly greying sunrise sky. For the first time in my life - here - I was fantastically (though not decisively) happy. I was content with simply lounging aside the Ionian beach bars or occasionally joining Kemi for a splash in the twinkling clear Mediterranean sea. I watched the beach-life unfold each day; the coffee-skinned Athenian women lay topless, the well-tequilla'd guys made eyes at the girls as they slept in the sun. I could roll off my laid-out towel and into the bar. When I looked upwards it was into a cloudless sky filled with unflinching blueness; it hung above us like an unrippled sea waiting to be crossed. When I looked downwards the sun glanced back at me all across the sands, its reflection shimmering across plastic water bottles, together beaming like one hundred dazzling fairy lights. All of this occurred to the crickets' constant soundtrack. Every single day felt ripe for miracles.

Unfortunately I am not Jesus Christ (although I do have the same initials) and I was powerless to change the dark direction along which my life was routed.

Kemi and Harry both kept in touch with England through the day-late tabloid papers on sale. I opted for ignorance, preferring the excitement and bliss of uncertainty. Newspapers were not to be trusted; the tabloid press was the all-seeing-eye for the world's misled pawns, a propaganda machine which systematically devised suitable opinions for its audience. I had no interest whatsoever, although Kemi said he was concerned that one newspaper was launching a name-and-shame campaign on sex offenders. Apparently it had already caused a sack load of riots, while England's new government was doing nothing to fragment the law of the uprising mob. I disapproved of all this, obviously, but felt little compulsion to act against it. For now at least.'

Instead, by day I simply lazed, vacating my mind. On the beach we were sun-lashed and sweltering. In the bars we were mere travellers, hiding from the heat in a shady haunt. By night, after going out, Harry, Kemi and I would debate topical questions, or sneak down to the empty shore for a starlit night-swim. There was nothing quite so beautiful as singing quietly with the deep-mouthed Zante sea. The three of us were isled in the unlit waters, clothed only by the ocean, wading slowly through calm watery space. Just tipsy enough to feel safe. Then, in the morning, when I awoke the window was decorated with mountains, palm trees and sea.

That was all I needed.

Sometimes, though, I wondered quite what had happened to Kemi. However close we were it was hard not to think that he should have made a much better person. I thought this as I watched him leer, or slur lascivious-nothings to unsuspecting young women. I thought this when he cut off deep discussions to comment on a passing car or a speed-boat - it almost seemed as if the sparkle had gone from his eyes... something that a man should never lose if he is lucky enough to have it in the first place. Once upon a time Kemi would probably have laughed out loud at the person that he later became. It was almost as if he was a clown from one of his own comedies.

Of course, I still savoured his company more than any other's.

I could never feel nearly so disappointed with Harry - I had so few expectations. As the holiday progressed he and I had come to a comfortable understanding with one another, but there was no closeness. His pointless mirror habits annoyed me. In the morning he would spend an hour on carefully waxed hair designs. Each night he would look in the mirror to check that his tightly packed genitals were bulging keenly from his trousers. I secretly wished a tumour on him to swell that proud package. It would surely impress the passing ladies. For such a disdainful, antisocial beast he spent a stupid amount of time on his appearance.

One of our final arguments took place on the ferry to Corfu: I was talking about slow, mundane schooldays when Harry dared to announce that all children were, in his opinion, no more than snivelling little monsters. Vampires of the classroom. Playground hobgoblins. Abject little bastards. "Utter nonsense," I protested, without entirely understanding why I was arguing with the man, "I have a lot of very good kids." My objection was erratic and involuntary. I had no idea how protective I felt towards my pupils.

In one beachside bar, while Harry was entertaining himself elsewhere, Kemi and I came across an unusual character, a hippy traveler named Robert. He was a perpetually slouching vagabond with long matted brown hair and a young - but shattered and unshaven - face.

"This guy is amazing!" Kemi told me after a short discussion with the man, "this guy is the ultimate non-conformist!" I looked across the bar at Robert whose feet were propped up by a wicker chair. His drunken smile stretched nearly from one ear to the other, with dimples somehow packed in at the sides.

"Hi!" he waved, clearly eager to speak to me. I groaned.

Despite my negativity Robert was, indeed, an amazing character. He had been a student at an art college in Cornwall but had dropped out a couple of years ago.

"Why did you quit?" I asked him.

"I went to Glastonbury," Robert slurred in a loud voice, "and I never came back." He spat out a raucous, rattling, fractured laugh which could almost have been the sound of him choking on his beer, "Hhech! hhech! hhech!"

Robert told us about the drenched festival fields of Glastonbury. He casually compared their oozing mires of muck and sewage to the muddy, bloody death swamps of the Somme. It seemed a crude analogy, especially when he spoke with fondness of the crackling festival fires or the ocean of tents that disappeared into a smoky mist. I remembered attending festivals myself, some seven or eight years before. I could still taste the charcoal of bonfire-burnt food and feel the heat of fifty thousand huddled bodies baying for music. I had almost forgotten.

Then Robert recalled how he had discovered hallucinogens, "They changed my life. They opened my eyes!" he ejaculated, leaning so close to my face that I could feel his eyebrows tickling mine. "After I came back from Glastonbury I decided never to return to college... so I emptied my bank account and took a one-way ticket to Corfu." He spoke in quick disjointed bursts and had a habit of filling the gaps between sentences with a loud, unhealthy wheeze. This I found to be intensely irritating.

"That's incredible!" Kemi enthused, spitting the cigarette from his mouth, "this is what we should do, Joey! We should just drop out and become non-conformists!"

I was not so convinced. Although I warmed to Robert I doubted that his blurry existence was much more interesting than my own life, even if he did reside in Zante. Nonetheless, I would never have dared question for a second that he was a far happier man than I.

"What do you actually do here?" I asked him.

"I drink!"

"Where do you sleep?"

"I have a bag... which I keep behind the bar... here," he explained, trying to swallow a mouthful of lager as he spoke, "in the summer I kip on the beach, in the winter I sleep on floors... sometimes they let me sleep in the tavernas."

I speculated that Robert was from a fairly wealthy family.

He had clearly never done a single day's work and yet he had seemed to have an endless reservoir of alcohol funds.

"That guy is the ultimate individual," Kemi declared, as we walked back to the apartment that night, "he follows nobody and he's completely free of routine. That's the way we should be."

"Are you sure, Kemi?" I responded, "I hate my weekly schedule as much as you do yours, but I think Robert has a routine just as ugly as anybody else's. His daily programme consists of waking up on the beach and walking fifteen yards to the bar! Once there he slouches behind his table - beer in hand - and talks constantly to, or even at, strangers all day long. Occasionally he picks up a novel and attempts to decipher a string of words, then it's back to the drink."

"But," argued Kemi, "that's the way he wants to live. And look *where* he lives!"

"I agree with you," I answered, "and he is a very nice man, a really fun character. But I bet that these beautiful surroundings will have long since lost their impact on Robert. He watches the world through the bottom of a beer bottle, just like the guys down our local. The sea, the sun and the heat probably ceased to impress him after two or three months."

"No. No way."

"Kemi," I insisted, "These surroundings are mere decoration to Robert. Bright, entrancing surroundings are like fancy new wallpaper - they look good at first but after a while people don't see the change. His way of life is no different to that of ten or twenty others down the Lion."

Kemi shrugged.

After our brief exchange we switched subjects, but as we walked back along the seafront I could not help but feel that I had been cold and dismissive. I questioned for a long time whether my judgement of Robert had been reasonable.

Not once on the holiday did I think of my day-trips with Agatha to Cromer, Clacton or Southend: grey days taking shelter from the rain below rickety wooden piers - those stumbling reminders of a proud but deserted nineteenth century heyday. Crowds of us would stand beneath, hypnotised by the pier edge's unsteady waterfalls - rainwater streaming off woodwormy planks and plunging in sheets or ribbons into the sea.

One thing I had not forgotten, though, was our visit to New York. The beep of yellow taxi cabs, the shade of soaring concrete towers, the smell of street food and coffee bars. Everywhere one looked the street was peppered with brilliant people, and between them steam upreared from any of a million drains. The place was poorly represented in my photographs; I wanted to return, so that I could taste the place again and Kemi was keen to join me. We talked of flying to J.F.K., buying a car and driving across America from coast to coast, over lakes and mountains, through deserts and valleys. We imagined ourselves looming in on San Francisco then rolling up and down its hilly city streets - trailing the Steve McQueen wannabes, glancing across at the Pacific.

For now though, we were in Europe and that was more than enough.

There had been times on our 'tour' when I had thought of Europe as *my* beloved continent, a part of me in the same way that America had been so firmly a part of Kerouac. Then, before long, the reality of my true existence would haunt me again; the loathsome home town with its Red Lion Pub, its insipid High School, its Whiplash Women and I. Yes, poor, languid, listless Joey Carlton. He did not deserve beauty.

There was a true communal buzz all about the Greek islands, and I felt it recede with each and every mile that we travelled on our route back to England. We moved quickly up through Europe with no time to recover any of the energy or enchantment that we had spent during our journey down.

Eventually we took a delayed midnight ferry home. I felt terrible; as if I was making a definite mistake. I stood on deck aside the booming funnel. As our vessel swayed towards the wide-eyed moon I felt like I was being taken slowly, but inevitably, to the gallows. Was it necessary to return? Were the demands of my comically dull routine really so unavoidable? Would it be such a crime to live like Robert? I was wrong to have come back.

We came into town in the early, brightening, but still-silent hours. Britain was cold, empty, immobile. Sunday had just turned into Monday, but few had yet come around to realise it. I loved Sundays. I despised Mondays.

I looked down at the grey, cracked, uneven pavement then up to the vast above. Clouds schemed across the sky like thin streams spilling into murky chemical water-beds, growing thicker with milky pollutants.

Finally, left alone, I unlocked the front door and faced my house once more. I looked in at the small but sparse living room with its thinning, faded beige carpet and its scrawny, tattered, threadbare sofa. I could smell the kitchen wildlife that had formed on stray scraps of food. I could feel, even taste the immovable damp.

Suddenly the holiday, that great respite, counted for nothing. I was back in Purgatory and it was about to get even worse.

Chapter 5

Disillusion

I was growing suspicious.

School restarted three days after my return and there was a letter waiting for me in reception. Its anonymous writer stated curtly that I was 'UNFIT TO TEACH'.

It was not too difficult to dismiss this threat on its own and, besides, I was in many ways unfit to teach. Perhaps some unknown close observer had chosen to state the obvious. However, in conjunction with a vicious mobile phone message all became a little hard to explain. 'We're onto you...' warned the grimy, fast (and oddly distinctive) Cockney voice. I decided that the best option was to delete the message and pretend that it had never been received, as opposed to storing it, reporting it and torturing myself over it.

All around Britain the firstlings of change were beginning to turn. War had been declared on some distant, random opposition. The new government had found itself a battle to fight, an empty cause for its subjects to rally behind. In every town street I perceived myself as an enlightened man among the multitudinous unknown soldiers; so many lost souls imprisoned by a cause that they would never understand. Yes, the nation had the purposeless war that its people demanded. It was a channel for their animosity.

Of course there were new, different 'wars' shooting up everywhere, all of the time. Internal struggles. Day-to-day conflicts. The new government seemed happy for ill-advised, tabloid-wielding mobs to lead those petty local crusades that they considered most important. An outspoken priest was hounded from his home. A careless heart surgeon's family were besieged. A suspected sex offender's house was fire-bombed.

I was growing concerned for Kemi - and even for myself. I felt curiously insecure and it was not simply because of the threats. They were a mere smudge on the bigger cesspit.

In all of the most obvious fashions the world was the same as ever - the people had not changed, they were still scared of anything they did not understand and urged constantly to destroy whatever that may be. Yet this right-wing regime appeared content with the nation descending into an impious war of mob rule. The Press thought it fantastic - every week they created new enemies for the people, and the people duly agreed to fight them.

Every time I faced my class or set foot in a supermarket, I could see these sad lacklustre lemmings each becoming players in the populist war machine. I feared that intolerance soon would be liberated and all hope forlorn. The planet was in conflict with itself and suddenly the very fabric of society seemed uneven, unbalanced, unsteady. I felt ill at ease with the world around me.

Of course, I was too far too fixed in my life's little station to act on such fears. I much preferred to pretend that they did not exist, or find something infinitely more trivial to worry about instead. Kemi was eager to move away, perhaps to the rural obscurity of Norway or Finland, but that was far too drastic for me. How could I possibly leave town? I had spent most of my adult life – seven or so years - walling myself into the place with steadfast familiarity. I knew the town, I understood it and even though I would probably have been much happier in Finland, I could not bring myself to break the pattern. There was something in the British earth that was holding me back; as if I was immersed in the concrete and clay of my hometown streets. I hated myself for being restrained by banal routine. It made me a sad, foolish, helpless creature, like a wingless magpie stubbornly rejecting a lift home in favour of slow, painful demise in the ditch.

I had quickly returned to my accustomed state of disillusionment after the short-lived respite of our European tour. Once again my mind was all stale beer and curriculum criteria. Zante was a distant dream.

One chilly morning before school I decided to go out for a

walk. It was a chance to kick through the frosty gravel on country dirt-track crossroads, and breeze past silent streams as if they were not even there. Then I sat down on a bench in the park to consider my plight by daybreak.

I had been having dreams about sitting in a small plain amid dense woodland. It was another perplexing but maddeningly convincing dream; it led me to spend the first twenty minutes of the day distinguishing between sleep and the real world. In the vision I was often sitting next to a beautiful girl and was too shy to speak to her. Occasionally she would say something to me, but I would never hear it, nor care to say 'pardon?' The air in the plain was summery at first, it made me sneeze, but then grew hotter and closer. I gradually became uncomfortable and, then, quite suddenly, was aware that the woodland all around us was snaking in. The branches were reaching up to my face and thorns were starting to wrap around my limbs... after a while the girl was gone, her face lost behind a mesh of brambles. The strangest thing about these dreams though, was that I always knew that I would escape in the end.

Back in this cold morning reality, however, the wildlife was scuttling about me; I was being bugged by cockchafers but felt too tired to strongly protest.

Then I watched a magpie close in on a worm - swooping in on its earthy arena and slicing the thing in two with just one swipe of its pointed black beak. The bird pecked into the soil, nagging at the two demi-worms in their bootless struggles, one doomed half of the earthworm's form flapped blindly in search of its burrow, in search of its home and safety. Still the magpie nagged at the damned annelid, its white feathers browned by the thrashing soil. The vile bird persisted till it had swallowed down the nearest of the worm's two desperate halves. The other half remained, at first rolling in agony then flailing uselessly, and for a few frantic seconds this holy duel filled my entire planet... there was nothing more in my eyes than the two creatures; the ground's faceless, blind, foolish servant versus its merciless black slayer. Surely there could be only one outcome. Then, something odd occurred. The magpie turned briefly away and the frantic worm, its severed body already mending, suddenly composed itself. Slimy cords of fresh new body were already sprouting from the creature's severed end. This was the Newborn: a finer, stronger and brighter invention. The worm turned and in one calculated movement dived away from the bird and back into the earth. The magpie was shocked, left choking on this new worm's condemned brother, but not knowing where in the world to look for its canny second portion. The bird was beaten.

I turned away from the battle and across the park I saw a labourer cutting across on his way to work. He was a teenager of sixteen or seventeen years, with untidy blond hair and with eyes like the acute rifts in two unripe pistachio nuts. His unwashed baggy jeans and plaster-caked t-shirt left behind them a trail of yesterday's dust, beaten from the boy by a harsh morning breeze. He stopped to grapple with the bag on his back, and at that precise point that I realised him to be the campest labourer that I had ever seen! His limbs were like pipe-cleaners with wrists limping like a willow's branches. I smiled, involuntarily, as he fished through the contents of his dainty black satchel. Perhaps he was searching for some lipstick or mascara.

I remembered when Kemi and I had spent a few winter weeks on a building site. I recalled those endless rainy days, slaving incessantly in collapsing trenches, and how we had to breathe pavement dust as slabs were sliced in two by relentlessly whining diamond blades. I remembered how we had talked the language of the construction worker; in trestles, akrows, lintels, picks, shovels, squares, spades and blades.

The only thing that we actually enjoyed was when we walked into the Red Lion Pub after work. In this town nobody wants to know you if you are dressed in a suit and tie. However if you are Carl The Plasterer then you immediately become accessible and interesting. As soon as we walked into the pub covered from top to bottom in cement dust and mud, people were interested. Two good young boys doing an honest day's work, learning the time-honoured skills and plainspoken ways of the building trade. And though they may spend their whole lives covered in muck, at least they are straight-talking workmen. That is enough. Well no, it was never enough, not for us.

By the end of our labouring days Kemi had grown tired of the name-play on his Islamic roots; "Come here Ranjit!"... "Oi, macaroon get me a lump hammer!"... "Where's that bloody nig-nog boy got to?"... It was ridiculous - Kemi was talcum white and there was nothing more than his shortened forename for these plebeians to work their ignorance with, but that was sufficient. Appallingly, I found myself laughing at these jibes. In the end we both left the job after being lambasted for accidentally smashing a porcelain mains drain. The damage was more costly than two days of our wage. We had to run for miles from a mob of irate thuggish builders, all brandishing trowels and bellowing at us. Despite our rattling lungs we outpaced them through the alleyways, leaving the angry workmen - and three days' wages - behind with an expensive pipe to fix. It did not seem to matter. As I looked back in time I asked myself when, exactly, that defiance and decisiveness had deserted me.

I recalled how I had become bored of being 'nigger boy's mate', and how I was even more weary of the mindless unchanging work, such as sweeping ballast from the road-side and into a heap. 'What harm is it doing to the road-side?' I would ask myself, 'if I sweep it into a pile, then I'm only going to have to move it all over again tomorrow.' It made no sense, but if you questioned the builders you would be told 'not to think, just to do'.

I looked back over the field at the pathetic, queer labourer as he disappeared into the cold dawn haze. I felt a small amount of sympathy for the pointless work and cruel abuse that he faced in the days - maybe years - ahead. Yet, at this stage in my life I had not even started to appreciate how significant such men as he were to our world. I did not understand the importance of his role in society's great machine. I was detached from these folks and their pitiful lives; to me they represented no more than the comedies of mundane existence. I was better than them and they were created, I felt, for people like me to laugh at. In fact, I was not altogether keen on mankind in general.

Meanwhile an evil, cloudy sky was grumbling above. It occurred to me briefly that I had almost forgotten those wonderful sunshiny weeks in Europe already. They were a world away from this. More than ever I wanted to be someone else, free of the shackles that I had set for myself. Yet I knew that if I ever awoke as a different man I would only recreate the same old chains for a new identity.

I took to my feet and left the park, although I felt more like calling on Kemi and getting drunk than readying for a day-load of work.

Back in school all of the nation's subtle changes were lost on its dreary student populous.

I spent three of my five lessons that day robotically removing figurative speech from classic texts, but not before another anonymous threat had appeared on my mobile phone. I was quite unsettled, irritated even, by this and was slowly growing intolerant of the faceless intimidation. I deleted the message and decided that I would punt the mobile phone into oblivion as soon as I could find the time, not thinking that my unknown enemy might find a more damaging medium through which to cow his thoroughly confused victim.

In the staff room at morning break I found myself sitting alone in a corner with nobody to speak to. I looked up for the clock; in the staff room it was always set three minutes 'slow' so that teachers could in one small way justify their overdue arrival into lessons. Meanwhile in all of the classrooms, clocks were set 'fast' by the pupils so that, even though it meant that they were always late into lessons, they could be packed and ready to leave a few minutes before time.

I decided to check through some specific curriculum criteria. I wanted to understand the difference between a pupil's 'competence' and 'incompetence' in using figures of speech. The closest that I could find was:

'En3 Writing 4B

Pupils should be enabled to considerably increase their competence and overall familiarity with figurative language. They should be able to distinguish between the imperative figures of speech and apply these precisely to a wide variety of valid evidence, showing an understanding of their effects and purpose. Their ability to analyse work from a range of sources through figurative devices should become coherent, and sustain a relevance to the author's perspective.'

What on Earth does this MEAN? The diction was tortuous and almost nonsensical. If a pupil of mine had ever produced such a piece of meandering, verbose textual vomit then I would have asked them to flush it down the toilet. I dropped my copy of the document and went to make a cup of tea.

Standing aside the kettle was the head of my department, Mr. Jackboot, a dapper old gentleman with a loose grasp of received pronunciation and an ever looser grip on reality. He was an honest, unassuming but infuriating old fool. Agatha claimed to have been taught Maths by him (before he turned to English) when she was a student at the school, and had considered him to be an imbecile ever since. In my days as a trainee teacher Jackboot had been my ineffectual mentor. "Oh! Hello there Joey, h-how are you?" he asked in his ridiculous thespian stutter.

"Very well, thank you," I answered dutifully.

"O-o-oh, jolly good," he returned, with a pathetic, sincere smile. I could not understand how his pupils let him get away with such irritating mannerisms.

"And how are you?"

"Well, not bad at all. Not bad at all. I've just jogged from the canteen, so I have to catch my breath I'm afraid Joey."

"Oh dear."

"I mmmet a bit of a frosty reception there, I'm sssorry to say. I think the dinner ladies have something of an axe to grind with me, Joey."

"Really?"

"Yyyyyes. Yes. Am sorry to say. Coffee debts, I fear. Anyway, remember the department meeting tomorrow. Old soldiers must stand shoulder to shoulder with you young - er - cadets. What was it I was saying to you this morning, over coffee, Joey?"

"About the theatre trips for Macbeth and Kes?"

"Oh yyyes, of course it was. Think we might have to toe the line a little over that one. Not sure the budget can quite afford two trips in one term. Sorry about that, Joey."

I told him that there was no problem and politely poured

41

the boiling kettle water onto his coffee. "Milk and sugar?" I asked him.

"Nnn-n-no thank you Joey, as it is please, absolutely as it is."

I handed over the coffee. "There you go."

"Oh! Thank you so very much, Joey. How very good of you. How kind." The man was utterly comical.

There was some deep - but forgotten - reason for my disdain towards Jackboot, but what I consciously hated most about him was the remarkable effect that he sometimes had on his pupils. Although most students were indifferent to his peculiar brand of disordered ramblings, a number of his classes - sometimes the most difficult - overachieved to unthinkable levels. Then there was the unusually good rapport that he kept with his adolescent audiences perhaps, I concluded, because they were entranced by his irksome singularity. Whatever, I envied his effortless popularity.

Back in the lessons I was systematically dismantling as many great writers as the syllabus could get its vile mitts on. I sat on a stool and leaned back against the wall for support, slumping like a cadaver while picking out slice upon slice of figurative language. My weary pupils were dragged through anaemic analyses, constantly chattering above my tired warnings.

"This," I said, "is an example of Transferred Epithet." My exhausted, unhappy marker pen finally ran out as I stabbed it into the whiteboard. "Then this," I whined on, "is an example of Pathetic Fallacy." I glared at the countryside that dipped down and rose up beyond my classroom window; it was made bruise-brown by the thick smoke shooting up from some chimney below. "And that... that we call Litotes." 'I continued, while still grappling with the mild sensation of bemusement.' "This here is Antithesis" I announced. The kids were getting everything they would ever have to know about literary review, and yet they needed to know none of it.

Why, I wondered, did I have to teach this nonsense? Did the writer even know what was meant by 'litotes' or 'dramatic irony' or 'oxymoron' or 'lacunae'? In what way, exactly, was any of this important to the STORY? It wasn't! This was a science, not an artistic appreciation. It was the science of understanding what made something work, all through a tiresome array of bland terminology.

Before long all of the definitions were blurring into each other and they, in turn, into the curriculum criteria. I stopped mid-sentence, wondering what on the planet I was waffling about and whether it actually meant anything at all. For a few moments my mind stood still. I could feel my neck growing warm, my facing blushing red and my eyes squinting awkwardly out at the class. All of these young faces... All looking at me... All waiting for me to conceal a piece of unblemished literature with dull, bloodless labels...

Then, thankfully I thought, my mobile phone began to buzz. The nagging beep sounded for once like a death row reprieve and this time instead of turning it off I answered the call, without apologies, behind the desk.

"Mr. Carlton," the voice started, and suddenly my heart stumbled again; yet another threat. "We will be paying you a visit soon." I could barely believe it.

I switched off the phone, swallowed and looked up at my class. I was not sure why but I felt sure that I was about to burst into tears. It was not as if I was petrified by this latest threat, more so vexed and only very subtly spooked. For a few seconds I began to question what, specifically, was happening to me and why on Earth I was being targeted by this lingering irritant. It occurred to me then that the calls and threats could concern something from deep in my distant past... but then I soon discarded the possibility. Surely nobody could be interested in my past. I instantly went back to my undirected panic. If there is a God that could possibly love me, I said to myself, then the school bell will surely go right now. Please.

The bell rang.

Without a word I waved the pupils out of my classroom and dashed off to the toilets, just outside my door. These were especially unclean student rest-rooms and rarely used, except for by pupils caught short in lesson-time or the most desperate of young smokers.

I sat down in a cubicle and tried to contain my thoughts. I looked around at my surroundings, trying to divert my mind with the scrawls of obscene, misspelt graffiti: 'Dwayne 4 Charlene D' and 'Kieron Woz Ere' had pride of place on the back of the door, while 'I Luv Sharon Betts' was dabbed across the toilet-roll holder in correction fluid. It was not nearly enough to stop my mind from falling back into the rambling curriculum language and the benumbing English terminology and the threatening phone calls until... 'MR. JACKBOOT SMOKES COCK'... Just below the lock on the door, hard to see in thin green ink. Quite immediately a smile swelled across my face and a deep breath of agitated air evacuated my lungs. I was well aware that I should have considered the insult to be foul or juvenile, but my true feeling was that I wished to find whoever wrote this and shake him firmly by the hand, maybe even give him a few pennies to spend on alcohol or, who knows, crack. I rose and left the toilets with a wide grin.

From then on the whole day was terrible. I walked back to the house at lunch time and found another two threatening messages on the answer phone. For some reason, this time I fell quite aghast. It occurred to me that there was somebody out there who, for whatever abominable reason, wanted to trouble or even destroy me. They knew my home number. They knew my work number. They must have known where I lived. I was not safe.

I left the house in a hurry that afternoon and decided that I should make the most of the remaining school day, there in the sanctuary of the school grounds. Who, I wondered, could be as unholy as to feel such vitriol against me? What had I done to deserve it?

When I got back to school I was too shaken to teach, I felt as if I was waiting for a nuclear strike, so I engaged my class in a series of pointless conversations. Some adolescents will seize on the chance to recount an episode of dull juvenile degeneracy, so we discussed alcohol, tobacco, sex and drugs. They seemed to enjoy the exercise, even if their teacher soon grew bored and fell silent. While I was forgetting the threats and refocusing on my more general depression, they chatted amongst each other.

Aaron, who was in the group, produced an array of lascivious remarks which could well have got him suspended and eventually he over-stepped the threshold. "Aaron get out," I barked, much to his astonishment.

"What?"

"Get out." I could feel my face cheeks sparking red.

"Where do you want me to go?"

"You know the drill Aaron. First, you go to the office. Then, you tell them what you have just said. Finally, you come to me on Thursday after school and then we will see if you can keep your libidinous witticisms to yourself for an hour."

"Don't worry Mr. Carlton, you're safe with me."

"What was that?"

Aaron did not answer. He kicked the desk forward, pulled his bag strap from beneath a chair leg and picked himself up. He turned first to me and then the class with a mocking smile as he left the room, "Be scared everyone, Carlton's reasserting his authority," he uttered almost imperceptibly, as he walked out.

"That makes it two detentions," I responded, even though the remarks hardly deserved the discipline. In fact, my overreaction served only to confirm Aaron's allegation. In addition I was sad at having to punish my favourite pupil, although quietly pleased with my use of the word 'libidinous'. I looked it up in the dictionary as soon as the lesson had finished.

The rest of the lesson was marked by minor disturbance. There were more licentious comments and more brags of decadence; at the back of the room a young couple disappeared in a clinch. I longed for the bell to go, but did not really want to return home.

I hated my life. Zante was gone.

I was so immersed in my own disillusionment that I could not address that very real, very present danger in my life. Looking back I struggle to understand how any man could ever have been so blinkered.

Whenever I faced the threats it was with a sense of helplessness and bewilderment. I spent more time feeling annoyed that somebody should have taken a dislike to me than I did being concerned about my safety.

There was, from my past, a very good, a very clear reason for all of the harassment, but I was far too blind to consider it.for so much as a second. Once or twice, like that lunch time when I heard the answer phone threats at home, I had a faint, slippery notion of what the menaces may concern, but I always dismissed such thoughts. Then like so many other things it was all erased from my memory, until the next time at least.

By this point in my life, all traces of youthful recalcitrance had been snatched from me, thieved by the wearying, sterile swings of time's slow pendulum. Long, long gone was the will to spit, snarl, kick and hit in protest. Nowadays I was too dull to be vicious. I did not even remember what had gone wrong before. It was no longer relevant to the man that I had become.

My pernicious past had become a pallid, treasureless present.

Then later that evening, I would learn what fear could truly mean - and how deep into the soul its icy drives could spike. This was no fleeting snack of alarm. It was unbounded horror.

First, though, came the walk.

I needed to escape the house and wander alone. I paced through the town. It was a night on the dawn of winter with every facade turned to frost, and the whole place was so white that one could not imagine it ever wearing colour. Freezing fog was everywhere and leafless branches dripped on every hooded head.

There was a fair on the green outside the council offices. I decided to walk down and have a look, despite being worried that some begrudging ex-pupil might recognise me with fists clenched. When I arrived it was immediately clear that I would be meeting few ex-pupils; the fair's populous seemed to be comprised entirely of my bottom set English group.

"Hiya Mr. Carlton," one girl screamed as she soared up into the haze on the huge, flashing, primitive ferris wheel. Its chairs swung and croaked, its engine coughed and groaned. It was full of juvenile lovers, swaying back and forth into the swirling foggy sky where neither I – nor anyone else on the ground – existed anymore. It was entrancingly innocent.

It was there at the fairground, across a hectic bumper car

ring, that I spotted Aaron and Gemma huddled together in line. I watched them on the dodgems, the g-force, the candy floss store and then the rifle range where Aaron had to show off his fine shooting skills to Gemma.

Through it all I listened to the fairground radio, dished out on a treble-heavy public address system to the chattering proletariat. They loved it all. Some of the kids were dancing, but I preferred to laugh at the sounds - rock music full of three/four rhythms, top string bass and whiny shoe gazing singers. Then there was the B-boy music from the ghettos of Colchester and Chiswick. Here, the market salesmen and duck watchers of the future were in the prime of their adolescence... but it got no better than this; an uninspired melee of bodies and lights.

I sensed, though, how easily these surroundings could be corrupted by the recent mutations of our society. I deeply feared that our new government would wish to bring these comically simple, merry scenes to a quaking halt. I worried that they might systematically replace pure unsullied celebration like this with something entirely more sinister and vitriolic. I foresaw the cropped grass as overgrown, the bright lights struck down and the fairground rides dismantled, discarded and locked away. In my vision those young, unblemished faces on dodgems or spinning teacups were scarred and mean; all marching in line for a 'worthy' military cause that they could not comprehend.

Thankfully that was, so far at least, only a distant concern - but still enough for me to suddenly see something quite amazing in that unoriginal fairground scene.

At one point in the night it began to rain viciously. I left the park and found myself in a crowded bus shelter. I always enjoyed a good storm; to be warm, dry, safe inside while the Gods grouched above and whipped the land below in anger. Under cover, though, we were mere spectators to this purgative ceremony. The winter's night light was cut short to brief brilliant flashes - houses' yellow lamplights and the garish fairground sparkle were all struck dead.

I had always loved a summertime thunderstorm when, in between the cracking jolts of fork lightning one could momentarily wonder, if only for a few seconds, whether the streets and homes that were lost in the darkness were really there at all. This, however, was a frosty, misty winter night and when the storm subsided the streets refilled with the shivering rabble. Aaron passed by with Gemma and I decided to stalk them. I left just enough distance to remain lost in the dark, while still being close enough to hear them speak and taste their tobacco. They were arguing.

Through all of this I had too much time to reflect on the toils of the day. Whenever the answer phone message and the threats came into mind I had to quickly blank my thoughts and listen to the young couple ahead.

In moonlight we passed the street corner where local townies convened to plan nothing much. In a few years time the juvenile mobs would leave this spot and take their meetings a little further up the road, to the Red Lion pub. Then, they would start to buy their food from the shop next door, rent one of the neighbouring flats and, once they had begun work at the top-town hosiery (where the workhouse once stood), they would never again need to leave this hundred yard stretch of road. Finally they would be laid to rest in the cemetery, behind the pub, near their flat and next to their parents and their parents' parents. Many of these people forget what the world beyond even looks like. Aaron, I hoped, would turn out different, but I only had to look at myself to see where it could all go wrong.

So on we walked, past the more fashionable bars where hipsters unite to discuss their dreams through oily uncombed fringes. Once upon a time I would drink there, but now I understand how easily the hair becomes cut and how the dreams are aligned.

Now I drink at the Red Lion.

From what I could gather, Gemma was angry with Aaron because he had been dating an older woman. I found it all quite amusing, especially as my star pupil seemed firmly unapologetic.

We went on towards the park. The young ex-lovers were kicking up sand on the soiled, park-edge path - the mud on the concrete was like the chocolate stains on Gemma's sea blue jeans. They strode on, ignoring the moon and ignoring me as I spied on each word or exchange of exasperated glances.

Finally tired, I turned away and walked back towards my house down a side-alley. It was then that I began to feel that I was being watched, and sensed that there were footsteps splashing in the puddles behind me. I lacked the courage to turn around but simply paced on at a feigned leisurely pace, telling myself that the sounds were either imagined or those of some innocent pedestrian. Up ahead on the path there lay a giant orange smile, street-lamp-lit, where the alleyway's vanishing point was hidden by the weedy grin of the undergrowth as it jungled onto the path and up the fences on either side. I focused on this and, for the first time that day, longed to get back to the house.

Having opened and shut the door, I was quick to bed. The light over the staircase was left on - this made me feel more comfortable - but my room's sliding door nearly shut so that I did not have to face any shadows from the landing on my room wall opposite. I felt insecure...

I think I had fallen asleep and could not be certain whether or not what happened next was in my dreams.

There was a cold, stern gust of wind into the bed, from which the covers had fallen. I was naked, shivering, and sure that a vague silhouette - cast by the night-light outside - had ghosted across my pale wood-chip wall. There was a clatter of cutlery downstairs, but I lay still.

The bedroom was a long and dark place and the landing light had started to flicker. I could hear its unhappy buzz from my lying place. From the churchyard I heard the clock chime in some early morning hour; I hoped for five o'clock and the promise of morning light, but the bells stalled at three.

I listened intently, suppressing my breath and remaining unmoved. I could hear the boiler's on-off drone, I could hear the wind as it tackled the trees. The light bulb crackled, then fell dark and silent. Suddenly there was no noise whatsoever - and this was worse.

The silence bothered me the most so I got out of bed and picked up the knife that lay in my bookcase. I kept it there because I always feared having a weapon at my bedside in case

Agatha should ever be overcome by some fit of discontent and attack me with the blade.

The staircase creaked, whined and moaned as I descended. I could see as I came down that the back room was empty, so I switched on its light and moved, slowly, towards the living room.

I stood in the doorway, with the electric light from behind throwing my shadow down onto the floor before me. I was eye to eye with the full moon through the window ahead, everything in the room was a dark disarray of objects, all only half-lit by the moonlight. I walked up to the window and looked through. My heart shuddered.

Outside there was a lone figure, staring fixedly back at me. He was tall and thin but thickly dressed, facing away from the moon, countenance black with nothing clear but for the whites of his eyes. Unblinking, unflinching he remained - simply staring at me, shamelessly. I was incapable of crying out and, besides, who was there to hear me? The neighbours would only roll over in bed or bang on the walls.

I turned away, thinking immediately that I should leave the house through the back door then run; across gardens, over fences and through fields to find a place to hide, beneath a dense hedge or inside some deep ditch that could conceal me from the moon's torch.

It never happened. As I prepared to start, the light from the back room was switched off and I heard the door to the under-stair cupboard thudding shut. Somebody was inside the house after all and now I could neither escape to the front nor to the back - I was trapped.

Two or three terrible seconds passed and nothing happened; not a sound, not a move. The room now seemed quite light and I could smell the damp as well as recently fried onion. I remembered Agatha's phone call when she had told me about the men rummaging through our rubbish. I wished that I had listened to her warnings and the innumerable threats that I had received. Now, it seemed, somebody had come for me.

It was at that moment that I suggested to myself, quite conveniently, that I might just be dreaming - that this could be nothing more than another nightmare. Remembering the knife in my hand, I tiptoed silently across the room. With each motion I feared that, at any second, the stillness all around could erupt into vicious animation.

Quietly, quietly I trod, and yet there was still little more than the distant shush of trembling branches outside. Perhaps, I told myself, this dream is not so bad. The man outside could be a lost local drunkard on his late night stumble-around and the noises inside could be muffled echoes from next door. I repeated this to myself as I moved back into the doorway and flicked the dining room light switch back on. Then, there in the dining room, in definite and palpable materiality, stood the unavoidable proof.

"Mr. Carlton," said the man in a deep, untroubled voice. His deep-set eyes were wide and blue with impossibly small pupils burning into me. His skin had a buttered glaze, almost jaundiced, with thin red blood vessels running like barbed wire down from his bulging cheekbones to his concave temples. His lips were thin and drawn back to unveil a glimpse of yellow tooth. His tangled, fading blond locks were sprawled about his time-worn forehead and invisible ears. The man was large - both taller and wider than me - but with a look of composure and intelligence about him. "Mr. Carlton," he said again, this time louder and tilting his head slightly to one side. Then he turned, ready to leave through the back door.

"How did you get in?" I asked him.

No answer.

"Are you from the Press?"

He stopped, and looked back at me over his shoulder. "I'm from the Government Mr. Carlton. The Press have already nailed you," he answered. Then, with a monstrously uneven smile he added, "I'm here to finish you off..."

"What?"

"...When the time is right."

"What?"

"Goodbye Mr. Carlton," said the man, finally, and then he left the house.

"What have you come here for?" I called after him, "what

in God's name are you doing here tonight?" I wished not to sound too aggressive lest the man turn back around and murder me at once, but he did not. He was gone.

At that moment I was too shaken to feel scared any more, but still I locked the door, fastened the windows and considered setting a few pathetic little traps; a rubbish bin at the top of the staircase, perhaps, or a trip-wire between the kitchen and dining room. But I did not. As I returned upstairs it occurred to me, only very briefly, that I had at one point asked the stranger if he was from the Press. When I woke up the next day I had no idea why the thought had ever come to me.

I did not even know if any of it had actually happened.

Chapter 6

Invigoration

I still have no idea why I took the drug, but feel sure that my reason had something to do with my upsurging disregard for reality.

Over two months had passed since that night – almost long enough for it to be forgotten - and February's empty promise was upon us. The country, I knew, was changing into something even more abysmal, and I felt less welcome than ever. Our far right revolutionary leaders had made clear to their subjects that popular policies would prevail; 'dangerous' suspects, ex-convicts and minorities were to face swift 'on the spot' justice administered by roving 'Community Courtrooms' (or, put succinctly, lynch mobs). Capital punishment was not only to be revived, but returned to the suburbs, where prison funding could be cropped by swiftly killing off the incontestably evil. Most worrying of all, however, was that the electorate actually adored these policies. There's no room in the world for murderers and rapists... Forgiveness is weak... Revenge is strong... Reject any religion which is not attuned to the ways of the patriot... Everyone must integrate... Everyone must conform... Any dissenting voice was derided.

The thugs were suddenly storming from the jails to serve their perfect new part in society's unruly flow, while the most evil or disturbed of our inmates were labelled 'irrevocably bad' and quickly extinguished. It seemed to me that the only people left in the jails were the thieves and young drug addicts. Our revered new ruler promised the land that no man who had tested positive for illegal narcotics would ever be released until he was 'clean' enough to fit in.

All of this was so understood by the media that very few fathomed just how drastic the transformations were. The population was too fixated by Britain's faraway crusades - the

53

furious new foreign policy - to be particularly interested in civil rights back at home. Anyway, the proles agreed that the rights of a criminal suspect were not especially important. To them, the concrete and clay beneath their feet seemed as firm as ever. The objections of Britain's disquieted neighbours in Europe were immaterial. Besides, they all had problems enough of their own to be dealing with.

I was gravely concerned for Kemi. The government had not gone so far as to sanction the execution of each and every petty sex offender, but they had agreed to publish the names and addresses of every registered paedophile in the tabloid press. That, of course, included my good friend.

In addition to all of this, the authorities had been somewhat sluggish in their response to vigilante attacks on sex offenders. Angry crowds often clustered around paedophiles' houses to harass the troubled minds within. Sometimes a member of the multitude would throw a brick in the name of their endangered offspring who were, no doubt, busy playing alone and unguarded in the park at the time. It was an excuse to riot and on at least ten occasions since Christmas people had died, none of which in the least bothered the Home Office.

Vigilante attacks were becoming more frequent and a local throng of thugs were already onto Kemi; he knew it would not be long before something happened. I told him that he should move away - and he agreed with me - but Kemi was never the type to decamp.

What we had arranged, though, was a five day trip to France during the February half-term. Secretly, I had fantasised that we could simply remain there together in some solitary shack in Brittany - but then, quite suddenly, my plans were thrown madly afield.

Marc had been a friend of Kemi's for a good few years. He was only twenty-three but was highly-esteemed in every local drinking hole, which is probably how Kemi made his acquaintance. When I had been with Agatha she would only ever come to the pub if Marc was out. The ladies worshipped him - even more so than they loved Kemi - and they took turns to share brief but ever-ebullient moments talking with the boy.

The discourse seldom got further than football, cars, sex or beer, but Marc was forever smiling and ceaselessly upbeat. He looked like a slim, fresh-faced fourteen year old with untidy golden hair, deep-set dimples, olive skin and gaping green eyes. I always worried myself when he spoke a word to Agatha because I was sure that he would bed her in a second without the fuzziest notion that what he was doing was wrong. Of course, he would have needed to be both blind and senile before even considering it.

Marc and Kemi had been drinking at the Red Lion on the Sunday night, and I had dropped in for an hour myself.

Early the next day Marc left his house to drive down to the newsagents for a can of gas lighter fluid. The shop was only a ten minute walk from his house but the path was cold and icy, so he took the car. On the way back, with a dense fog descending, he swerved suddenly to avoid a stumbling drunkard... and piled into a parked van, headlong.

All for a little lighter fuel.

As usual, I had a macabre concern for the gory particulars, but Kemi refused to listen to even the slimmest of details, from the broken bones to the grim and lingering demise. All Kemi wanted was a single photograph from the depths of my collection; of a punch-fuelled house party that had taken place at his house five or six years before.

It featured five youths slouched about a lounge - some on the sofa, some on the carpet - with Kemi and Marc slumped back to back on the floor. Neither of the youngsters were looking at the camera nor grinning politely. Instead their stoned, vacant gaze was racing somewhere into oblivion. It seemed that then, at that point, their lives were laid out before them... but Marc would never live to become old and worn. This would be him. Forever.

The rest of the group in the picture, I among them, smiled compliantly.

Marc's death had rocked us all. At the funeral, Harry and I had been forced to stand up because there were not enough seats for all of the mourners. People often talk of having had a colourful young friend taken from life in his prime, but to actually see it happen shook me thoroughly. I cannot begin to think how thunderstruck Kemi must have been.

When the casket vanished behind the curtains I tried to think of Marc and my memories of him, but could only ask myself how many people by comparison,would come to my funeral. I knew that I would be lucky to find ten mourners and wondered why it was that I would never mean as much to as many people as Marc did. Did it mean that I was worth any less than him?

It was with all of these thoughts fresh in our minds that, to my bitter dismay, Kemi suggested we cancel our holiday and instead spend a couple of days binge-drinking at his house in town. I still have no idea how this was any more appropriate in the wake of Marc's death than a few days in France.

So, it was in this state of general disillusionment that I agreed to take the 'drug'. I never for a second thought that it was going to change my life forever.

The day began with a cool, muddy-skied six o'clock rise. The sink was blocked and the oven alarm had switched itself on. I remembered agreeing to make my way over to Kemi's for midday and immediately regretted the promise. I felt slow, awkward and so bored that I almost wanted to take up alcoholism or chain-smoking. I called Kemi's mobile to find out when we were meant to convene and where. He answered that he had spent last night at the abode of a 46-year-old grandmother called Rosette and that an old friend of ours, Baz, would be picking both of us up in his car before we went over for the drinking marathon.

Baz arrived at about one in the afternoon and rapped on my porch door just as I was finishing my third cheesy chip sandwich. I brought a six-pack of beer and an old green sleeping bag with me into Baz's car, which was a rusty old number with neither wing mirrors nor hub-caps.

Baz was a year younger than me and a year older than Kemi. We did not see a great deal of him because he was a born drifter, inclined to saunter from county to county and from house to house without ever settling. I doubt very much that he had ever so much as rented a property and I feared that he would use this meeting as an opportunity to find a new sleeping pad at either Kemi's or mine. I had always admired him, despite the fact that his dark alluring countenance had long since surrendered to the effects of long-term substance abuse. He was untidy and unshaven with frequently dyed hair and eyes that had once glowed permanganate purple, but were now dimmed to ashy graphite. Baz was the master of acid-induced rumination; he had a drug-related interpretation for every film plot and song lyric. He was always reading either Aldous Huxley's 'Doors Of Perception' or 'The Tibetan Book Of The Dead', and had listened to Syd Barrett until the real world made very little sense indeed, regardless of what was or was not presently swimming through his bloodstream.

Baz had, apparently, also spent several nights with Rosette recently, so he knew the way to her house. "I think we'll meet up again this week," he revealed.

"Aren't you annoyed with Kemi for nicking her?" I asked him.

"Yyyyyy-no. No I guess not. No. Not really. Not at all in fact." Baz seemed very uncertain, but I knew that if he was angry with Kemi he would not let it show.

Rosette was sitting on her doorstep with Kemi when Baz's car drew up. He banged his horn, she called out. Baz jumped out and spoke with her for a few moments while I sat in the car with Kemi and listened to him prattling on about his conquest as if he had just discovered a new toy. Then he told me just how easy it would be for me to fix myself up with Rosette. He seemed to think that I would be interested.

"What would I want to do with that old tart?" I asked him.

"Well, she says that you went round to the flat where she hangs out. She knows who you are."

"She knows who I am? How?"

"You called for her mate - Gwyn, I think. She says Gwyn's the wrong woman for you. You need some good loving."

I suddenly remembered. "Oh!" I ejaculated, "she's one of the Whiplash Women."

"Eh?"

"Yes I do know her friends. I met them on the election

night, I went to the flat before I went to see you," I gave Rosette a long look, "but I can't say I remember her." I thought I had already told Kemi about my uneasy night with the Whiplash Women, but either way he seemed quite surprised.

"Whatever," he shrugged, "I think you're in with Rosette."

"Rosette is a whore," I muttered.

"Now there's no need to say that," retorted Kemi, sounding but not looking affronted. It seemed strange that he was still so merry, in spite of all the things presently threatening his unbound existence.

We got to Kemi's after a long delay but proceedings opened badly when Harry turned up to join us for a beer. We watched television for a while and, to my dismay, a programme about disobedient High School children came on. Not a minute passed without Harry remarking adversely on the state of the nation's youth. I despised these discussions because I usually felt obliged - as a 'liberal-minded' teacher - to defend the young generation, no matter how wayward I considered them to be. Of course I thoroughly disliked most of my students and utterly detested the teaching profession, but there were still enough likeable kids - Aaron, for instance – for me to remain partially hopeful.

After the documentary – and just before Harry left - the news was aired. It was suggested, in the day's main story, that the government could ultimately turn to conscription in its bid to win the war. As a teacher there was little chance that I would ever be called up but Harry, Kemi and Baz might all be candidates. As such, the breaking story was shattering for the three of them.

"There's no way I'd go," Harry insisted.

"I got the impression that you supported the war," I said, in a masked effort to be contentious.

"I didn't say there was anything wrong with the politics of the war," Harry replied, "but that doesn't mean I want to fight in it."

I wanted to tell him that actions count for more than hollow words, but I opted for a diplomacy of sorts: "If everyone in the country shares your attitude then Britain will lose the war."

Harry looked at me for a moment, "On the contrary," he

argued, "if everybody was a draft-dodger then there wouldn't be any wars to win or lose." The response infuriated me, partly because I knew that he was correct, and I wished that I had said this myself.

By the time Harry left the moon's light was already peering in through Kemi's front room window. I knew that he had something illicit for us and after a few hours of putting up with Harry I was urgently keen to partake, but I also had little clue what substance this might be or even when we might be taking it.

In the meantime we talked about anything and everything. It was in the kitchen that Kemi turned to me and said, "Joey, have you ever wanted more from this life than what you've got?"

I was silent for a few seconds, and then nodded.

"What then?"

But all that I could think of were nagging changes; I wanted a tidy house, a submissive wife, a differently shaped nose. The real problem, of course, was my inability to act upon my instincts and as such I remained hopelessly indifferent to everything. However this state of affairs was all about to change.

Matters moved on hastily after dinner, which consisted of synthetic bacon in four long strips served with baked beans. (Kemi was not a vegetarian, so I assumed - correctly - that this meat-free meal was a sign that he had recently tried to seduce a woman who was.) Kemi and Baz went into the kitchen to make some tea and it was with this that we took the drug, at around a quarter to ten. I had my doubts right up until the last moment, but the substance was only a centimetre square of coloured paper - it seemed harmless - and besides, I did not want to be left out.

We sat around the table, sipping our hot drinks. The gaps between each of us formed an equilateral triangle and the naked light bulb beamed down at the centre of the bare wooden table below. We sat silently for a long time.

I noticed no difference for the first hour, and actually felt slightly annoyed with myself for having been so easily led.. When it came to sex and drugs education I had always been almost as apathetic as the adolescents that I was lecturing. Now it seemed as if I should have either listened to my own advice, or been less hypocritical.

We were watching television - a wildlife documentary - when I noticed the first changes. My back was sensitive, I could sense its curves and bumps bedding into the sofa and straightened up immediately. Suddenly the television was dipping, drifting between two and three dimensions. I stood up and looked for a time at my friends. They were slouched in their chairs and seemed quite normal to me. Perhaps, I thought, my brain was feigning effects for this substance. I shrugged and walked towards the kitchen but found that I was negotiating my way through ramps in the floor below my feet.

From that second I was loathe to leave the company of Kemi or Baz, I tied myself to their presence and could feel their absence whenever I left for the bathroom. That horrible, lonely, silent bathroom...

While I understood more than ever that these sensations made up only my perception and nobody else's, I also found that my friends were sharing in these observations. We agreed that there was no real reason for the recess at the back of the lounge, nor a purpose to the immiscible shapes trancing across the room's wallpaper.

As the night progressed, Baz's face grew ever more contorted and radiated warmth, while in the mirror my face was lined with fear; each wrinkle a deep, groaning stress-trench. When we listened to music we could all hear the same ghostly gasps breaking out from the mix, which sometimes slowed to a groan and sometimes skipped to a strange Egyptian whine. Sounds concealed by the producer's console were recovered from beneath stammering beats and mechanic, crackling guitars; the tinkling symbol, the humming mellotron, the soaring harmony. All in perfect solitary existence. All alive. Each piano chord was struck with a resonant supremacy which at times grew confused with everything else and, at others, stood alone like never before.

The room itself was becoming hectic.

I still felt happy with the company of Kemi and Baz, but more scared than ever of what lay outside the front door. Thankfully, with the curtains drawn and the sky's light dimmed to night, one could almost believe that nothing lay beyond. Eventually we had to check.

Outside the streetlights sparkled into light rain. I saw not only their orange, but rather every one of their colours reflecting in the oily water and merging like faint rainbows crossing swords.

The houses seemed vacant in their unmoving sleep, but none of us knew whether or not midnight had passed. For a second it all reminded me of being a young child to whom the whole world is shambolic and alive. Each paving stone breathed and each tree's sway was intoxicated with life. I think it must have been about three in the morning by then, but the time did not really register. We went to rediscover the places we already knew so well. We could see the debris of a Friday night on the town; on the doorstep of each shop lay a vast spray of objects yet to be cleared up by the silent, shadowy night workers. Every burger box, drink carton, serviette and pamphlet was particular to the place from which it came. We walked along the empty street, looking at the objects left behind by the living. Each half-chewed chicken sandwich had a story to tell. Each puddle of blood was riddled with fear. These are the things that pass people by.

We were struck by the meaninglessness of cheap decorations, odd street signs and long, empty cul-de-sacs. We became offended by the inexpressive and overwhelmed by the subtly beautiful. It seemed wrong that the old Roman wall should be uncaringly glued to the red brick enclose of the old barracks. It seemed obscene that the glittering shop faces should be dulled by flaking paint jobs and moronic graffiti.

My strongest feeling, however, was for my own vulnerability. While I was, indeed, drunk with life once again, I also realised how easily it could be taken away. Yet I was scared of much more than the flimsy dripping scaffold that we passed under, or the ugly green river bridge rails that we refused to lean on, or even the high-speed vehicles circling the roundabout. Up until then I had failed to perceive with fear the dull upholstry, the lifeless backdrops to our society, but on that night I understood their potential for destructiveness just as I understood my own vulnerability. I was alarmed by the occasional passers-by; almost sinister in their bland, silent being. From time to time they would turn and stare at us, wondering what exactly was the matter. And I shivered whenever I reflected on the threatening phone messages that I had received.

The world seemed full of possibilities and infinite brilliance. Whenever I moved, the shapes from one object splashed fantastically into those of the next like prismatic clouds spitting into each other. We could smell, taste, touch, feel and hear the wonders of the world right before our eyes; unthinkable beauty in our very own street. But there was danger as well; the feckless and the dishevelled demons were creeping up on the fragile world.

Is this how life had really been for us before we grew up and old? Had we been blind for so long that our eyes were made to ache by the land's true vibrance?

We went back to the house, where the surroundings were far more organised than they had been previously.

It terrified all three of us when a fist came hammering down on the door. Kemi got up to open it but I knew already who it was. Harry walked in.

He had been struggling all night with a headache and had just embarked on a long, late walk when he saw us on the path to Kemi's. Harry was always too dull and cynical for me to write any great amount about, even in my hallucinations he seemed dark and difficult. I think that I must have been extremely aggressive and uncouth towards him, for he left the house very quickly. I remember him looking clearly unimpressed when we told him what we had been doing, but I have no idea what I might have said to so upset him. Whatever it was, Harry never spoke to me again.

Yet in Kemi the colours were thriving, revealing hidden ordeals and beautiful secrets. I remembered what I had first liked about Kemi; from his boundless curiosity to his unaffected lust for life. I was tempted to re-title him 'the explorer that stayed at home' but quickly thought better of it. The true depth of his soul had suddenly been unfurled, and an intoxicating sense of humour upreared itself again.

"Joey," he said, with a slight slur.

"Yes?"

"You know Agatha?"

"Yyyyyyesss. Of course."

"Agatha would have been alright if you gave her a head, body and personality transplant."

"That's harsh."

"Well, she was a dull bitch."

I started to chuckle, and that is exactly what the three of us spent the next hour doing; rolling over, crying out loud with laughter. At times I would ask myself how maniacal it would all sound to the neighbours; to a normal person, to a plebeian.

"Joey," came Kemi again, "I can imagine your sexual fantasy would involve erotically pouring tea over a bevy of naked supermodels, then asking them to play chess with you."

I was hysterical, aching at the sides in a way that felt new to me. My tonsils and vocal cords were shattered with laughter.

Then, wondrously, the three of us began to talk. By this I do not mean more lazy pointless prattle, but discourse so profound that we never wanted the night to end. We talked about religion and I actually felt that God was present - right there in Kemi's living room, of all places. I wondered whether the feeling was exclusively within me and at one point I quietly asked the big man to say something to me, but he was not listening. Kemi, for his part, occasionally said that he thought Marc was with us, but I did not share in this particular notion.

We went on to talk about how we feared the world could change under the new government. We discussed nanotechnology, clone armies and state-sponsored disease.

Kemi and I agreed that we should leave the country and seek sanctuary abroad. Both of us felt unsafe in our homeland, but Kemi in particular faced imminent danger. I promised to quit my job and move with him to Italy, an idea which would have seemed preposterous (to me at least) even a few hours before. We were both wilfully out of control that night, and in a way that I had not felt myself to be in a long time.

Our conversation knew no bounds: I told Baz and Kemi about Franz Kafka, then Herman Hesse, and they were both intrigued. Kemi showed us a book of visual illusions and we all toiled with Dallenbach's fragmentary cow and the Ames room illusion. Normally we would all routinely expel such stimuli.

Periodically, Kemi would baffle Baz and I with a dose of his deepest dumb philosophy: "Have you ever noticed the symmetry of human groups and races? Have you never noticed that?" At such instances, instead of simply dismissing him, we both tried our best to decode the man's nonsense as if it would reveal some deep, life-defining treasure. We must have wasted hours on this and I should have quickly ended this futile pursuit but for Baz's seemingly blinkered regard for the abstract.

The three of us listened to music and watched the sun come up in the purple morning. As the early hours slid by we considered the reality of the evening - that we felt as if we once more understood the all-encompassing life of the universe - the motion and function of everything that we took for granted. For the first time in many years, I had thought to look for the creaking cogs behind existence. As a result, I just wanted to lay open my soul and wash it in a blazing, Heaven-sent fountain of sunlight... I wanted to smoke my skin away and purge the mysteries underneath. For that, however, I would have to wait.

Most importantly though, as my mind began to steady, I found myself realising just how much Kemi meant to me as a friend, and how terribly I was going to miss him if he ever left us.

Chapter 7

The Brilliant Litter-Sweeper

With every corner that I took, the story would turn stranger and stranger.

It was not long after our surreal evening that I finally handed in my notice at the school. I decided that it was time to act on my intuition and make a bold move for once. I am still not sure what form of hallucinogen it was that I had taken that night, but its effect had been to open my mind to a few of the world's possibilities.

Oddly, I had begun to almost enjoy my job again and was certainly going to miss listening to the adolescents moan, bicker and fight. The school found a quick replacement for me, a belligerent and misanthropic idiot by the name of Iain Duncan of whom Jackboot could not speak without stammering out ridiculous plaudits. Whereas I would usually have had to wait until the end of the school year to leave, I was instead ushered out as quickly as possible. I was suspended for some minor breach of the school code, which allowed the disdainful Duncan to step in for me. I was quite reluctant to accept these terms of departure, because in those final days I had just started to rediscover my original reasons for becoming a teacher: I was interested once more in what made my pupils tick and wanted to thoroughly understand all of them, rather than just Aaron who - on my last afternoon - broke up quite publicly with Gemma. He failed to say goodbye to me, so I never had the chance to pry further into his personal affairs, but ascertained that the reason for the split had been Aaron's immoral fling with 'the older woman'. I was going to miss a lot of things about school - that is, until enough time passed by for me to forget all about it. Then again, there were a great many matters that would not be missed, such as teaching English to stupid people and trying to hold polite conversation with the unbearable Mr. Jackboot.

On the day that I finally negotiated an end to my contract I half-expected my friends to congratulate me on my escape; on discarding a diseased limb from my blistered past. That failed to transpire and I was a little disappointed that all I received was a pint glass of cheap white wine from Kemi.

My life was veering into a spell of swift transmutation. I had, remarkably, awoken my capacity for change; my ability to act on impulse. Baz moved into my house for a while - without invitation as far as I can recall - and justified his occupancy by making me cups of tea every morning, although they were usually too weak or too cold for me to consume. At one stage I panicked that he could be spiking my morning drink, because the after-effects of our hallucinogenic evening were lasting far longer than I had expected. For at least one whole week the lined paper of students' essays seemed to wave when I was marking. Of course, I never mentioned any of this to Baz and I am glad of that, in retrospect, because I actually enjoyed his company. I liked the fact that he erased the threatening answer-phone messages and deleted the forewarning e-mails (a more recent development). Plus I enjoyed coming home into the cannabis haze and trying to figure out what narcotic he was under the influence of this time. I would decipher this initially by methodically measuring the pace of his speech - was he prattling on speedily, or slurring lazily? Then there was the matter of his eyes - were they gaping wide like two cavernous black holes? Were the irises dulled and the whites wrinkled red with angry blood vessels? In addition to these clues there was the sweetness of the smoke in the air and the extent to which mellotrons or psychedelic organ solos featured in the music he was playing to himself. This could give away a lot.

Poor Kemi's situation seemed to worsen by the day. We never did move away to Italy - as had been suggested before - and he was presently facing daily hate mobs outside his front door, keen to make him pay for his long gone crime. Bricks were thrown through each of his windows, none of which were repaired, and the local police made it abundantly clear that they would not side against the mob. Baz believed that Kemi was not long for the world if he remained in town; the local lynch mob had placed him at the top of their hit-list and he felt that it was only a matter of time. Kemi, however, was suddenly quite determined to stay exactly where he was. He was not the type of man to be bullied.

Unfortunately for Kemi - and any other 'wanted man' - our land was turning ever more anaemic; its judicial heart had grown cold and bloodless. In these days, no suspected or former criminal could leave the country legally, yet he or she stood a strong chance of being attacked at any moment - and with no warning - if they stayed. Many a marked man, knowing that he faced an unpalatable end if he remained in the provinces, either plotted a brave escape or took the trip to London where he could at least face a dignified 'trial' and execution. Kemi was not yet in the mood for surrender and I supported him in this, for what it was worth, because I honestly expected the land's distasteful torrents of change to freeze and a normal state of affairs to resume. Besides, our retreat to the continent hardly seemed a viable option now.

Despite this, I was beginning to enjoy once more the minor details of menial existence and was finding new things each day to boost my enchantment. Although the British spring was barely upon us and the trees still naked, I felt as if I was back in the Mediterranean summer sun; immersed in a fragile happiness that I wanted to enjoy for as long as it chose to last. My former disillusion was presently as lifeless as Marc's rotting carcass, and the grave-worms had long since devoured anything else from the past that my conscience deemed distasteful. Like a reluctantly reformed addict I was quite sure that my misery would one day return, but at intervals I was also prone to fleeting fancies that I could look to the future, erase the inauspicious yesterdays, and begin building another 'New Joey'.

I clearly remember sitting in the park on a blustery March morning. The sky was still a dark seven o'clock grey and the only human noise was of the early dog walkers calling their Labradors and Alsatians over. I stayed in that park for a few hours, breaking briefly to buy a football magazine which was soon carried far away by the wind. I saw it dancing farther and farther off across the plain; a rider on the breeze. At one point, later in my meditations, I saw a litter-sweeper struggling with his brush on the park-side footpath. I tried to empathise with him and understand how important that job might have been to him. To this sweeper - I told myself - the road has to be the cleanest and barest street in the land. He wants to purge the place of litter, leaves, papers and wrappers; to clear away the mess and then look upon what he has achieved. He dexterously manoeuvres that broom - the weapon of his trade - and together they tangle with tricky kerbs and uneasy drains, pulling up sludge and rubbish that would otherwise congest the road forever. The litter keeps coming back at him but he is quicker and knows, all the way through, that he is good at what he does and that somebody in the world needs to do it.

It was at that precise moment - while under siege from my milder 'schizophrenia' - that I resolved to get up and find myself a job; something ignoble but unspectacularly useful, just like the brilliant litter-sweeper. On reflection, perhaps I could have chosen to be less servile to that changing and ever-more malevolent society of mine.

Later that day – having been employed as the Red Lion's newest part-time kitchen runaround - I decided to join the builders and the labourers for their after-work session in the pub. On the way I knocked on Kemi's door in an attempt to lure him back out into the open, but he refused and jabbed the door shut with uncustomary haste. It saddened me to see a fine man so unusually despondent, and I could no more than guess at the measure of his inner melancholy.

Once in the pub I propped myself up against the bar where I had spent many a younger year with the likes of Baz, Kemi, Marc and Harry. A burly builder to my right was trying to avoid conversation with a vest-clad, raw-boned tippler who was standing aside him and slurring vexatiously. The builder was in his fifties - a chain-smoking man-mountain with a plaster-coated green jumper on. The muzzy fool next to him was only a little younger, with a crooked blond moustache, a green truck-driving cap and a jumble of home-made tattoos scrawled across pale, thin biceps. I wondered, while I looked upon his tattered black tracksuit bottoms, what it might be like to go clothes shopping with the man.

"Yyyer shee shir," he slurred, almost indecipherably, "the problem ish... the probbbb-er-lem ish..." I almost forgot to listen as his mutterings stuttered and stumbled to a stop, but then - with no warning - they suddenly sprang out with such impossible haste that I could not make out one single word of what followed. I watched the builder carefully as his unwelcome companion dribbled on; the big man kept glancing uneasily towards me, sometimes smiling and rolling his eyes. He had not yet opened his mouth to me, which meant that I so far had no taste of his belligerent - but comical - nature (although I should have expected it from my previous experience of his kind). Sometimes he would answer the idiot with a few lines of his own, to which the fool would always reply by saying "Preshishely! Preshishely!" This was about as much as I could understand from the drunkard; he spoke in one long nonsense word and any crooked breeze-block of intent was mostly conveyed through the singularity of his slur's tone or volume. The individual segments of his speech had all melted into one another like tightly packed chocolates at above room temperature. The result was something shapeless and ugly.

Eventually the builder became bored of the drunkard and threatened to furnish him with a 'flat face'. After that he turned to address me, and for a short while I took some perverse delight in his detailed building jargon, although I understood very little of it. This man's language was formed around trestles, akrows, lump hammers, levels, pointers, spots, saws and barrows. Eventually, after telling me about the many dreary particulars of his trade, he asked me what I did for a living. I replied that I had until recently been a school teacher, only to grow tired of the profession and opt instead for good honest bar work. He did not seem very interested and decided that he would rather tell me a joke.

"What's that?" he asked me, pointing to the bar code on a cigarette packet.

"I don't know, what is it?"

"An Ethiopian family!" he cracked, in the loudest and most raucous voice that I think I have ever heard. I had to smile - not at the joke (which I had heard one hundred times before) - but at the terrific eruption of laughter that followed from the builder. After that we talked with some ease about various subjects - some serious and some not - always in simple and straightforward terms. In fact up to that point most of the multi-syllabic offerings (and malapropisms) had been from the builder:

"I'm not depravating your character," he promised me before embarking on a rant against teachers. He then told me that charging high prices for doing a proper job was a "paradox" in the building trade - "because nobody wants to pay for it." All of this was before he expounded the break-up of his marriage, describing how his wife - hearing untrue rumours of an affair - had ignored all of his "desperate implications and extrications" and left him.

I fancied that this builder was some kind of modern hero; like Robert or Gwyn, a free spirit unshackled by the bestial system and cosily enveloped in an artless nirvana. I liked this man, for a short time at least.

Regrettably, conversation soon sheered into darker matters - "I'm not too keen on these bloody wogs," he snarled at one point, before preferring to spout off about recent tabloid scare-mongering over child-killers and rapists. "I'm sick to death of seeing them every time I open the newspaper!"

"I don't read the papers," I told him.

"Then you must have seen it all on the news."

"I've probably watched the news five or six times in the last year, and even then I instantly ignore a lot of it. I used to watch the news and I used to worry about it, but these days I find that anything important comes to my attention soon enough. As far as our new government is concerned, I know a lot more about them and what they stand for than most people without even reading a single tabloid."

"How do you do that then?" asked the Builder.

"I listen to what people say about them."

"Well don't they read the papers?" he quizzed impatiently.

"Yes," I replied, "but I'm interested in what people think about the government, whether they read the papers or not."

"Hmm. You're talking like a bloody teacher now!" he laughed. "No. Personally I do like this new crowd up in Parliament. They're giving us normal people the chance to defend ourselves and punish these offenders properly. I think it's about time we're allowed to castirate" - (he meant castigate) - "these child killers and rapists us-selves, especially when they live on our own doorsteps."

"We've all committed our crimes though, haven't we?" I returned instantly, "surely you - or someone you know - is guilty of something that this new government would happily see you hang for?"

"No!" he bellowed back, his voice quickening and eyes widening a little in a faintly baleful manner, "I've never killed a child, or raped a woman, or mugged a granny, or sold drugs - have you? And what about these paediatricians, what do you reckon we should do with them?"

"Paedophiles, you mean?"

"Yes whatever. What kind of person has sex with a child?" he thundered, half addressing the barman and half addressing me, "Another pint mate" he added, to the former.

"I agree that they're sick people *if* they're having sex with eight or nine year-olds, but some of the sex offenders that people are targeting were young men when they committed their crime, and their victims weren't pre-pubescent either."

The builder gave me a confused look. "To be honest with you mate, these blokes are getting what they deserve. Did you see in the local paper? Round here there are loads; perverts, sex offenders, whatever you call them. The mob are going to go out and get the whole bloody lot of them and I don't blame them."

"You think it's okay to kill them because of something they did a long time ago and probably never repeated?"

"Of course I do. What you don't understand is that most of them do it again and again. They go round in all these duffle coats and sunglasses and berets, and they sit on swings and invite babies back home to play exotic games with them. Of course these people deserve to die!"

"Not all sex offenders are like that, though! There are people who've committed one sex offence with a minor and are going to get killed for it."

"They deserve to. Do you have kids?"

"No."

"Then you don't understand. Now I do have kids and if someone touched mine then I'd kill whoever done it myself. Well... saying that, my youngest is twenty-eight now, but you still know what I mean."

"I don't know!"

"Have you seen the two blokes who've been in the local paper the last few weeks? The two paedos?"

"No. I don't read the local paper. I don't read any papers."

"One of them went on the run but someone grassed him up and he got taken down to London. You know what'll happen to him there? He'll be executed..."

"-Yes," I interjected, "but the government much prefer to let ordinary local people do all the dirty work-"

"...The other lad - used to drink in here - can't leave his house. The mob have found him, they've done his windows in and, all being well, he'll be dead within a few days. And I hope the bastard rots in Hell with all the other bloody sex offenders - the whole lot should be extenuated in my opinion."

The Builder was talking about Kemi of course; it was not difficult to deduce. I felt furious for a few seconds and I could even feel my face burn a seething red. It was people like this builder who were responsible for what was happening to Kemi, and what was *going* to happen...

I turned to my right and, with an immediate shiver, realised that one of the men standing behind the Builder was none other than Kemi himself. Before I had the chance to admire his bravery for being here, or worry about what he must have heard my new friend declare I realised that he was looking at me and grinning unshakably. I blinked, looked up at him again and, yes, he was still beaming away. Then he gave me a speedy wave and left the bar without uttering a single word.

"Do you want a drink?" the Builder asked, dumping a pint on my beer mat before I could either answer him or run after Kemi. With a spurt of discomfort leaping up from my stomach, I politely accepted the gift.

After a couple more hours I went back outside for the last light hour of the day. I went out to the edge of the town and stood at the top of a short hill, overlooking the jagged patchwork countryside and untidy woodland. Sundown strode away with brilliant bronze footsteps, and as it went it stripped away the glow from row after row of the oak trees below me. Then, everything was gone, and the land left entirely grey.

That night I spent a while on the phone to Kemi, talking of nothing more than football. Afterwards I turned out the light and passed upstairs with my bedtime reading. The house was soundless because Baz was out at a party. Within a few minutes my eyes were shut and my head nestled in the pillow.

Chapter 8

Regression

That same night, while reclining into sleep and before beginning the routine shamble through my dreams, I felt a sense of comfort unlike anything that had befallen me for several years. It was a pure and contented moment that, within twenty-four hours, I would yearn to revisit. And yet, as with my return from Europe, I was soon to find that such hastily constructed rejuvenation could be quickly razed.

It was as I descended into sleep that the voices started up: First they came from somewhere beneath the bedside table drape and then, anonymously, from below my calendar. Lights were out so I quested frantically for the matches, only to empty my glass of water over the box and my tallow candle as I fumbled in the dark. I was not scared at first; not until I remembered that Baz was away that night and I was alone in the house.

My pupils outstretched as I gazed into the terrible blackness before me. Outside the window a dormant streetlight convulsed back into its usual pumpkin orange and I could see all about the room. I peered up at the unevenly plastered ceiling which seemed to slope down towards the far wall into which, two thirds down, the uncurtained window frame was cut. I looked at the wall to the left and then at the wall to the right, onto which a quivering dance of expiring light from the landing opposite had recently played. Then I looked down, past the bookcase and - sensing that there was something unwelcome soon to meet my eyes - across to the middle of the bedroom floor... and there they lay.

It was almost with relief that I laid sight on the creatures, because I knew quite instantly that it was fictional and that I must be dreaming. The two demons were wound about each other, each about three feet long, angular and bent-backed like spineless human bodies with coarse, deep brown skin. The eyes of one were a quarter open, offering only a glimpse of the whites, while both animals were purring and twitching as if each was resounding the other.

I was struck with panic; unsure whether to tackle the beasts or beat a rapid retreat out of the room. I opted instead for a diplomatic approach - of bargaining with the fiends and persuading them politely to exit. At this stage I had already decided that I was definitely asleep because, had this been reality, I would most certainly have hidden beneath the sheets in an attempt to forget that the beasts existed.

"A-hm, excuse-me," I said, in a whisper which began as a teacher's command for attention.

I was sure that this was not enough to wake the demons and, for that moment, felt fairly glad of it. Then, suddenly, "Joey..." snarled the second beast, whose face I could not see. "We're awake. We've not come here to sleep." The words were hushed so quietly that I could barely decipher them.

"What have you come here for?"

The eyelids of the first and closer creature opened, unmasking two wholly dove-white eyes. "We've come to stay, Joey, we've come here to watch you."

At the exact moment of that phantom foreboding my eyes shot open, my body jerked up and I rolled swiftly away from the circle of sweat on the sheet beneath. I turned on the light and the floor, mercifully, was clear of demonic beings. However, there was no chance of me going back to sleep that night, so I walked downstairs and uncorked a bottle of cheap white wine from a rack which Agatha had stocked.

I opened the front door and felt much safer sitting on my doorstep, sipping from a half litre glass of wine. It was a little cold, but at least I knew that I could easily get away should any devilish entity emerge from the lounge behind me. After finishing my wine I darted upstairs for some clothes and left the house, vowing not to return before sunrise.

I passed aimlessly through the streets; I monitored the grains of the concrete paving slabs as they passed below me, following their cracks, their sudden dips and their curiously differing shades of grey. I pondered over the meaning of my latest nightmare, and how the euphoria of the day before already seemed like a distant shadow in my past. These thoughts were volleyed from wall to wall, through channel and chamber of my brain as I walked alone in the dark. I looked up to see an old woman who must have heard my footsteps switch on her sulphurous yellow bedroom light and peer warily down at me. She cut a solemn figure in that window frame. Poor old dear, I thought. The only noises left to fill her empty nights are the occasional taps of anonymous footsteps outside. The one single highlight of her pointless day - apart from the first game of Patience - is her lethargic hobble over the road to randomly accost busy construction workers. Perhaps one of them finds the time to slip down off the scaffold and talk to her for one precious minute. Maybe she saves her finest cream bun for her favourite young labourer, and then savours his gratitude as far into the remaining day as her brain can recall it.

I was just approaching Kemi's road when I felt the first freezing cold hailstone rap unkindly on the back of my neck. A few more followed in quick succession before an arctic flurry burst from the sky. I fled towards my friend's house, in shock at this sudden downpour, but by the time I reached his porch hail pellets were melting down my neck and shooting through my frosty veins.

"Joey?" he called, from somewhere.

"Kemi," I answered, pushing open his front door and making my way inside.

Kemi, it became clear, had not managed to sleep either that night and was watching the weather with his favourite dark rum. It was before I had even managed to take my coat off that he said, without warning, that he had decided to travel down to London the next day.

"Why in Heaven are you going to do that?" I asked; genuinely astonished.

"Apparently..." he began, before pausing to strip the wrapper from a new cigarette packet and unload a smoke. I noticed that the 'lucky fag' ritual which he usually followed (by flicking the bottom of the packet and saving the cigarette that shot out the furthest until last) was absent this evening. "...Apparently the mob are coming for me tomorrow. That's the day they've set. They're going to kill me if I stay here."

I had no idea what to say. I knew very well what he meant and could do nothing more than stare at the putrid yellow composite carpet, speckled as it was with shards of wrathful glass from the broken windows. I felt abysmal.

"They're going to kill you if you go to London, Kemi. Why don't you go on the run? At least try to escape into the countryside."

"They'll find me wherever I go. You know that - it's inevitable - there are mobs in every town, city and village. Any newcomer is immediately monitored and even if I go into hiding they'll find me, then they'll torture me. In London I'll at least give the government the inconvenience of having to execute me themselves."

"There is that, I suppose. But, Kemi, if you're that sure that they'll find you anywhere else in the country, who's to say they'll let you get as far as London?"

"I don't know."

"It's a gamble."

"I know."

"And there's not much of a reward at the end of it, is there?"

"I might manage to stay undercover for a few months in London, who knows? And I can keep my dignity when it does end."

We both became silent. I could not believe that it had come to this. Kemi handed over the rum and then switched on the television. The adverts were on; first up there was a military tank to advertise toilet roll, trailed by a magpie to advertise insurers and a stampeding water buffalo to promote sanitary towels. After that there was a follow-on from the first advert and, as a serial hater of repetition, Kemi turned the television off again. "We could have gone on the Internet, had a look at dodgy midget porn or something, but they've cut off my connection," he said.

There was more silence. This time I laid my eyes on Kemi's

fruit bowl; a dish-shaped web with myriad wicker junctions. Any distraction from the difficult stillness would suffice. I handed back the rum and instead picked up a can of expensive lager. "May I?"

"Of course, it's all got to go!"

After a short while Kemi broke the silence with a peculiar rant about how having his windows smashed had made him aware of how the glass panes had acted like mirrors on the inside, even by day. "Do you think they were designed that way to keep us indoors, you know, by hiding all the brilliant things on the outside from us?" I considered this to be an exceptionally strange line of questioning and, sensing a diversion into one of Kemi's awful 'dumb philosophy' cul-de-sacs, I darted into the kitchen to make us some tea. However, that crazy line served to propel us into conversation, after which we spent the rest of the night talking without stint. I forgot about the hailstorm outside and the fact that this would probably be our last night together. We simply sat down, as two best friends, and talked.

Kemi told me that he had been thinking about old Robert from Corfu and how he was probably still zipping from one place to the next, waiting until the summer when he could sleep out on the beaches again. "I bet he's drunk and happy right now," he said.

"I bet he's asleep or dead," I returned dryly. Kemi replied with nothing more than a dismayed glare.

We discussed and debated through the dark hours until about seven o'clock when the sky was bright and cold and we were both inebriated. We reminisced about our time at university and about happy days at the Red Lion with Baz, Marc and stupid Agatha. We talked at length about our last summer's excursion with Harry. It was raining fitfully outside but Kemi said I should go home for my own safety. I refused and instead borrowed a sleeping bag from him. He slept on the sofa and I on the floor, looking up at the ceiling and out to the awakening world; all to the backing-track of Kemi's unhealthy snore. I heard the friendly tumult of neighbours packing children off to school, and I could feel the time of our parting grow wretchedly closer. As the sun flared into the room, soaring up above the semi-detached houses opposite, I could see the signal for my friend's departure and told myself, sadly, that each of his snores might be the last that I would ever hear. I knew for certain that before the sun sank back down that day, Kemi would be gone forever and yet, I thought to myself, the serene morning both looked and sounded like any other.

Eventually, long before any mob had found the time to gather outside, Kemi rolled off the sofa (and, at first, onto me) before preparing for his final adventure. He grabbed a green t-shirt and some baggy, torn jeans. We hardly exchanged either word or glance that morning, instead preferring to set robotically about rummaging through belongings and packing bags. Finally, and a long time after Kemi had originally intended, my friend was ready to leave. Wearing an old man's flat cap - which only he could know the cause for his possessing - and blue-tinted sunglasses, he slipped out of the door with me in tow.

Most of our walk to the bus stop took place in silence, but every so often Kemi would search my patchy memory for some random happy event that we had once shared. At one point it was in a sweaty, hectic festival crowd, then it was on the empty streets after the pubs had cleared, with the two of us clasping bottles and bustling untidily beneath an inky blue-black sky.

Finally, it was the time to part, and I was already feeling distraught. The bus was already late and a small crowd had gathered to wait. Kemi, with a green baseball cap pulled down low to darken those infamous eyes, dropped his possessions at his feet and looked up at me. I leaned into him, "Don't go. Don't go," I begged, with a desperate and senselessly tearful whisper. "I don't want to lose you."

For a few moments Kemi was unmoved - almost stoic - but then he clutched my jaw in his right hand and I could suddenly see how wretchedly upset he was. "Don't worry about me," he said, "I'll turn up again." I looked straight through him and we both understood that he was lying. "You'll think I'm dead and then, in twenty-six years time, you'll be in a casino with your third wife and I'll shuffle in wearing a buffalo-skin coat and a beret."

We hugged each other. Kemi's oft-suppressed

sentimentality was now laid bare; singing deathlessly through his routine, dauntless exterior.

"This is all getting rather homosexual, isn't it?" I remarked, trying to be upbeat but still choking out my words as if three slices of half-chewed bread were plugging my throat. At that point I heard the bus's distant rattle straining up the hillside, swinging round a tight bend then, lastly, rolling down the hill in and out of the obstinate potholes that prickled the road surface. I longed to be joining him for the journey but, sadly, this could not happen.

"Joey," said Kemi, "look at me."

I was looking at him anyway. "Yes?"

"You know who I am... you've known me longer than anybody."

"Of course, yes, of course."

"Joey..." Kemi was struggling with a matter of grave importance. He had forgotten about the bus, which had now stopped and flung its doors open outwards. "It was you... it was you wasn't it?"

"I don't know what you mean," I replied, suddenly the more composed - and certainly the most confused - of the two of us.

"I've known you for longer than you've known me, Joey. Don't you remember me? From before?"

"I don't know what you mean," I repeated, but this time I was lying. For just one solitary second in time I understood precisely what Kemi was talking about and, despite my shock, I could remember exactly what he was referring to. "Why are you bringing this up now?"

The bus driver called out for any last passengers. Breaking instantly from our curious farewell, Kemi picked up his belongings and prepared to turn away.

"See you Jack," he said, with a wry and knowing smile. 'Jack... Jack...' it was a name that I had answered to a long time ago, but never since. Somehow, I realised, the true reason behind almost everything that was happening to me was in that name and what came with it. For those few terminal moments - as Kemi passed finally from my life - it made sense... then suddenly, inevitably, the clarity lost itself and I was confused once again. The last I saw of Kemi was him disappearing into the bus, and by the time he was gone I had already forgotten what it was, of such importance, that he had said during our strange unhappy parting.

Our friendship - occasionally enchanting and always immutable - was gone.

The bus bobbled away across the uneven road and off to my right; its bumpy passage beclouded by my weeping eyes. There must have been eighty other passengers on the bus - with a story to tell for each one's journey - but to me it felt as if Kemi alone was on board as the vehicle moved away. Nobody else mattered.

I walked to my house alone, missing my friend more with every stride. I was only ten metres from my door when I spotted a man in a suede jacket, notepad in hand, pounding at my front door. Baz had obviously not yet returned.

"Can I help?" I asked curtly.

"Mr. Carlton is it?" he said, in a fast, high and ugly voice. It was not familiar to me, it possibly should have been.

"Who are you?"

"I'm from the Press Agency. We're planning to run a story on you."

"Well I'm not going to talk to you about me. And you can go now." I was angry at this rude intrusion into my mourning and tried to put my key to the door. The unpleasant hack, eager for the early kill, blocked my arm and inadvertently dropped his pad in the same movement. "Is there anything else?" I demanded, forgetting to keep my voice down.

The newspaper man tried to clear his throat but I gave him no time to answer my question. "I've got better things to do than talk to scabby little reptiles like you. Do I make myself clear? Get back to the zoo before they realise you're missing," I seethed.

"Yes okay, I heard. Maybe you'd like to talk about your paedophile friend then."

I could feel my torso boiling and my mind beginning to bulge with rage. "What?"

81

"Your friend the child molester. If you aren't going to answer questions about yourself, maybe we can start by talking about him. Besides, we've got plenty on you already."

"Who are you working for?" I stormed, barging the fool out of my way and unlocking the door. Then I stood in the entrance to my house, glaring savagely back at my vile customer.

"Your friend is going to die for his crimes, Mr. Carlton. Do you think that's fair?"

"Of course I don't think that's fair you horrid little imbecile, he's my friend - you said that yourself. Now get off my property before I set my bulldog on you."

"You haven't got a dog. You see, Mr. Carlton. we know more about you than you know about yourself."

"Then you'll appreciate that it's in your best interest to go away now before I put a blade through your bastard neck!"

"I'll take that down," he grinned, reaching to pick up his pad.

"You *can* take that down. And you can add that Mr. Carlton lodged his fist inside your throat, dragged you indoors by the tonsils and trampled you to death. Go on! Put that down you slimy little weasel!"

"Listen, Carlton," replied the hack, recoiling slightly with shock, "I have a story to write about you and your pervy mate. Now if you don't want to tell your side of the tale then I'll let the facts speak for themselves. We can negotiate over this."

"Negotiate? You can take your grubby story and shove it up your anus for nothing. And when they pull it out they'll have to remove the pickaxe I put there too."

"What?"

"Listen," I ranted, now entirely out of control, "if I ever see you again - after what you rancid bandwagon-jumpers did to my friend - then I swear that I will MURDER you. I will rip your throat out with my own teeth. I will cut off your genitals and mail them to your primitive, inbred little family. I am serious about this. Now GO!"

To my immense surprise the odious little creature turned and fled without further warning. I had managed to be far more menacing than I could ever have imagined myself being. He had actually been scared by me… but why? I turned into the house, shut the door and then delayed a moment to arrest my pulse. I think that I may well have delivered on my threats had he remained in my sights for any longer.

For truly forty-five minutes I stood in the kitchen, staring back at my face in the mirror and wondering how the sallow countenance before me could have produced such terrible words. I looked deeply into my face; at the lines around my eyes and the irremovable pits across my forehead. I was growing older every day and forever sliding further down the inescapable funnel into seniority. I could not, it seemed, revisit the days when my eyebrows never needed separating and my flaking cheeks never needed creaming. My eye-whites were tinted yellow, my neck was creased unevenly- and this only started to depict my inner decline. Not so long before I had been beginning my life again, but now it felt as if there were few places left to go.

I was lonely, scared, uncertain and purposeless. After a long, still silence I decided to go back outside.

Nothing much happened on that walk. I felt as if my life was hopeless and that it was time for me to deliver its inevitable, imminent end. I wanted to die.

I had taken a lot of my money out with me in the hope that I could find myself a pitiful beggar worth giving it to; I thought that I might have a better chance of going to Heaven if I committed one final, minor act of generosity. I was praying that Saint Peter would gaze down and consider this final slice of goodwill to be a foretaste of what I intended to do with the rest of my life, before impulsive suicide stepped into my path.

In fact, charity was something that I should have given more towards, and I knew it. I justified this by pretending that my taxes were a form of charity and that I was therefore already going beyond my duties. I did not like the idea of funding some worthy cause advertised on the television or the Internet. I preferred the idea of giving my money to a useless vagabond in the street, even if they were going to spend it all on cocaine, heroin or methadone. I would rather see the reaction of some hopeless beneficiary than imagine the delight of some desperate

African orphan, who would probably starve to death anyway; I wanted to be gratified by the knowledge that Joey Carlton could effect such happiness in a useless dropout. This feeling of empowerment was more important than the sense of being pleased to give the needy a fillip. Naturally, I was glad to do that as well - only not so much.

I decided that this was probably how most Christians operated anyway.

Unfortunately I never found the Lucky Stray and eventually returned back to the house. Baz was not home and I sat for a while devising a suitable suicide note in my mind. It became steadily more obvious that I lacked the backbone to kill myself, but nonetheless I fancied the idea of Baz opening the door and seeing my lonesome legs swaying through the empty middle space of the back room. I guessed at what it might feel like to look outside and then draw the curtains finally on those familiar sights forever. And I liked the idea of a hundred distraught mourners in the crematorium.

Sadly, few people would have been moved by my death. I abandoned that notion and stumbled instead on another - far more desperate - plan. After a brief fumble through my half-empty address book, I began to dial Gwyn's mobile phone number.

Chapter 9

The Whiplash Woman And I

Gwyn's phone was turned off, so, after briefly returning to the idea of suicide, I decided that I must leave the house once again to meet her. I remembered the address of the so-called 'Whiplash Women' but decided that I should settle my uneasy stomach with a few glasses of port beforehand.

My stomach was stilled but my head swaying by the time I began my walk. Over a year had passed since the last time I had trodden this path on a mission for sexual relief. So much had changed since then, and this time I was in search of something very different. It had also been a year since I had felt Agatha's cool sweat under humid bed-sheets, or caressed the undulating thin ripples of skin above her bony waistline. Still, I missed none of it and was certainly not lusting after a woman's warm blood.

My journey to the Whiplash Women was, this time, all about survival. I had initially perceived Gwyn as a dirty old whore, but after that uneasy election night I had come to respect her free spirit and liberal conscience. Now I hoped that she may, somehow, be able to help me. It had occurred to me that if there were a few more political 'prostitutes' like Gwyn in the world, then perhaps these terrible changes would never have seized our land.

Night's boundless blackness had already cloaked the street's brickwork patterns by the time I began my walk. I wandered through each silent lane, from home to the flat where I hoped to find Gwyn. Gaunt and gangly concrete blocks shadowed my walk as I passed through the town alone. The sky's stars were all put out, neither distant sun nor moon offered me a light. Factory chimneys pricked the earth and dim orange streetlights leaned menacingly over the pavement below. Ugly factories flanked the first part of my journey and evil black-shadowed houses lined the second. I thought for a few moments of the pains to have unfurled behind those doors; stories of hopelessness, hatefulness, discontent and demise. To one side the street was flushed with a greater, hollow darkness where the wall of houses dipped away and was replaced by vacant park-land choked with giant, tremulous yew trees. I looked deeper and saw a few shuddering leafless willows and a skeletal orchard. As I approached my destination there were push-bikes slumped on walls and children huddled upon doorsteps; shambling drunkards under sinister arch-ways and bellowing adolescents on splintering benches. Yet none of it actually felt real - and I wondered whether every child and every stone and every house and every man might just disappear if I put it to touch.

Finally I arrived and, mercifully, the lights were on. Gwyn opened the door and faced me with the very same all-enduring smile that I remembered from before.

"You know Joey," she said immediately, miraculously remembering my name, "I was sure I was going to see you again one day. Come on love, sit down. You've come for a chat haven't you?" I felt comfortably mothered at once, and thought again that Gwyn was certainly no conventional prostitute.

As before, there were a few forty-something Whiplash Women sitting in the lounge but not one grubby old pervert with horn-rimmed spectacles, moustache or trench coat. I never did ask the exact nature of Gwyn's illicit occupation, and she never chose to tell me. I found the lady far too attractive to befoul her name with labels like 'tart' or 'slut'.

Over the next hour - to the nameless muffled soundtrack of sex nearby - I explained everything to her; about Kemi, the dreams and the horrible local hack. She was confused by this and failed to understand how, precisely, I had come to be in so much trouble. "You must have done something to be getting threats like that," she insisted unsympathetically.

"I honestly don't know what I've done wrong," I rejoined.

Eventually, remarkably, Gwyn offered me a viable solution. "Tomorrow," she told me, "I am taking the bus to London. My sister owns a flat there and she's just moved up north. She's trying to rent it out, but if you want to stay there and if you can pay me the money, then I'll take it out in my name and you can stay there until you run out of cash."

I nodded eagerly. The idea of upping and moving on was definitely radical, but I gave myself no time to weigh up my few remaining options. I gave myself no choice in the matter.

"There's a few conditions, though," she continued, "for a start, I am going to be spending a lot of time in that house so I don't want anybody to know that you are there as well. If anybody finds out, then I'm in bother, aren't I? You've got to lie low. If you leave the house, then you do it by night or else you go dressed-up and disguised. You get me?"

"Yes."

"Right then, Joey, finish your cup of tea and your biscuit and get back home. Tomorrow morning meet me in the park. Nobody's to see you leave here tonight, okay? And I think we'd better get you a shave and a hair-cut when we get down to London. Okay?"

"Yes."

"Tomorrow at... let's say eleven o'clock. Yes?"

"Yes."

"And perhaps we'd be better off not taking too much stuff. Do you think you can manage with just a rucksack?"

"Yes. Probably."

I could not understand why Gwyn, who had only ever met me once before - over a year ago - would want to risk her own safety to look after me. She should really have shown more surprise in my choice to nominate her as my saviour. On reflection, it was almost as if she had been expecting me. In fact I could well have been suspicious of these efforts but I was so mesmerised by her lexicon of assurance that I never thought twice. Besides, I was desperate for help and somehow I had known that only Gwyn could offer it. She was perfect company for my escape - attractive, independent, dominant and deceptively sharp. Anyway, who else was there in the world? Kemi was gone; Harry hated me, Agatha was impossible, Marc was dead and Baz was seldom sober enough to be useful.

I returned home at about ten o'clock and Baz was back. He told me that he had heard, from a friend, that there was going to be a story on me in the local newspaper tomorrow. He had come home early to see if I had heard and, if so, how I had received the news. I felt honoured by his concern.

"I've heard what they're going to say about you," he told me. "I don't care whether it's true or not, Joey. I don't care."

I know that Baz wanted me to explain to him exactly what I had done, although he never asked directly. What he failed to understand, though, was that I simply could not tell him. I was confused about everything that was happening to me. Joey Carlton had never harmed a living creature.

"Are you going to leave town?" Baz enquired.

I was wary of giving away too much information and settled for telling him that I was taking a long holiday on the east coast.

"Are you going to miss me?" he asked with a grin.

"Oh no!" I exclaimed, "humans spend so much time with good company that they forget the value of silence. Only when we're forced into solitude do we accept that nobody else in the world is worth talking to."

Baz replied with a bemused glare, "Where did you hear that?"

"I don't know," I answered, feeling reasonably pleased with myself.

I agreed for Baz to remain in my house until he was offered some other place in which to diffuse his bottomless supply of drugs and pornographic magazines. Before I went to bed that night we shook hands with a cool formality.

I slept badly, troubled again by vicious illusions.

I found myself wrapped tightly in a narrow black pall, and shaken as I was carried along some anonymous rocky path. Finally I was laid down and the sightless journey was over. Then I rose, opened my eyes and looked all about me. I found myself sitting upright in a coffin and glancing about a crematorium chapel. I shuddered with deja-vu and climbed out.

There were only three mourners and none of them had seen me stride from the casket. It was as if I was invisible.

One of those people was Baz who was lighting a huge,

carrot-shaped reefer which he had assembled on the hymn-book. The next was Agatha, weeping falsely and shrouded ridiculously in undue black garments, milking every theatrical moment for what it was worth to her.

The third was a young boy - and harder to recognise - so I advanced closer.

The child was veiled in still black shadows, with his head hanging limply so that the chin was nuzzled into the chest of a burgundy red t-shirt. I kneeled down so I could look up at his face, then arched my neck, slowly, forward.

I recoiled in sudden horror. The child was all of three or four years old, and a dead smile hung on the lips of its pallid face. Fine gory locks laced the boy's bloody, mangled temple and lay tangled among jutted skull fragments in the shattered left eye socket. The nose was crushed but the cheeks were still dressed with a strange heavenly innocence. An ear was missing, but one bloodshot eye was intact and gave its deathly gaze to the stone floor below.

I fell back on my kneeling left leg and felt the sudden strain on my ligaments. As I lay flat on the crematorium floor the boy's wounded face moved slightly and his shattered bones moaned at the motion. His one lifeless eye and his one smashed socket gaped straight towards me. His mouth moved. He spoke something, although I cannot remember what, and the unsteady neck fell limp again.

I turned back towards the coffin. Without properly taking to my feet I ran, ran and ran towards the curtained inferno that lay beyond my casket. I felt the heat blast cruelly against my face, then my eyes bulged open and I escaped the nightmare.

Chapter 10

London

There was no option but to go away. I was fearful and miserable after Kemi's disappearance. My life was in imminent danger for as long as I stayed in town. Gwyn had offered me an instant getaway and there was no choice but to accept gratefully.

In our new 'society', as soon as a marked man left his hometown a portrait would be bandied about every police station and local newspaper in the country. If he fled to an obscure hideaway then he would be rapidly traced. Marked men went to London because they could at least hope for a trial and a dignified execution when they were caught. It was only in the capital that the judicial system bothered to deal with their 'outlaws'. Anywhere else - even in the cities - they would face persecution, torture and primitive annihilation.

I felt certain that Kemi had made it to London and hastily found himself a temporary abode. His landlord was probably a regular police informant and would inevitably be suspicious of him from the beginning. It would take a few weeks - maybe a few months - but eventually Kemi would be tracked down and terminated. Of that there was little doubt. The reality, for once, was unavoidable.

Ultimately, my fate would be a similar one. My story would hit the local newspaper, the mob would descend on my house and, when they discovered that I had left, my photograph would be distributed all across the country. I would probably survive undercover in London for a while; possibly longer than most with the added advantage of having Gwyn to take care of my public obligations. Eventually, however, there could be no escape from the law unless - as I prayed - our right-wing government suffered a sudden demise.

For me, I was sure that the end was near but felt - somehow - that it was going to herald a strange and wonderful beginning.

Gwyn dressed me in a blue woolly hat and - despite the endlessly grey sky - thick mirrored sunglasses for the journey to my new home.

The bus journey to London was a torturous one. The best that I could wish most of the passengers was an early death. The driver was a peevish, belligerent imbecile who shouted at everything before and behind him on the road. His face was permanently purple with rage, his eyes green and listless. I gave myself reasonable odds on him dying before the journey was through.

At the back of the bus there was a vocal young man who could well have been a comic genius of the Blackpool Pier variety. At one stage an obese young woman was standing at the front of the bus, waiting to dismount when it came to a stop. "Eh up!" shouted the young fool, "take a tight bend with 'er standing to one side and the bus'll tip over!" I had to listen to all of the classic one liners from that loud-mouth, especially whenever anyone was about to alight from the bus.

Then there was a lovey-dovey couple sitting just behind the driver, dribbling shallow vows of devotion over each other. I would prefer Agatha's cold indifference to such sugary falsehoods.

Later in the journey I overheard a toe-stitcher and a spastic trying to hold a conversation just in front of me. It took me ten minutes to ascertain which of them had the higher IQ. They both seemed to be on the same level. By this stage my final shards of faith in the human race were falling away.

My favourite two characters on the bus were a couple of old men who spent half of the trip sleeping and the other half making some of the most insignificant observations ever to be iterated, all in brief predictable bursts:

"Do you have one of those mobile phones, Cyril?"

"Nah. Can't stand the bloody things."

"No me neither. All the kids have 'em though, don't they?"

"Ay. They only use 'em to say pointless things though. They'll phone someone up on the train and say 'Hello, it's me. I'm on the train.' What kind of bloody fool wants to know that you're on the train?!"

"Yes you're right Cyril, you're right... What about the Internet? Are you on the Internet?"

"Nah. I'm not into all of that."

"Neither am I. My granddaughter Tammy's on it all the time, mind. Can't get her away from it."

"Yeah well, there's no need for it. Kids'll spend all day long staring at their computer screens trying to make a friend off one of these web chat doo-dahs. Haven't you thought that if you didn't spend so much bloody time on the Internet you might meet some real-life people?!"

"Yes you're right Cyril, you are right..."

Through all of this Gwyn sat in the seat ahead and to the left of me. Occasionally she would turn around to check that I was well, but for the most part we had little to say to one another. Whereas I could normally have spoken to a relative stranger about their occupation there was no such option with Gwyn. In that respect, I considered it rather impolite of her to be a whore.

It seemed like a thousand years before Gwyn and I got to the second floor flat. At one point we got lost and Gwyn stood in the road, trying to find her way. I patiently beheld her imperfect grace, set against the ragged and black street.

The flat was in a run-down area on the north-east of London which I initially - and incorrectly - thought to be Stratford. I had only been to London once before (I could not remember when) and had few clues about the geography of the place. I was keen to try out the underground, but Gwyn said that it was a bad idea.

The city appeared to be a colourless, rotting sprawl of ugly tower blocks and flaking paint-work. The odour of industry hung in the air and mingled with a melee of chemical mists. Hunched, leather-coated muggers of all creeds and colours marked every shadowy recess. Vehicles bustled past with merciless permanence. Beggars lounged on ash and litter cushions in the doorways of dead-faced shops. There were primal hoots from bunched ragamuffins as we paced through the myriad streets.

Opposite the flat was a stack of high rise buildings, each as grey as a stripped tin can and peppered with flaccid washing lines. Sad faced women peered through windows and, below, angry tattooed young men came charging out of cars. Through our side window a dusty needlework labyrinth of traffic-blocked roadways could be seen, winding hopelessly like a maze of clogged arteries. Closer to the flat was a chunk of terraced houses, each with a thin strip of garden into which I could easily have spied had they been less overgrown with weeds, brambles and stooping trees.

It was a chaotic, soulless jumble of lost purpose, yet I never asked myself why it was that I had made the trip.

I had not even found the time to look around the flat when Gwyn said to me, "I know you're not going to tell me what you did. You probably don't even know yourself." I nodded. "But I'll definitely find out someday soon and I don't want you to worry about me turning on you. Whatever it is you've done, it's for God to judge you and not people like me." I found this possibility far more concerning than the primitive hate mobs back at home. This was because I well remembered the 'drug night' at Kemi's house; how I had sensed spiritual realisation to be so tangible and close... how I had reached out, called out and found no reply from the God I was looking for. I was scared of what he had to say to me.

The flat was very sparsely dressed with threadbare brown carpets or cracked cream tiles vying for floor space. There were two wooden chairs with grubby cushions slouched back into them and a battered, blackened gas heater. The kitchen had a few cupboards packed with inedible pasta and, cryptically stored in the oven, a disused and probably dangerous white microwave. In the lounge there was a soggy red bean-bag and a stylish old rickenbacker guitar, propped against an incongruous lime green wood-chip wall. I picked it up.

"Can you play?" Gwyn asked me.

"No," I told her, but, sitting down on the floor with the guitar on my lap, soon found myself picking out a few chords as if I had taught myself to play in a subconscious moment. I played Gwyn a few segments of some old songs, all of which contained the same four chords (which I now understand to have been A minor, G, D and C). She said that they were bad songs but that she liked the way I played them. I received this as either a great compliment or - more likely - an unconvincing fib.

For ten days I did not leave the house. Gwyn mastered my disguise with a haircut, a little chestnut-brown dye, some full-mooned lensless spectacles and a clean shave. I had grown a beard about two years before when my efforts at 'designer stubble' had got out of control and it felt strange to see the pallid skin of my cheeks again, just as it felt unusual to see my ears freed from locks of unkempt, straw-like hair. I could not recall having had my hair shorn so short before and I had never worn glasses, so it seemed unlikely that anybody would recognise me from an old photograph.

By the eleventh day I was already sick with the thick morning air of fresh tarmacadam and exhaust fumes. I was half-weary of watching my own lonely shadow tacked to opposite walls and could not see the point of my new disguise when I was never out of the house.

Gwyn, my sole companion, was usually absent on nameless endeavours. Yet there were times - like when she smiled across the low table at breakfast - that I truly wanted her and, occasionally, I would thrill at the thought of coming close to her; of being touched by her, of being loved by her, of absorbing her shadow into mine. Seeing her before she left the flat in the morning, and after she returned late at night soon became the two brief highlights of my day. The rest of the time I slept, with my alarm poised either for "Good morning" or "Good night". Without the presence of friends, enemies, colleagues or pupils to dilute Gwyn's effect on me, she quickly became a pathetic obsession.

On the eleventh day, though, I missed breakfast and was so maddened by my own inattention that I decided to leave the house and test my new face on the streets.

No matter how many times I repeated short whispers of reassurance to myself I still felt insecure. My eyes were immediately screwed up by the bright spring sky, which dazzled me from all angles like an inverted ocean of magnesium light. My jacket kept blowing open untidily, my lip-skin was cracking and my hands were colder than they should have been. It was sufficient to make me believe that I was ungainly enough for people to stare cynically in my direction. I never once looked up at the sun-struck, greening trees, but instead chose to stare down at the dog faeces and fractured sidewalk slabs.

After summoning a little courage I stepped into a Chemist to buy a pair of cheap dark sunglasses for my sunlight problem. I made a quick decision on a pair, without daring to remove my specs to try them on, then went up to the counter - with the correct change in hand - and paid the owl-eyed lady in blue uniform behind the till. I stared ahead while I waited for the receipt, trying to look nonchalant as I chewed on a bitten-off nail-piece, but just then came a jab and I was stabbed in the back with a bony forefinger.

I had been recognised by somebody, but the store-lights were too bright for me to recognise in return. Then the hand gripped my jacket, and I was pulled out of the shop.

Once outside I shakily put on my new glasses and dropped the old ones to the ground in the same movement.

"Joey," said Baz, letting me go and looking as if he was unsure whether to laugh or sigh, "are you okay?"

"Baz!" I gasped, suddenly craving a cigarette and a triple malt, "I thought you were... emm... someone else." He was one of the last people on Earth that I had expected the bony finger and the firm grip to belong to.

"Your disguise is alright," he told me, glancing around and speaking a touch too loudly, "I think I'd better tell you what's been happening, Joey. Let's find ourselves a pub, shall we?"

I was certain that something must be wrong. Baz could have few reasons for being in London; for grabbing my arm with such uncharacteristic firmness; for looking at me with eyes that were so curiously solemn. His expansive pupils were now thin and focused, his red vessel-laced eye whites now as clear as milk. He was here, I knew, on a weighty matter.

We went on a long, silent walk then took a bus into the city centre. We went into a pub - I forget the name but know that it was near Chelsea Bridge - and sat down for a little dinner.

"I assume you've not come down to London just to find me," I ventured, as two steaming shepherd's puddings were laid on the table by a slim, smiling brunette.

"No. I was surprised to see you here," answered Baz.

"Why are you here?"

There was a pause. Baz picked up his fork and stroked the flaky pastry surface of his dinner. "Kemi."

"Why? What's happened to him Baz? Is it bad??"

I knew the answer already. And yet I needed to hear it, if only to formalise the matter.

"Kemi's dead."

Then there was another pause. I was unsure how I was supposed to react to this news; but inside I just felt blank. I looked across the table at Baz who, I guessed, must have spent a day at least assimilating the news and growing used to it. His face was like an earthquake ready to open up.

"Dead."

Quite suddenly I felt an immense, throttling hunger in my stomach. Without looking up again I began to eat my lunch in huge chunks, mouthful by massive mouthful. When the meat was all gone I would quite happily have chewed my way through the food bowl if there was a chance of getting away with it. On reflection, I understand that this was the only expression of grief that I was capable of at the time - and the single, solitary clue that I gave to the level of my devastation.

Baz had actually come down to London for Kemi's funeral. News had passed around town that our mutual friend had been executed within a day or two of leaving for London. We knew nothing more, although Baz had found out that the service would take place that afternoon in a chapel not far from where I was staying. "Are you going to come?" he asked and, without thinking of the frightening consequences, I said that I certainly would.

So we had three or four more beers in the pub until the hunched human bar furniture no longer seemed to be staring at me distrustfully, as I had initially perceived. We relaxed together, laughed together and for just a while talked freely, as if the country was not clamped into a fascist stranglehold and as if neither of us had anything to fear in life. Then, suddenly, I was reminded of the reality of my situation when Baz explained that my face had been spread across the pages of our local daily almost every day since my departure. He sensed my discomfort on this issue, however, and thought better than to delve any further into it.

I felt happy inside the pub. When I ignored the Chelsea and Fulham football shirts pinned to the wall and when the Cockney bar-talk was hushed to an unidentifiable murmur, the surroundings could have belonged to anywhere in the country. There was the unclean but friendly stench of old ale, the neighbourly poison of tobacco smoke and, above it all, the type of discussion between two old friends that can make most pubs in most places seem entirely indistinct.

By the time we left we had lost track of the time and forgotten to be sad or worried. We shambled, stumbled, whooped and meandered through the ragged, colourless jumble of city streets until we found ourselves a bus then, finally, found ourselves the road we were looking for. We were so late that we had to sprint the final three hundred metres from the bus stop to the chapel. We ran so fast and with heads so drunk that the subtle contrasts of the world all around us melted into one another. The urban backdrop became a galaxy of molten metal - aluminium, tin, silver and mercury. We got so hot that our lungs felt sick while our hearts leapt like gazelles and swelled like over-ripe pods. We cut across the chapel lawn then onto the path, looking down at the pebbles underfoot and the thin gravel that took our footprints as we galloped inelegantly over them. Then we arrived, with not a moment to ponder how dangerous it was for me to be there.

Looking back, the place should have been crawling with the police. They were chasing me and had a good idea that I was in London. They knew that Kemi was my best friend and that if only one person was at the funeral, then it would probably be me. As it happened there were only two other people at the service and one was the priest. The other was Kemi's mother; a short, thin and hairy white woman with deep brown eyes. She was wearing a black outfit and a dense grey veil that suited her better than anything she usually wore. The old lady - who had been forty-six years old when she conceived Kemi - had always hated me with an irrational passion, simply because I once spilt tea into her long-defunct record player. She had little time for her son and even less time for anybody who happened to know him. In return I secretly desired for her to suffer a painful and (if possible) humiliating destiny. It was the sight of that cold and bony brown-eyed warlock in the empty chapel that finally rammed home the finality of the situation. My heart constricted then, for just a moment, it shivered. Within sixty seconds of our unnoticed arrival, the curtains had drawn and Kemi's casket had been sucked into the terminal furnace. Baz and I were - from that second on - free to leave the place, forget everything, and resume our binge elsewhere. We pushed what we had just seen to the backs of our minds and, from there on in, spoke rarely of our departed friend, using only the present tense when we did.

I remember few details of the following two and a half hours: Baz and me ate cheap vodka jellies in a park, then drank brandy Alexanders in a claustrophobic cocktail bar packed with the overwhelming stench of joss-sticks, the mindless throb of club music and the constant raving of unsteady adolescents who should have been at school. I thought better of taking Baz back to the flat, partly because I knew that Gwyn would reprimand me for bringing an outsider into her home, partly because I feared that he would see my new accommodation and then accidentally relay the address in a tipsy moment.

Instead of inviting Baz over to my new home in London, I found myself agreeing - without really engaging my brain beforehand - to join Baz when he caught his evening bus back to town. I wanted to spend one last night under my own roof. It was a doltish and ludicrous plan, but one which I was too drunk to dispel or even question until it was too late. It turned out that there were many hours of ecstatic ignorance still to come that day and they were disturbed only very briefly by a short-lived spurt of unease that darted through my chest when we were homeward bound.

Chapter 11

The Last Escape

Our legs were so tightly packed in the bus that they felt stiff and swollen by the time we jumped out. The journey was predominantly a silent one with the most common exchange between Baz and I being the furtive trading of rum and gin bottles. We got back to the house without even thinking that anybody would be waiting for me. Besides, I told myself, I would be unrecognisable under night's black cover, especially in my new disguise.

We drank on for no more than twenty minutes. Almost as soon as we sat down I sensed that our binge had been left behind in London, or on the bus, and that the night was dying on us. Baz rolled himself a goodnight joint, but was so inebriated that it took him a toilsome forty minutes before he could finish the job. Then he fell asleep on the sofa and left me to collect my emotions. I stared through the window onto the remote street outside and began to realise the extent of my hazardous stupidity. As the mixed drinks lifted from my stomach I felt the Titanic plummeting through my gut, and as my eyelids shut I sensed a tremendous fear opening up in my heart.

In my sleep I dreamt of Gurkha troops chasing students through London's gaping-wide carriage-ways, and clone armies surveying streets that had been strained of life by evening curfews. It was not a nightmare this time. It was too close to our land's new shadowy existence. Britain, these days, was staggering through the heavy ashes of its former glory.

I woke up at three in the morning with my head still weighty but my stomach loosened by a flurry of wind. It took no more than a second of looking across at the pointless wall-plates and flaking ceiling of my house to realise, quite suddenly, that I was in a position of grave danger. I bolted forward from the chair-back against which I had slept like a man who had missed his alarm call on interview day. My heart bustled and my body bundled to its unsteady half-numb feet, then without delay I left the house for the town centre station, under the insane premiss that I could catch a bus to London before the safe dark of night had exhausted itself.

It was then that I walked around my hometown streets for the last time. I was tussling with a snappy wind which charged against me in contemptible fits. Debris from the evening before swirled, swooped, dipped and drifted through the cool summer air. Nobody was there. The world was clean of people. There was only the discordant noise of a breeze sizzling high in roadside trees and a fiery wind hissing over chimneys, under bridges, into open windows and out of dark pathways. I still felt uncomfortable. I walked into the town centre, my mind overwhelmed by the stupidity of my decision to return home, and walked past two tramps wrapped around each other, sleeping loudly in a shop doorway. One was hunched over the other so that they were rolled into a single ball with a solitary pair of tattered legs reaching out into the street. I checked the bus timetable and found that my bus was not leaving for London until eight in the morning. I felt tired, idiotic. My ears were cold, my throat sore and my legs weary, but the cold airstream was merciless. Why had I come back here? Why was I in town at this hour? I had been a terrible fool and knew very well that I might not survive this mistake. I had, in a moment of my wildest schizophrenia, made the most foolish decision of my life. Now I had to walk on, wrestling with the wind and toiling against my own tiredness. The streets seemed to be getting quieter, and the snarl of rustling leaves was reduced to a distant whisper. The wind began to fall, replaced by an expectant serenity.

Then there was a familiar moan from somewhere to my right. I looked across and Agatha, of all people, emerged from the churchyard ranting at an invisible partner. On first glance it was obvious that she had tried to dye her dark hair red - only for it to turn out ginger - and if there was a world record for the most denim worn by one person at once, then Agatha would have had a good chance of setting a new one. Although I was close enough to see the glow of her fake tan in the street light, I felt sure that I was far enough away not to be recognised. I slowed my pace and strained my eyes to get a glimpse of the younger lover for whom I had been spared. "I'm never going there AGAIN!" she howled like tortured banshee. I wondered what she meant and waited for her man to emerge from the shadows.

"I didn't make you come," answered a familiar male voice, "you said you wanted somewhere romantic." Where had I heard him before? I stood still for a moment.

My question was quickly answered when out of the night walked Aaron, my favourite former pupil. I felt myself sinking with disappointment - not with Agatha, but with Aaron. I could hardly believe that he had hated me enough to date Agatha. It was obviously a dare with his friends; a conscious attempt to both humiliate me and pull an older woman. I felt immediately distraught, devastated that even my favourite pupil could despise me so deeply. I ran hastily back to my house, crying much of the way and caring little if anybody saw me.

I returned to the house at about five o'clock with Baz still snoring away on the settee, although I noticed that his mouth had acquired a bubbling froth of saliva since my departure. I lay down on the floor but was too cold, damp and uncomfortable to sleep for the next hour. Finally I did sleep and woke up shortly after, with the bright sun showering down on me just as it had on Kemi's last morning in town. It was the same deluge of thick, eye-blistering yellow light that had burnt holes through me in Florence and Zante. It was all that I could see in the window above me, and for a moment I felt like a soldier in the trenches looking up at the skyline before clambering over the top. And this, here, was the self-same skyline; the same universe. I was waiting in the silence. There was no sign of life outside. The clock strode on, its handle gliding through the one, the two, the three, then the four, five... six...

Seven. I had to get up, I had to go outside. The danger was unavoidable now. I felt sure that they must be waiting for me out there and, even if they were not, people would see me. The clean shave, the sunglasses and the cropped brown hair would hide little from the locals; they knew how I walked, how I talked, how I nervously fingered my ears and tapped my cheekbones. I had been snared by own imbecility.

I left the house for the final time, not bothering to wake Baz before I left. I knew then that I would never see him again, but I had never cared for lingering farewells. It was a normal morning. It felt the same against my skin as any other would at that time of the year, although I was sure to keep my head low and my eyes fixed mostly on the ground below. At one point I had to veer away from two obnoxious ex-pupils of mine who were preparing to start some menial community service in the park - clipping trees and sweeping litter. I momentarily relieved myself of fear by questioning whether the world would be a poorer place without them.

I expected the bus station to be crawling with police officers, but it was completely empty. My coach arrived early and left on time with only the driver and I aboard. I watched passing towns unravel as sweet morning light greyed to midday. I knew, from the beginning of the journey through to the end, that I would be greeted in Victoria with a mob of coppers. I prayed that they would be looking for somebody else. Irrational thoughts blundered through my brain; at one point I even asked myself whether Baz had lured me back into town simply so he could win himself a sizable reward. It was, of course, a ridiculous notion. Yet, as our bus drew closer to London and its overhanging skyscraper shadows, I could not remove these thoughts from my head.

When I stepped down from the bus it felt as if I was dropping from an aeroplane straight into the sweltering naked June sky instead of a dark, claustrophobic bus station. I closed my eyes in fear. As it happened, Victoria station was indeed peppered with police officers, but none of them even noticed me alighting the bus. As soon I stepped into the terminal's ruthless white light I was just another figure in the crowd. Occasionally I imagined a curious gaze to be aimed in my direction, but it was quickly clear that nobody was interested in my presence there apart from, perhaps, the young pickpocket who made off with a few coins hanging loose in my jacket.

The most trouble I got into that day was with Gwyn, who

was infuriated by my reckless endeavor. She reprimanded me with an angry whisper and refused to join me for breakfast the next day. It all left me feeling miserable and alone. I peered up at the sun by day and the moon by night, wondering what Baz might be doing far away and under the same sky's light. Probably drunk, stoned, slumped in a bush or dribbling over himself on the sofa at home.

I envied him.

Chapter 12

H i d e a w a y

The months passed slowly. April showers were delayed till May. Gwyn found herself a boyfriend; a suave half-cast Londoner called Zane. I had to listen to them romping every evening, night and dawn, each time imagining that it was I instead of him poised beneath the bedsheets. I hated him before we even spoke and wished that she was sleeping with strangers for money instead. By the time we were introduced I already knew his voice well from the primitive yelp of sexual triumph. Gwyn tried to avoid talking to Zane about me and my situation, but she grew to trust the man, then fairly soon it slipped out. He came to talk to me about my plight, and expressed his empathy as a 'devout liberal', but I had little faith in him. I found him slimy, dull and strangely reptilian. I hated Gwyn for trying to impress the man with hair dye, make-up and moisturiser. My cordiality towards the newcomer was purely because I feared the consequences of being cruelly, brutally honest about the vitriol I reserved for him.

Gwyn would welcome Zane into the flat and then he would smile smugly and say 'hello' to me, but as soon as he and I were alone there was seldom anything more than a silent, suspicious stare.

I began to lose touch with events outside the flat. I lost interest in the contemptible whirl of neo-fascism. Gwyn spoke of the ongoing war abroad and the imminent threat of biological or chemical warfare. Hospitals were ordering smallpox vaccines and Londoners were buying gas masks. I was more concerned by Zane's sinister presence. He had made the Gwyn that I loved seem strangely impure. She lost all of her untouchable dignity. She rarely surfaced for breakfasts, instead she gasped gladly as he thrust and grunted atavistically against her bare body in the room next door. I lay awake and listened.

I spent my days watching local lives slip by outside. Throughout summer the morning air was overripe with pollen, and the evening air was charged with a foul stench of undercooked sausage meat, sizzling away on a hundred barbecues below. I watched life pass by; the woman opposite with a hanging basket obsession, the builders next door drinking cup upon cup of tea and then passing water into the flower bed. I kept up with the urban gossip through late night walks to the off licence. A lot happened in those months. Across the road a major business went bankrupt and its twin-towered premises were controversially demolished. Locals bleated about the effect it would have on people's lives, but I suspected that they were really more bothered by the aesthetics of their neighbourhood being altered.

I soon became bloated through a combination of cheap cider, bacon and prolonged inactivity. I gave up meat and took to chain-smoking in an effort to lose weight, but this drive was quickly ended by vegetable intolerance and asthma. Gwyn bought me some sea kelp tablets and I convinced myself that these alone would be sufficient for a return to shape.

My nightmares continued. I dreamed once more of clone armies - a thousand identical faces stomping through unidentifiable suburban streets. Yet I also imagined that these mechanical, man-made beasts still had within them that irremovable mortal insurgency; the desire to revolt and to form opinions that lies within all human beings. No matter how real and likely my nightmares seemed, I retained my faith in the power of human rebellion. Despite my overwhelming despair I felt sure that there was, at least, some hope for mankind. All they really needed was enlightenment, and that could only come from people like Gwyn and the Whiplash Women, people willing to risk their own well-being in the name of freedom. Perhaps, I hoped, a great new leader would emerge from the political shadows to challenge and usurp our fascist oppressors. I could feel it coming. I just wanted it to hurry up.

I was fairly certain, from the time of our first meeting, that Zane was nothing like the man that Gwyn held him to be. Then one morning, after their routine wake-up romp, Zane emerged from the bedroom to finally confirm my suspicions.

He strutted out of the bedroom with a red towel wrapped around his brown, hirsute middle and he drummed clenched fists aggressively against his sides. He stopped in front of me and, as a blast of cigarette smoke was blown in my direction, released a heavy, primal grunt.

"Are you okay, Zane?" I asked, impassively.

He looked down at me with bulging bluebottle eyes. His mouth undulated into a slithering viper smile. "No, not really," he lied, "but then, neither are you, Joey, are you?"

"Obviously."

"And that's why I'm not okay. See?"

I knew exactly what he meant and I was perfectly aware of the game he was playing. He fully understood that I could not afford to upset or insult him, no matter what games he played with me.

"See?"

"Yes. I see. Is that all, Zane?" The confrontation was starting to arouse him. I knew that Gwyn would suffer for this.

"I don't like your kind. I'm not into all of this hippy stuff like her in there. If they find you and shoot you full of holes then it'll be more than you deserve."

"Why is that?"

Zane looked a little confused; the contours of his face deepened and he stroked his left temple ponderously. His black hair was doused in so much gel that his fringe was crawling onto his forehead like the legs of a huge, dripping-wet spider.

"Well," he replied eventually, "you deserve to die because of your crime. You did what you did and now you have to take your punishment."

"And what did I do exactly?"

"I don't know what you did," Zane snapped, careful not to speak loud enough for Gwyn to hear, "but she knows."

"Gwyn? What does she know?"

"She knows what you did."

I told myself, then, that Zane must be lying. "No she doesn't."

"Don't you argue with me," he ranted excitedly, prodding

106

my nose with his stubby forefinger, "she told me that she knows exactly what you did but she wouldn't tell me because it's so bad I wouldn't want to know you if I heard!."

I shook my head and laughed quietly underneath my breath.

"She did! She said one of her friends from home read it in her local newspaper. Do you realise that as soon as they connect her with you they'll track you down and kill the both of you. Gwyn will die because of what you did."

"And do you care about Gwyn that much, Zane?"

He paused again. "That's none of your business," he answered, before turning back towards the bedroom. I felt as if I had won the argument without being offensive or bitter, but I was far from certain that I had gained anything from the exchange. Almost immediately, though, came screams of sexual torture from Gwyn in the next room, and I knew then that I had, at least, enraged Zane.

I was unsure whether Gwyn would be aware of the row that had taken place. When she emerged from the bedroom, later than usual, she was strangely snappy and choleric, as if her mood had suddenly been sieged by an army of angry termites. Zane followed her, grinning and raising his eyebrows smugly. I almost wanted her to know what had happened, but as soon as she reached into the cupboard it became clear that her short temper was due to nothing more than the early stages of influenza. I felt disappointed and lonely. I prayed for Zane's sudden death and, briefly, thought of killing him myself, but I never truly took the idea seriously. Instead I dreamt of a thousand far-fetched and brutal slaughters that might be suitable for the man, in a parallel universe.

Before long Gwyn warned me that people back in town already suspected me to be hiding in London, and that the Metropolitan Police would soon be sticking up 'wanted' posters. Gwyn, thankfully, was not implicated in any of this. Far from it. It appeared that hardly anyone - apart from, perhaps, the other Whiplash Women - even knew that Gwyn and I were friends. As far as the public were concerned, we were both away on (very) different business. Besides, lots of people have perfectly legitimate reasons for going to London. I, of course, was not among them.

The consequence of this was that I was impelled to limit my cherished evening walks. I still ventured out onto the streets - albeit infrequently - and decided that it would probably draw no more suspicion if my rambles took place by daylight.

On these occasions I would stride alone through a maze of identical roads and alleyways; past indistinct laundrettes and liquor stores - anywhere to avoid Zane. The sooty, red-bricked terraces that once stood tall over Victorian squalor, cholera and despair now sat sadly under the breath of graphite-grey flats, piled high into the sky, blotting out sun from the disheartened streets below.

I used these walks to reflect on my life both past and present: I tried to recall why, precisely, I had originally become a teacher. I failed to remember my original reason, but concluded that it was probably through a desire to inspire people. It is, after all, impossible to be an inspirational accountant, I.T. consultant or bar manager, even if they do earn much more money.

I hated the city more with every minute. People come to London to escape small-minded mentalities and conventions, but the capital offers no improvement on this. People expect enlightenment and prosperity but even if they attain the latter they can never find the former. Why? Because London is a hundred small-minded towns rolled into one great cataclysm of narrow-mindedness.

On my lonely wanderings I found, an old cleared-out bargain store - 'Kathleens' - with its splintered insides half-choked out onto the pavement and its dignity deeply gutted. The place stood forlorn at the end of two terraced blocks, a red-bricked corner shop with its slated roof stumbling in on the final strewn remnants of a meaningless past.

To the concrete towers overlooking, this bleak and lonely place meant little. Neither did it matter to the neighbours who had quickly grown accustomed to Kathleen's absence.

So who was Kathleen? Her grammar was poor, that was for certain - it implied that there had been more than one Kathleen. Perhaps there were ten of them. So where had they gone? What pain or gust of ill-ease had driven them from this place? Where are their bargains now?

I imagined the labourers first at work on these streets, building something new. I could picture them, dipped down into the five foot trench and laughing... but now they are surely all dead and with not an echo left of the laughter. What might they think if they could see this ripped-up ruin? Would they care? Does anybody?

I peered inside. What had happened in here? Once this shop was the centrepiece of somebody's life, and a cross on the map for so many more. There was a story to each of its stripped-naked corners, but that had all passed. Its friends had departed. As I watched a woman drifted by, incidentally, but she did not turn to look.

Nowadays the half-empty hovel would be little more than an occasional hiding place for secretive young mobs of weed-smoking gigglers. I stared down at the shop's ancient, crippled facade - dropped to the ground - and at the font on its rotting nameplate. This place could have been empty for decades. Other stories might have taken place since then; some of its innocent tokers would be heroin junkies by now, others dead, others married.

So much for 'Kathleens', then, left silent here. Decomposing on death-row. I walked into the house, deeper and deeper. For just a moment I fancied that I could be safe if I stayed there forever. Then, in an instant, it occurred to me that I was in terrific danger. The neighbours would have seen me step inside the shop and probably assumed me to be a drug-user or a squatter. They could have called the police. I walked on a little further, but now the fear carried with me everywhere: as I tiptoed through the old shop - along corridors, up the short staircase, into the bathroom - it followed. I foresaw the armed officers kicking through Kathleens unglazed, crumbling door-frame, barging past dust-blackened shelves, trampling over memories and storming up the steps, trapping me where I stood. I had to get out. But then I calmed down and took a seat. It was peaceful here and after a while, I found the paranoia vacating my mind.

I gained a great deal from these fleeting adventures and observations. They set me free, temporarily at least, from the fear that was starting to take hold of my life. Whereas I would previously have ignored the danger that I was in, I presently found it impossible to be ignorant - and not least because Gwyn kept reminding me of my situation's dire reality.

On one other occasion I sat and, for an hour, watched as a lonely woman looked down from her bedroom window. She gazed, vacantly, onto the grey and emptying street down below and seemed so small compared to the vast, restless chunks of cloud above. Meanwhile the thinning crowds below - oblivious to it all - were politely waiting for smallpox to come to town, strutting about their aimless routines. I thought to myself, at the time, that only at moments like this can one fully understand sadness, insignificance and loneliness.

The loneliest excursion of all, though, was also one of the riskiest. I went to a football match for the first game of the season. I sat under the gaze of surveillance cameras and observed the mobs which flanked the pitch; full of primal chants and loosely channeled animosity. In this arena it became easy to believe that human aggression could be harnessed for political gain and - ominously - used to great effect. After about thirty minutes of the game I left my seat to go to the toilet and the burger stand. I chose not to return.

During my most desperate moments, I often called on God to help me. I imagined him up in Heaven, decked in white robes and surrounded by virgins, truffles and harps. I pictured him looking in on my prayers but then, when they went unanswered, I would grow angry with him, curse the almighty and pray for the devil to help me instead.

I had called on God once before - when hallucinating with Kemi in happier days - but now he was even farther off. He offered no protection against the swarm of nightmares which plagued my restless sleep.

One night, as I slept, I dropped back into the crematorium where I had previously dreamt of the young wounded boy. This time I was running back towards the coffin again, but I stopped next to it instead of running on into the furnace. I looked down into the casket below. There was a body inside - and it was my body - still flushed with life but shorn of expression. I stared down and looked at the face. It seemed to be changing, as if the scattered stress-lines that had mapped my face for years were loosening, contracting and - finally – vanishing. Yes, the face was changing; the skin colour deepening and the hair growing thicker. The stubble vanished and the skin tightened around the skull. The body began to shrink in the clothes until they lay slack like a mass of blankets. Eventually most of the cadaver's slim, boyish figure had fit itself into the breast of the baggy white shirt, and could be seen clearly through it, like a rotting cat in a wet paper bag. Then the change was over. I looked back at myself and then I realised what had happened. My corpse had grown short, slim and youthful. The body below me was that of a ten-year-old child.

Then, quite suddenly and with no further explanation, the dream was over.

All the while my hatred for Zane grew fiercer and my love for Gwyn more improbable. My temper churned more and more with every pallid morning to whiten the rips in our blinds, and with every taste of a neighbour's burnt supper to soar up through the flat's gaping windows.

I wanted to be with Gwyn. I wanted to live in her thighs forever and whisper lines of clumsy poetry into her ears. I wanted to be clamped safely into her arms while the roof above our heads was snatched away by the sternest cyclone, and the floor beneath our bed shattered by the fiercest earthquake. By night I wanted to gaze into her sleeping almond eyes and stroke her wild toffee hair. By day I wanted her calming company to soothe my vulgar shell.

I decided, finally, that I would try to seduce Gwyn. Partly, I understood, to consummate my simmering lust for her and partly, of course, to spite Zane. I wanted Gwyn to tell him that she had slept with me. I wanted him to punch me. The greater consequences of this were unimportant.

The details of how it happened are unimportant, but it did

happen. I approached her as subtly as I could and she accepted me with minimum resistance. I creamed the contours of her aging face and she unzipped my frustration. Our bond was alarmingly loveless. We awoke in the morning, side by side, but an ocean apart.

What it all meant, though, was that we had to move on. I wanted Zane to know what we had done and, within a week, Gwyn had told him. She seemed surprised at his instant promise to telephone the police and report us both, but I fully expected it and had already packed my bag. Zane never punched me - he probably felt no need - and I was hugely disappointed that the grin was still fixed to his face when he left the house.

Gwyn knew that both of us would have to leave. If she were to be arrested then her punishment would be little lighter than mine. As for me, I was ready to leave. I hated London.

Within five minutes of Zane's final exit, we were both back on the road.

Chapter 13

The End...

I could sense that the end was near, but was strangely conscious that it would also mark a new and fantastic beginning.

Neither Gwyn nor I were in any doubt that Zane would have immediately reported us to the police. It occurred to me that I should have murdered him before he left the flat, but it was probably best at that stage that I avoided leaving another scar on my conscience.

The reality of the situation was that Gwyn and me were in grave danger. We were at risk in London. We were at risk outside of London. It was decided that if we left the capital then, if we could survive for at least a year on the run, it might be possible for us to slip into the Scottish Highlands unnoticed. I wanted us to be David Balfour and Allan Breck Stewart in Kidnapped.

What made our situation all the stranger was that we never discussed how we had got ourselves into this position: I declined to consider what I had done to start all of this and Gwyn declined to blame me for pulling her in.

Our journey out of London was hasty and silent. Our recent, putrescent bout of intimacy had pumped our relationship full of discomfort and, I believed, we were only still together through a lack of viable alternatives.

We only saw one police van before we passed out of the city suburbs and into the flat, vapid countryside sprawls of Essex. We went as far as daylight would take us before the sunlight retreated behind spongy grey clouds.

There was, it appeared, a pop-music festival taking place nearby. We stopped in a lay-by overlooking the campsite. Gwyn pulled down her window and drew on a cigarette with emphysema-charged rigor. She emptied a half-empty aluminium drink can that had been lying in the door-bin and shuddered with fear. Outside, in the night, the fields were electrified by camp-fires, star-lit by random pearls of light popping on and off. Although the parties were by now almost invisible we could still taste the dense plumes of bonfire smoke, and hear all the boys, all the girls; their chatter loaded with boundless adrenaline. The intoxicated murmur of contentment was skipping across the plane. I got out of the car so that I could walk close enough to see the faces of the youths below - wide-eyed and each one fearless - and conceive that I was as free as them. These people, I told myself, are the future. They are free. They are the future. Now that was my mantra. For the first time in a long while, I was almost optimistic.

We moved on for the night, worried that we might attract the attention of suspicious security guards. We drove towards the coast and spent the night in a car park. We had to wrap our bodies awkwardly around the gear stick, hand-brake, reclining seat and steering wheel, but even among these obstacles we kept as distant from one another as possible. Neither of us slept, but neither of us spoke either and in the dark of the morning we drove wordlessly north to the seaside in search of accommodation.

When sunlight finally dropped through the inky dawn clouds I was sitting on the beach (of some or other east coast seaside town) while Gwyn went off looking for a place to stay. I was tired and happy to sit by myself. I propped myself up against a cold rock from which, to my right, a melee of electrical wires, pylons and generators cut into the cliff top landscape. To my left the sands grew pebbly, damp and grassy. They swarmed over the paved-red promenade, towards dormant donut stalls and amusement arcades.

I watched the waves soaring, the waves shambling, the waves clattering in - and then wimpering away again, as if there was another clandestine ocean tucked away in a box below the shoreline, urging them back out.

I could see for miles along the coastline and so, secure in the knowledge that I would still be able to see Gwyn when she returned, I went for a walk. I looked across the wet sands and rock pools, up towards the crumbling cliffs; where land's glorious green strides are suddenly cut off, where vast stretches of countryside stumble down into the ocean. This is the end of our nation, where it falls away. Beyond these rocks and reefs there is nothing left of England, apart from what its brown rivers spew out into the endless, open sea. Far away, where the sky drips down into the sea, there is little left of dark England to taste in the sea-water. Even from where I stood, looking out, the sand, the salt and the dead jellyfish could belong to any country, although the chilly sea air and Victorian piers were something of a giveaway.

I loved the piers; jutting out into the sea like giant decomposing millipedes. Nobody cared for them anymore. Their only purpose in the world was as a defiant reminder of black-and-white seaside photographs from the last millennium; of days when the beach was crowded with a thousand over-dressed families and as many sand-castles. Now they felt disconsolate, empty and exhausted.

A man walked past and said something, but I was deaf to him. I counted six airplanes, watched their six vapour trails and six times wished that I was up there in the sky, away from Earth, away from the country. The sky was growing white, and a pale fog was closing in on me.

I began to guess at what Baz and Harry might be doing back at home, or what Robert could be up to in the Mediterranean. It was only a year since I had met him on that beautiful, reinvigorating trip through Europe. I found it difficult to fathom what had happened since that journey and even harder to understand how my world could have changed so much since my first seedy encounter with Gwyn.

I knew, now, that I was going to die in this place, and began to wish that I could have gone like Marc in the car; suddenly, unexpectedly, instantly. Then I wished that there was somebody left in the world - other than Baz - who would miss me when I had passed over.

When Gwyn returned she was smiling and told me that we had a place to stay with single beds. We left the car on a local council estate in case it was identified and took a slow walk up to our new accommodation.

It was a single room which smelt a little like a workshed. It had two beds, one sink and a commanding view of the town's superloo. After briefly inspecting the shared bathroom I decided that I would choose between the public toilets and the sink before daring to experiment with the hotel's unwholesome facilities. In the meantime I entertained myself by counting cigarette burns and trying to identify a selection of suspicious stains on the curtains and bed blankets.

I only saw the hotel owner twice. She was an instantly loathsome red-headed fifty-something with a gravely voice, black teeth and a ridiculous pink dress. She coughed, snarled and wheezed but never uttered a single recognisable morpheme. On the first occasion I saw her she knocked on our room door, and when I answered she waved her bony yellow index finger at the shut window. "Open it?" I asked. She nodded with a foul sniff. Obligingly, I wandered up to the window and, subsequently, spent the next five minutes trying to prise it open. An hour later, when the window decided to swing shut once more, I was forced to go through the same ordeal all over again, with the old woman casting a critical seaweed-green eye over me as I toiled with her malevolent window.

I must have fallen asleep at about four in the afternoon while Gwyn was out buying us new clothes. We both agreed that it was safer for her to go out shopping and for me to sit in the room feeling miserable.

I awoke with a start at about five o'clock when the room door crashed shut and Gwyn hurled a box of shoes at my head. She was clearly alarmed and could not speak for breathlessness.

"What is it?" I asked her.

"Joey... We've... We've got to..."

"Yes?"

I sat up in bed, readying myself for the worst.

"We've got to... got to go now!"

"Why?"

Gwyn did not answer, instead she motioned for me to get up and get out of the room. I did not argue. Within a couple of minutes we were out of the hotel and running back towards the car. I ascertained, from Gwyn's sporadic meaningful gasps, that our host had identified us from pictures sent out by the police to hotel owners all over the country. Within a few minutes there would be no way out. We could only run. Run and hope.

We reached the car and were immediately on our way, motoring carelessly through the town streets with Gwyn again at the wheel.

We were two miles out of town and well into the country when the police vans began to pass. I was not even scared by this time. I already knew that we were inescapably trapped. There were police ahead, police behind and I knew that, given time, there would be police up above as well.

"Is this it?" I asked Gwyn. Her eyes were fixed, inextricably, to the road ahead. "Gwyn? Don't you think we should give up now?"

She was not going to listen, but I was eager for the end. I wanted whatever end they had designed for me to unfurl itself immediately. I was bored with futile escapades. I was braced for departure, desperate for death to come and be over, which made Gwyn's pointless attempts to avoid it all the more maddening. I pondered grabbing the wheel off her and turning us into the ditch, but did not have the courage to make the move. Then I decided that I must take the wheel - there were trees on either side of the road, if I could crash the car at this speed then we would almost certainly die on impact - it had to be done.

"Gwyn, let's just give it up shall we? I've had enough Gwyn. Gwyn! Gwyn, I'm going to take this car off the road, I've had enough of this, let's put an end to it all. Turn the car into the trees and it's all over. Please!"

She ignored me and simply drove straight on ahead. I began to count down from five, telling myself that when I hit one I would send the car hurtling into one of the great oaks to our right.

Five... four... three... two...

No, go again.

Five... four... three... two... Five... four... three...

I inhaled deeply.

Five... four... three... two...

ONE!

Then on cue I clasped the wheel and veered right, towards the flank of roadside trees. I shut my eyes, clenched my fists, gritted my teeth then waited for my oak of choice to slash through the windscreen, the bumper and the dashboard.

There was a huge clatter, then the sound of the car's engine skipping and underside splintering. I heard glass shatter and my hands were thrown from the wheel. I opened my eyes and turned to look out of the rear window. The long succession of oak trees was disappearing behind us while, up ahead, vast horizontal plains of boggy farmland were reaching out for miles.

"You managed to miss the trees," remarked Gwyn flatly, "I think you'd better steer."

However I had barely laid a finger on the wheel before the car swung again to the right, this time of its own accord, and straight into a deep, thorny hedgerow. We crawled through it and carried a few branches on our screen for a moment before, finally, our vehicle dipped down headfirst into a narrow stream and stopped.

I was shaking violently, but Gwyn was calm and still.

"What now?" I asked her, after a pause.

"We get out of the car," she answered, slowly pulling herself out of her contorted driver-seat, "and then we separate." She tussled with the car door until it reluctantly fell open. The passenger-side door was jammed so I followed Gwyn out of the car.

"Where are you going?" I asked.

"I'm going to run, and I suggest you do too," she answered. "Get as far away from the car as you can as quick as you can and don't stop."

"I've hurt my leg."

"Well then, hobble away from the car and lie low somewhere. Pray they don't have sniffer dogs or heat-seeking helicopters."

Amid all of the excitement of our ludicrous escape I had entirely forgotten about the futility of survival. Gwyn raced off in the opposite direction while, limping heavily on my right leg, I hopped down the stream for what felt like a mile. My left kneecap flashed with a searing pain whenever I moved it, so I had little choice but to stay in the stream and use it as a trench. At one point the water snaked slightly to one side which meant that I could no longer see the car from where I was. At this point I decided to stop and lay my leg out flat in the water.

"Joey!" called a male voice, from up above. I shivered.

"Joey, Gwyn, come out. The game's up. We know you're round here. You can come out now or you can wait until the dogs drag you out." The voice was getting louder. "Joey? Joey?" Suddenly the voice was directly above my head. "Ah, here we are."

I looked up at the face that was smiling down on me then began to shuffle my way slowly and awkwardly up the muddy, thorny bank-side.

"Hello Joey, good to see you," said the man, smugly. I looked up at the face for a second time and it was then that a bolt of realisation exploded within me: The amphetamine-yellow skin, the tangled blond locks, the pregnant cheekbones and the pinprick pupils swallowed up by huge yawning eye sockets. I had met this man before. I had seen him somewhere... but could not locate the face in my memory.

"Good day Mr. Carlton," called another, higher-pitched voice, accompanied by the shuffling of heavy boots on thick grass. Another male head peered down at me for a second, but it was wobbling unsteadily and the man had to retreat. "Do you think I might have my story now?" he added. After a few moments I managed to place the voice as that of the newspaper reporter who had asked me to talk about Kemi.

"Get lost," I replied.

"You said that last time, I think," he said, shuffling away.

Then the first voice came again, "Perhaps you should talk to him. Everybody deserves a chance to tell their side of the story."

"I'll do that in court then."

Laughter broke out up above. It was clear, from the noise out on the field, that the reporter and the man with the yellow skin were not alone.

"What's so funny?" I asked them.

"Well," answered the first man, "I think you know very well what's so funny. You've led us on quite a merry dance, haven't you?"

"Have I?"

"Yes you have!"

I was being taunted. "In what way?"

"Well, since the last time we met - at your place I seem to recall - you have been on quite an adventure. You've been off to London with your lover. You've been up the coast. Oh, and you've lost a good friend, haven't you? I forgot about that."

"Tell me. I'm gripped," I grunted lethargically.

"Do you really wish to know the gory details?"

"I already know what happened to Kemi."

"I don't think you do. As far as you know, your kiddy-fiddling buddy went on a bus to London, got to the capital and - after a few days or weeks - was caught and executed with dignity. That would probably be your understanding, wouldn't it?"

"If you can call being strung up without a decent trial dignified then yes, I suppose that would be my understanding."

"It's certainly a lot more dignified than being roundly tortured by the local mob, I'd say. Unfortunately it's also a lot more inconvenient for the government. You see, we in power don't like having blood on our hands. We prefer leaving grubby local affairs to grubby local people. Take you, for instance, it's much easier for you to be dealt with in your own hometown than it is when you're roaming through London. Of course, we caught you eventually, but if the local mob had caught you first then we needn't have bothered chasing you. And it also saves all the bother of putting people on trial, administering justice, organising public executions and so on."

"What do you know about justice?"

"We have to be seen to be just. We can't just go around hanging people, shooting them and cutting their heads off. Unless they pose an immediate threat or, as in your case and in your friend's case, you're in the process of getting away."

"How am I getting away? You've just caught me!"

"Yes you're right. But then, that's not how it'll read in the papers, is it Brian?"

The newspaper reporter laughed in acknowledgement. I could picture him shaking his head.

"Do you see, Joey," continued the man from the government, "that we have everybody on our side? The right-wing press adore us. The people adore us. By killing criminals like your paedophile friend, we're simply protecting ordinary folk."

"So how did you go about it?" I squirmed and squelched a little on the pebbly stream floor. A few small fish were gathering on my left where I was damming the water-flow.

"It was easy. We stopped that bus within about five minutes of it leaving town. We made everybody get off and told them that there was a dangerous sex-offender on board. People began to panic, argue and speculate among each other. By the time Kemi came forward the place was practically hysterical - we could have shot him there and then."

"But you didn't?"

"No, we let him run first. It's a lot less respectable that way. He hid in a ditch, much like you are now and - in the same way as you will in a minute - he was asked to crawl out of the ditch. It was very wet and slippy so by the time he did get out he had mud and thorn-cuts all over his head. Then, when he was out and on his knees, I shot his face off."

"You're telling me that you made Kemi kneel in front of you, in a field, then shot him in the head - and it didn't look like an execution?"

"Nobody saw it happen. At least none of the public. But they heard the gunshot and they were cheering by the time I got back. They ran up to see the body and, just then, you could have nailed your friend's coffin shut with the relief they were feeling. It was that tangible. They didn't feel any emotion when they saw his head spread across the grass - all skull fragments and brain, like chewed-up, raw minced beef spilling out of his neck. It didn't look human. You'd never have guessed that he was crying when I pulled the trigger."

"And is this your job? You go around from town to town killing suspected criminals?"

121

"Oh Kemi wasn't a suspected criminal! He was a convicted criminal. He did time! People like Kemi - and people like you - don't need a trial. Nobody cares when your kind get a bullet through the face. The only problem comes with the assumption that people are innocent until proven guilty - that's when it's difficult - but Kemi and you, you are already guilty. We'd rather the locals deal with you, but we can handle it."

"What am I guilty of, exactly?"

The man from the government chose not to answer my question. Instead he kneeled down, so that his face was staring straight down onto mine. When he spoke I could feel his saliva landing on my cheeks. "Time to get out of the stream, Joey. You know the drill."

I clawed my way slowly out of the trench. I lifted my head slowly, then delicately over the top, as if moving gently and steadily could somehow soften the bullet's impact on my fragile skull. Everywhere was silent. I looked across at everything; all that lay scattered beneath the blotchy overhead. I was struck verbless.

Men and women with pens and pads. People to the left, then across on the right. Cold mist on the grass, thin mist through the hedges, then mist in the trees. Expectancy all around. Endless dull green below, endless patchy grey above.

"Look at the gun."

I looked at the gun - a .38 double-barrelled revolver. I am not sure how I knew that, but I did.

Just then, spontaneously, the words uttered to me by that battered infant in my dreams came charging into my head.... then, in a moment, they passed straight back out.

Chapter 14

On The Road To Find Out

Initially I was senseless. Nothing to touch, taste, smell, see or hear. My mind was, for a time, bereft of thought. I felt unusually comfortable; oddly liberated.

Then I thought that I was in hospital; I saw the masked medics towering over me in blue and green. Perhaps I had been saved! Perhaps the bullet had, by some miracle, passed through some inessential part of the brain. Perhaps I had never been shot at all.

Those thoughts passed.

Then I reflected on all that had happened to me. Was it all a dream? My life had become so abnormal that I was beginning to doubt whether all of these events were really taking place, or whether the visions and voices from my dreams had broken into the waking hours.

I worried for Gwyn; whether she had managed to evade the government-man-with-the-yellow-skin and his sanguinary followers, or whether she had also slipped into a place as shapeless and inanimate as this.

I also reflected upon the nightmares that had laid siege on my sleep over preceding months: the funerals, the bloodied child and the demonic beasts were all, somehow, linked to this. I felt, then, that there must have been more substance to them than I had at first assumed. I knew, of course, that they had only been fictional night-visions, but it still appeared that they had been forewarning me of the terrifying times ahead and - I suspected - some fresh, unknown ordeal which was poised to throw itself upon me.

I had no sense of movement - or of time passing - during that period in the dark. I could not see my hands, I could not even feel them. I felt amorphous and unpalpable. All that I had was a numbing inactivity; spells of intense contemplation followed by complete nothingness. Apart from worrying over Gwyn, I was not in the least concerned about my surroundings (or, as it was, the lack of them). In addition, I was neither frustrated by my new environment, nor keen to be released from it. The reason for this, I concluded, was that I had no concept of the seconds, minutes, hours or days that I was spending there. This place, wherever it was, did not seem to exist in time.

Then the lights came on. A door flew open, I shuffled along and - after stumbling on somebody's foot - unwittingly found myself seated on a red plastic chair, looking straight up at a white, smudged ceiling. I was in a line of chairs backed against a corridor wall. I was clearly in some sort of waiting room and hoped that my appointment was next, because I was bored. I could feel gusts of fresh, clean air pummeling down into the corridor from a line of fans tacked high onto the wood-chipped wall opposite. This went some way towards combating the smell; something like a sickening blend of bleach and juniper berries.

There were five or six empty chairs to my right and then, further up, two other people rocking awkwardly in their seats. I looked across, as if to suggest that one of them should embark on a little friendly discourse. I wanted to test my vocal cords once again and find out whether that my face was adorned with bullet entry wounds. Not one of them looked at me, instead they gazed ahead wretchedly.

Then a glass door (which I had not yet noticed) was flung open - on my right, at the end of the corridor - and a mean-looking lanky man with a million keys strapped to his belt came hobbling towards me.

"Next one up is Monsieur Carlton," he snarled, in a thick French accent. As the creature loomed closer I could see that he was about twenty, with greasy black hair and long, deep scars in both cheeks where his dimples should have been. His slacks hung loose from around his belt, but fell at least four inches short of his tattered socks. Quite an achievement, I told myself. He wore a black and brown shirt that was probably once white and his scabby, half-chewed nails poked through a pair of fingerless gloves. He looked at me.

"You are Carlton, yes?"

"Yes," I answered in a timid voice, while trying to find my feet.

"Well come on then. This way," he demanded, turning away with such disgust that I began to wonder if I had upset him in some previous, long-forgotten encounter. As I followed the man he turned to his left, snorted and then spat a dessert-spoon worth of phlegm onto the white wall. It slithered down through the wood-chips like watery lemon jelly and in that moment I realised that the whole wall was covered in mucus stains. I followed the young man through the door into another corridor. He stopped briefly, bent down to pick up a minuscule trampled-on cigar butt then, after studying the thing for a moment, dipped into his pockets for a lighter and began to smoke it. In addition to the rich sickly smell of expensive tobacco I could detect the heavy stench of cheap cider on his breath, as I followed. We came to another door. He rapped on the glass panel, kicked it open and then motioned for me to enter. I obliged and he followed me into the room.

I had, up to this point, assumed that I was in either a prison or a police station and that my tall, smelly escort was some kind of jail warden. However, the bloated, bald fellow seated behind a desk in this room did not look like a policeman. He was wearing a white pin-striped shirt, a bark-green tank top and garish blue corduroy trousers. On his desk was a sprawl of paperwork, a framed photograph of his family and a plastic ice cream carton full of pens, pencils, crayons and other assorted stationery.

The walls of the room were painted an icy blue, decorated with nothing more than a set of fire evacuation guidelines and a crucifix, while the floor consisted of unvarnished, rotting wooden boards. The man, who did not even look up at us, was sharpening a pencil underneath his desk. His face was round and red, with a forehead that was encased by a swarm of large purple veins. He cleared his throat and put the pencil back in his container. I considered whether he was in the process of methodically working through the entire stack of stationery, meticulously ensuring that all of the equipment in his carton was clean and poised for use.

"Thank you Humbert," he boomed in a deep Yorkshire accent, still not looking up from his desk. He pronounced the name 'Humbert' in exactly the way that it would read to an Englishman, as opposed to the correct French manner.

"Just call when you're done with him, Mr. Flaxby," answered Humbert, pushing me unkindly towards a seat in the corner of the room, as far away from my host as it was possible to sit. I fell back into the cushioned chair. Flaxby looked up at me immediately.

"I don't remember asking you to sit down, young man," he commanded. "Don't your legs work?"

I stood up quickly, feeling quite exasperated. Humbert, across to my left, looked as if he was about to pounce on me.

"Okay, thank you Humbert," he called, again in an inordinately loud Northern English accent. "I'll give you a shout." Humbert saluted his boss and left the room.

I looked down at the fat little man behind the desk. He looked back up at me and then, evidently perturbed by being lower down than his inferior guest, motioned for me to sit down. Having done so I realised that Flaxby was in the highest chair that it was possible for him to sit in without being unable to reach his metal footrest.

"Now then," he started, glaring fiercely into my eyes, "you're a right horrible little bastard, you are. Yes, I've read all about you. A real nasty piece of work."

I was confused.

"Now," continued Flaxby, "I'm going to get all of the formalities out the way quick, like, so I can get on with the important part. No need to waste time with formalities, faffing about. Get it all out the way."

I nodded politely.

"So, you probably don't realise this yet Carlton, but you are dead."

Too right I didn't realise that… dead? How could I be dead? Was this a joke? I wanted to laugh, scream and cry all at once, but I was way too shocked to utter any response. I was simply struck blank.

"Yes, yes, you were shot in the face..." Flaxby made a crude gun shape with his hand and pointed it in my direction "...and you're dead. So now that's all out in the open, it's better that you get used to the idea as quick as possible."

I stared ahead, astounded. This had to be a dream.

"So now you've been transferred to a place that you'd probably tend to call Hell. My name is Ernest Flaxby - Mr. Flaxby to you - and it's my job to A) make sure you're suitably punished for what you've done and B) find a way to make you useful to us here in Hell. Am I clear?"

Again I did not answer. Flaxby looked back down at his desk, at some of the papers scattered about on it. He plonked a chubby index finger purposefully onto one of the papers in front of him and then returned to staring at me, threateningly.

"Don't you remember what you did to get here?" he thundered, bafflingly. "You don't, do you?"

I shook my head, perplexed, close to hysterics.

"No I didn't think you did. We get this quite a bit - people just blacking things out their memory. What we do with people like you is take you to a place called the Recollection Room and sit you down and make you watch your life - on replay, like - and look back over all the stuff that you've forgotten. We make you come face to face with what it was that you did, and often that's as good a punishment as there is for people like you." People don't tend to like seeing themselves fiddling with their kids and stuff like that. It's all a bit nasty. Not that they feel any remorse, mind.

I was alarmed by how matter-of-fact Flaxby was about my death and subsequent descent into Hell. I was terrified and bewildered enough by that declaration alone, before even contemplating what I might have done to deserve being in this place. As for being sent to the 'Recollection Room' and being forced to watch my life 'on replay'; it all seemed too farfetched for consideration.

"You'll be in there for quite a long while," said Flaxby, "and I'll be popping in and out. It's my job to monitor your progress and make sure that you're - err - digesting all of the information properly."

The room fell quiet, but Flaxby's eyes were still fixed on me.

"What are we waiting for?" I asked finally.

"Do I look as if I'm here to answer your questions?" he roared ridiculously, his eyes bulging furiously. "I will be the one asking the questions, not you!" He exhaled with a rattle. "The reason we're waiting is because I've got to wait for authorisation from the Area Manager. Should be here shortly."

I nodded.

"You know, young man, it's your kind that I like the least. People like you, you're the vilest kind of scum there is. You're bloody evil, but you manage to mask it with education. But you're still a scumbag at the end of the day."

"I don't know what you mean."

"That's 'I don't know what you mean, Mr. Flaxby' okay?"

"I don't know what you mean, Mr. Flaxby."

"Of course you don't know what I bloody mean. If you knew what I meant then I wouldn't be sending you to the Recollection Room. But once you're there you'll see exactly what I mean. You're a right horrible little cretin. Horrid." He shook his head, utterly sickened by me. It occurred to me that Flaxby must also have done something unpleasant or evil to warrant eternal damnation, but I decided to save that particular argument for a later date. Besides, I concluded wearily, it appeared that I would be having many more dealings with this obnoxious, belligerent, chubby Northern goblin.

It was then that the door swung open again and in came a slim, suited man with balding grey hair and a long pointed nose. He walked up to Flaxby, placed both of his hands on the desk and leaned forward. Flaxby's manner changed instantly; his eyes narrowed, his skin whitened, his voice softened and his hands disappeared back beneath the desk.

"Good day Mr. Anchors."

"And good day Flaxby," answered the impeccably-spoken Mr. Anchors. "Everything's ready for you now."

"Thank you, Mr. Anchors."

The Area Manager turned towards me and started to

analyse my face. "Is this the fellow?" he asked Flaxby.

"Yes."

"What's his name again?"

"Carlton."

"Ah yes, I remember." Anchors turned his whole body to face me, and rested his bony backside on the desk. "How long have you been here, Carlton?"

"I'm not sure," I answered hesitantly, "it feels like I've been here for twenty minutes or so... but I'm not sure... there was a bit before that, but I don't know..."

Anchors let out a quick, loud and cruel laugh. "Yes I see. I see. You're a teacher aren't you?"

"Yes. I was."

"What did you teach?"

"English."

"Oh dear," he gasped, "How disappointing! I don't like English teachers. I can only assume that English teachers are to blame for some of the awfully spoken young men and women that we get here. I was under the impression that you were a Maths teacher. Now I like Maths teachers."

"Oh. No I'm an English teacher. An ex-English teacher."

Anchors looked at me for a few moments, fingering his chin thoughtfully. "You don't say much, do you?"

"I'm still a bit... numb."

"Numb? You'll recover, Mr. Carlton. Has Flaxby told you about the Recollection Room?"

"Err - yes."

"He has, has he? I think you'll find what you see fairly alarming. You were quite an unpleasant young man, in your day."

"People keep saying that." I wanted to hit somebody. "I don't know why."

"Oh, you will soon. I quite enjoy watching people in the Recollection Room. They go in absolutely mystified as to what they've done wrong. Then they come out making every single excuse imaginable. Every excuse you could think of - 'I didn't mean to kill my mother, it was a mistake'; 'I wasn't thinking straight, it was the drugs wot did it'. And you'll be the same.

They all are. 'It couldn't possibly be my fault'. No doubt you'll shed a few tears because you've actually been brought to justice for what you did."

"I still haven't got a clue what on earth you're going on about."

All of a sudden Flaxby's mouth opened, as if about to reprimand me for being so disrespectful to the Area Manager, but Mr. Anchors interrupted him with another malevolent chuckle. He stood up again, fastened one of the buttons on his charcoal grey suit jacket and walked slowly towards the door. "I'm hoping that you're not going to let us down, Carlton. At one point we weren't even positive that you were going to be coming to us."

"What do you mean by that?"

Mr. Anchors did not answer me. He acknowledged Flaxby with a smile and a wave of his hand, then vanished through the door. I was left, once more, alone with Flaxby who had resumed his attempts to bore through me with an eye-bulging stare. I glanced at him lazily, then looked down at the floorboards.

"Humbert!" he shouted, still glowering at me. "Humbert!"

I considered Mr. Anchors' last line: 'At one point we weren't even positive that you were coming here.' What could he have meant? Maybe I nearly survived the shooting? Maybe.

The door opened and Humbert was towering over me. "Get up then," bellowed Flaxby. "Follow Humbert and I'll come and see you when I'm ready. And next time you see Mr. Anchors you can speak to him proper, else I'll belt you. Understand?"

"Yes."

"'Yes, Mr. Flaxby'."

"Yes Mr. Flaxby."

"Okay. Now sod off."

I followed Humbert, who alternated between spitting, smoking and breathing as we walked, and went back the way we came, along the white phlegm-stained corridors. He stopped outside a painted-green wooden door. There was nothing to indicate that it was the 'Recollection Room', nor anything else besides.

"Is this it?" I asked him.

"It is. I think Mr. Flaxby is going to come see you later. When you've finished I will come back and take you to the canteen. Yes?"

"Yes, thank you Humbert."

He nodded back at me, possibly to acknowledge my correct pronunciation of his name. Then he spat on the floor and kicked open the door. "Go in. Sit down," he told me, curtly. "That's all you need to do."

I followed his orders; walked into the dimly-lit room and sat down in its one chair. In front of me there lay a large screen, to the left a tin pot of hot tea - and very little besides that. I tried to make myself as comfortable as possible in my bony wooden seat, then I sat in the dark, waiting for pictures to come to the screen. There were no head clamps, or handcuffs or devices to pin my eyes open (like in Clockwork Orange). The architects of this place had clearly been of the opinion that, placed in a black room for long enough and with enough caffeine pumped into their system, nobody can ignore the light show going on before their eyes.

I felt empty, alone and totally - terminally - helpless. My spirit was ravaged. I was still shuddering with shock; the shock that I was dead and the shock that I was in Hell. It sounded too absurd to say aloud clutched onto the one, solitary hope that I had left; that I may at least be able to find Kemi in this frightful place.

While I sat there, in that dark and soulless room, there was nothing else to cling to. Yet it occurred to me that I had, once before, felt every bit as devastated and desolate as I felt then, there, in the direst place in the whole universe.

Then the show began.

Chapter 15

Remembering Jim

My name was Jim. Short for James.

James Thomas Barrett, the first son of Grace Patricia and Graham John Barrett, was born on a windy autumn morning in the back bedroom of a suburban semi in Cambridge. It was a cool, silver-skied Wednesday with tree leaves browning and poised to fall. The midwife was late, the ambulance never came and it was left to my grandmother, Mary-Jane (Mary to friends), to complete the delivery.

I was raised on the bare, desperate streets of a dreary, half-deserted council estate. The inhabitants were everything that one might expect of poor people in a rich, esteemed university town; resentful, indelicate and incurably bored. They were bereft of ambition and swollen by vitriol. When I was about three my grandmother, who lived down the road, would take me in the push-chair to a small green. She would sit on the bench and survey the overgrown park land; a thin, ragged rectangle strip compressed by the vile clutter of council houses, some with stone-cladding, some with hanging baskets and all with identical flaking royal blue doors.

Grandmother would smoke cigarettes and stroke my chin. "How's my little Jim-boy?" she'd repeat, blowing rings and plumes of white smoke into my scarless face. Then she would sit back and gaze, along with me, at the swings, the scattered branches, leaves, crisp wrappers and needles. This was our home.

I saw very little of my mother. She was a devoted poet with little time for anybody or anything apart from her beloved rhymes. I remember, when I was too young to understand, her reading poems to me - but they never seemed to make a great deal of sense. The only time that I ever found my mother interesting (or useful) was when she plucked splinters from my fingers.

My father was even less approachable. He was a belligerent, gruff Northerner with broad shoulders and breath full of pipe smoke. He was a 'frozen foods supervisor' at our local superstore and always wore his work clothes - white shirt, blazer, blue tie, red braces, shiny black trousers - even on a Saturday. He despised my mother and her miserable poetry, preferring 'honest' pursuits such as pub darts, dominoes or ale consumption. The only topics on which he could hold conversation were work (which he adored) and black people (whom he detested). These were the subjects that my father brought up every day at dinner; gazing intently through my young eyes, ranting noisily about inane shop-floor dramas, exotic new food products and the evils of immigration. By the time I was two years old I was using the words 'nignog' and 'wog' as often as 'mummy' and 'daddy'. I doubt that father even noticed. The only times that he acknowledged my existence were for five minutes, from seven AM, at breakfast and for fifteen minutes, from six PM, for dinner.

He spent most of his spare time in our local pub, The Marlborough. He never went out to get drunk, rather to repeat the same dreary monologue, on stock-checks, papaya and coons to a new audience. On other occasions, perhaps after one of the exasperated locals had told him to shut up, he would ask my grandmother to make him some marmalade sandwiches which he would take down to the local canal with his fishing rod. There he would sit and sulk alone for a time, perhaps grumbling under his breath to the birds or the trees. They, like everything else, were unresponsive - and I believe he liked to keep things that way. He was scared of what people thought of him; of what uncommon views they might hold. He was fearful of intelligence and education because he knew that it might show him up for what he really was; a lonely, narrow-minded, indistinct little man with a frozen food fixation.

On one occasion, when I was only four or five years-old, I decided to take the short walk down to the canal and watch my father fish. When I finally found him he was sitting on a bright green case, smoking his pipe and staring into space. His rod lay on the ground by his side.

"Why aren't you fishing, Daddy?" I asked, to which he looked down at me, blinked, snarled, grunted and then turned away again. At the time I felt slightly deflated and walked away wordlessly. Yet, on reflection, that may have been the only time in my life that I ever saw anything exceptional - or even remotely noteworthy - in my father. He simply sat at the waterside, alone, gaping at something that lay far away; across the canal, through the bramble mesh opposite, under the sky, over the sun and well beyond his reach. Something impossible, intangible.

He was neither a bright nor a well-travelled man, so he was destined to suffer eternally in his deplorable world of freezers, ale houses and pungent brown canals, without ever learning that, elsewhere, a better life was attainable.

He knew that his life was pathetic, but he did not know how to improve it. In fact, the only thing that he truly knew was the superstore.

We never had holidays. Not until I was five years old, when my father finally turned down the overtime in favour of a trip to bleak Hunstanton. At the time I resented him for taking us there and not to Bude or Yarmouth, where all of my friends went, but now the images fetched a fresh poignancy.

It rained every other day but Father still took me down to the beach to get away from my mother, with her whiskey, cryptic poetry and incessant wretchedness. He rolled up his trouser legs and fetched water from the sea in an old yellow pail, then brought it back for my sandcastle moat. Some days he would stumble into the sea, some days it would not matter because we were so wet from the rain anyway. Then we would go back to the caravan and punch its windows until Mother came around and unlocked the door. It was the only time in my life that I could not hate him for his silence, and the only time in my life that he actually mattered to me, though I still felt more for my disaffected mother.

In the Recollection Room I saw, once again, my father standing on the promenade; his white shirt blinding against the sun's naked beam. He stood there, throwing a battered green tennis ball down to where I stood on the beach. I never managed to catch it and my attempts at throwing the ball back all went awry, but he still persisted with a smile on his face. He never said a word, just chased my loose passes, running awkwardly from one side to the other in his best office clothes.

On reflection I could see the love in him there; the love that never dared to unveil itself to anyone.

Whilst on holiday we would take long mundane walks along the low cliff-top paths. I would be looking down and thinking that I could tumble over the side and still survive. I watched below as the sea rose and fell, exhaled and inhaled. That vast blue-brown body of water was sucked again and again under the rocks, then into small caves, leaving snakes of mucus-like water trails on the reefs as it went. It battered the cliff face repeatedly; great claws of water lurching up from the blue towards the path. I yearned, privately, for one of those oceanic arms to leap up onto the path, clutch both of my parents firmly and drag them down into its endless heaving gut. Yet the reality, inevitably, was less spectacular. My parents' eyes were fixed on the path ahead, avoiding the dog poo, with my mother hoping for the walk to end and my father praying that something, somehow would come from all of this to make everything better.

It was a week after we returned from Hunstanton when I discovered that my mother was pregnant, and three days after that when my father - finally shorn of patience - beat the unborn baby to death in her womb. It was the first time, though not the last, that I saw my father slam his bony fist into my mother's pale, fragile face. It had seemed oddly out of character - far too spectacular for him. From the moment he snapped he became unstoppable; hurling my mother into the wall, cracking her head against the bookshelf and slamming a porcelain pot-full of chrysanthemums across her breasts. I stood back in the dark hallway where I saw the thin snake of blood on the white wood chipped wallpaper and the uncompromising crunch of delicate skull against skirting board. "You deserve to die!" screamed my father while he cried into my mother's gaping wounds. As much as I loved her, I decided that he was probably right. He was justified.

Mother became pregnant again two months later. She finally gave birth to my sister Lucy on the first day of April, nearly a year after her first 'good news'. Her disposition - saturnine at the best of times - became suddenly very grave after this arrival. At first she grew even more deeply entrenched in her dusty world of unpublished poetry, but then she lost the will even to write. Instead she would sit at home in her chair, beneath the brown sprawl of nicotine-stained ceiling. She sat there watching television, smoking cigarettes and playing solitaire. I wanted her to die. I loved her more than anything in the world and never doubted that she in turn thought much of me, but I still wanted her gone. She deserved to be dead. At that stage though, in many ways, it was already over.

Father left us and moved out of the house on several occasions. Mother always said he had a fancy woman, although I found it hard to believe. Nonetheless, he always returned eventually, hoping hopelessly that something had changed in his absence.

I had always been my mother's favourite and yet she thoroughly despised everything, everybody, so being her number one actually meant very little. On one occasion she said that she preferred wine glasses to people; because they never leave without warning nor fight back, and you can always smash them up if you grow bored of them. My father, meanwhile, much preferred Lucy to me. From the time she learned to talk she was pretty, submissive and dumb: less intelligent and more malleable than me. I was increasingly bright, talkative, curious and, to him at least, threatening. She was none of those. Whenever Father left home he took Lucy with him, obviously harbouring some ill-considered thoughts of starting a new life with his little angel, but lacking the vision to know where or how. So he always returned and he always resumed his routine as if nothing had ever happened. He still spent all of his time fishing or droning on about supermarkets and 'wogs' or, perhaps, beating my mother senseless in a vain attempt to knock some life back into her.

It was on Christmas Eve, just days after my tenth birthday,

that my life was turned on its head. Father, Lucy and I had gone to spend the day with my grandmother just down the road. My aunt, who had been given just two months to live, was also there. Father had wanted her to stay with us for a few days, but I had complained fiercely about having a terminally ill woman there, on the off chance that she decided to die while in our house. I had always liked the woman, but I was of the opinion that it would be unpleasant to live in a house that a relative had died in.

It was a fairly ordinary Christmas Eve. The turkey was fresh from the freezer and our Christmas twig was dressed with a few pitiable fairy lights. A cold wind swung low in the air. Pallid clouds hung sparsely in the black and white morning sky. Everybody else - friends, neighbours and cousins - felt full of yuletide cheer; decking their pines with tinsel, baubles and chocolate treats. My mother had stayed at home. Long gone was her energy for family festivities.

Then... I should never have forgotten what happened next.

My grandmother was out of cigarettes and, as her foot was swollen and my father too deeply entrenched in a rant about bogus asylum-seekers, it was decided that I should go back to raid my mother's bottomless tobacco stash. I stepped back into the house, pulling the door behind me, then trod carefully towards our 'lounge', the ever-silent hovel where my mother and only my mother commonly resided. The living room door hissed as I tentatively nudged it open. Spider webs, too long gathered, were stretched apart as it edged, slowly, open.

The first thing I noticed was that she was no longer in the chair. She had reached, possibly even lunged, towards the door which I now stood beside. Her skin was the colour of thick chalk scraped over grey rock. Her eyes were wide open - wider than I had ever seen them - to reveal the irises' true blueness and the newfound crimson of her bloody, bulging eye whites. Her body was twisted so that her breasts lay flat on the carpet, squashed beneath her chin, while her thigh had fallen against a table leg - sent an ashtray sprawling - and turned her thin grey legs sideways. Because of this I could see the patch in her grey skirt where she had wet herself. She could not have been dead for long, because the puddle of urine next to her body was still steaming away in the winter cold.

By the time I found my mother her heart had stopped pumping blood across the living room floor. The blood clearly came from a slit in her throat, where a glimmer of razor blade could be seen deeply buried. From her position it looked as if she had done the deed, changed her mind and tried to find help.

I moved closer to her, leaned down and picked up a packet of her cigarettes from next to the still mass. I was glad she was dead. She deserved to be.

At the funeral I did not cry. To me she had passed on long before.

Father surprised me by throwing out all of my mother's stuff after the funeral and so, consequently, I had nothing left with which to mark her existence. Things could have been different, though, but for something that happened a week to the day after the service, when I was spending the afternoon at my grandmother's. She wanted a packet of cigarettes and so gave me a little money to take down to the local shop - which always served me - and buy her twenty. Fishing into my pockets I suddenly came across the same packet of my mother's, which I had previously taken from next to her corpse. Being young and naive I showed them to my nan and, fancying the money for myself, said: "Buy them off me!"

The old lady, instantly indignant, slapped me around the face and boomed, "Give them to me! What on earth would your father say if he saw you with a pack of fags?" So she took my mother's cigarettes, kept the money - and that was that.

The door surged open and Flaxby strode in boldly; banging on the light switch as he did and flooding the Recollection Room with dazzling whiteness. "Well?" he demanded, as if I was meant to sum up the first ten years of my life in a simple sentence.

"Very sad," I replied honestly, after a short pause.

Flaxby groaned, banging shut the room door as he did. "Can't stand your kind," he said, shaking his miserable head. "You think that having a university education gives you the right to be horrid. You've got diplomas and O-levels and degrees, like, and silly bloody letters after your name, but you're still a nasty little thing."

I chose not to answer, for I saw that Flaxby was not going to be placated by anything that I could possibly say. Instead I began to reflect on what I had just seen; on the forgotten minor details of my unspent infancy. It made dour viewing; a catalogue of utter hopelessness, a dictionary of dejection without stint - fairly miserable stuff - and yet it was all reminding me of something else... something terrible... and something which happened after... I just could not place it.

I began, for a second, to think upon the nightmares that had haunted me during those months on the run, and upon the reason - whatever it was - for me being pursued by the government in the first place - but Flaxby interrupted me. "You were a right revolting little brat, weren't you?" he roared, drumming loudly on his teeming gut to the beat of his tirade.

"Why? What did I do that was so bad?" I asked him, growing tired of his unrelenting abuse.

"Aren't you ashamed of yourself - aren't you ashamed that you never cried at your mother's funeral? That you stole cigarettes from next to her dead body and tried to sell them to your grandmother? That you wouldn't have your lovely old aunt round your parents' house because she might dare to die while she stayed there?"

"I was a kid."

"You were a vicious little beast."

"Whatever, Flaxby."

"Sir to you."

"Sir."

"Aren't you sad now? Aren't you sad that your mother died?"

I was not certain at first, but then I gave the matter a moment's thought and decided that, yes, I was sad. Yet this was not the time to express my feelings; I had not even had the time to digest these images from my past, long since abandoned by memory.

Fed up with waiting for a reply, Flaxby ranted onwards,

"You're the same as everybody else. Full of bloody excuses."

"Well if you gave me the time to think about it..."

"Oh you'll have plenty of hours to dwell on it, young man, because time's up for you in here for today. We've got other people to deal with you know."

"I never said you hadn't. I never even suggested..."

"It won't make any difference anyway. You'll go to bed. You'll sleep on it. But you'll still be a nasty bastard when you wake up in the morning. It won't make any difference."

"What's the point in all of this, then?"

"It's punishment."

"And what do you get out of it?"

"Don't you dare question me, smart-arse. Now - get lost. Go on, get out."

"Where to, may I ask?"

"Follow Humbert."

At that Humbert appeared at the door, accompanied by the tinkling noise of his key-ring and a heavy sniff. "This way," he grunted despondently, and I followed obligingly.

Chapter 16

The Crime

I spent two or three hours in a thin, low and dark cell, wondering more than anything else how I had managed to forget so much. It was a foul night in a foul place and yet, despite the lack of room service I decided that I had probably stayed in worse places than Hell.

After those solitary hours I was ushered back into the Recollection Room. Flaxby informed me, with his customary incivility, that I was about to watch the most abhorrent of extracts from my short, pitiful life. I offered, first, to tell him just how much time I had spent since my previous visit to the room thinking about my mother, and how I had just started to realise - for the first time ever - what she actually meant to me... but he could not have cared less. He just glared back at me, which made me feel as cold and emotionless as ever.

So I sat back down in the Recollection Room's splinter-riddled chair. Yet again the green fields and sprawling red-brown suburban rooftops of central England flickered back onto the screen. In those days the country was free, but its image - crisp, clear on the screen before me - only served to bring back memories of being pursued through the foggy East Anglian plains, chased by the Press and government officials.

This 'free' England was gone now, replaced by a vile and manacled mob-led hate state. I felt like crying for a lost friend... then wondered once more upon Gwyn and what may have become of her. Then what about Baz or Aaron or Agatha or Zane or Robert, all of those - good and bad - that I had left behind... there were too many of them.

The picture show resumed in the March after Mother's suicide. Most of young Jim's days were spent with his back propped up against the lounge sofa, near the spot where he had found her stinking carcass.

I saw, once again, how I often laid there - usually when I should have been at school doing brilliantly - and spent hours gazing vacantly at the seamless array of porn and horror videos which my father had bought to keep me quiet (without, I dare add, ever understanding the nature of the subject matter with which he was educating his son.. During these empty, silent hours alone I would often be more engaged in the cobwebs and plaster craters on the ceiling than in the contents of those video nasties, but their ongoing noise provided just a little mesmerising company. They became a backdrop to my everyday oblivion. I became used to the naked thrash of male and female forms, tossing mechanically about on the small screen; pressed together, undulating uneasily as one. I grew quickly accustomed to the staged horrors of man slashing man, tearing through cosmetic flesh as if it meant no more than paper. The mangled cadavers and gory bodies were not shocking to me. After a short time they seemed as ordinary and dull as the cobwebs.

During this time my father disappeared almost entirely. He began to take every second of available overtime at the shop, only now he had less interest in relaying mundane details of shop-floor politics. Even his dinner table monologues about immigration were replaced by a deafening quietness. I wanted him to roar across the room, to strike me in the face, to scream and bellow about rowdy customers and 'bloody wogs' but he never did. He was just silent. Or missing.

I think my desperate state of mind had more to do with his absence as a father than the final departure of my mother. I was left with nothing and nobody in my life. Of course there was my sister Lucy, but I detested her more than anything, I blamed her for everything going wrong and wanted nothing better for her than a painful death. When she was alone with me I would pick fights with her; hurl her across the room and throw books in her direction. Yet she seemed strangely inclined to attach herself to me, as if I was the most precious thing in the world. No matter how many times I struck or shouted at her, Lucy never seemed to grow bored of me. In a manner I found that the most irritating thing of all.

Then there was my grandmother. I had once been close to her, but now I was growing weary of her vexing presence. All of her conversations came from soap operas and her philosophies from daytime chat shows. I could see little of interest in her anymore.

The only character of any interest to me was my sixteen-year-old cousin - also Jim - the son of my dying aunt. He was, for some reason, everything that I wanted to be in life; he had smoked cigarettes from the age of twelve, had sex from the age of thirteen and dropped out of school at sixteen to become a happy barman. He was bright but not so bright that it became a burden and was content instead with cannabis and alcohol. I wanted to be like him - simple and happy. His parents - my aunt and uncle - cared for him yet gave him the liberty to discover the world - and it worked! Jim was a joy to know and, what is more, would never harm a soul.

Everybody remarked that I was 'doing well' after my mother's suicide, but they never understood how little she had meant to me by the time it happened. I was becoming bored by the chore of mourning my mother with dignity.

I tried so hard to play the part - to seem affected and melancholy - but could not halt the feeling that I wanted a better role. There must, I kept assuring myself, be something far more exciting than this out there. I began to spend my sleepless nights and restless moments planning to be famous; to be recognised as something special and spectacular. At times I dreamt of being a hero, a legend - then at others I fancied myself as a despicable miscreant. I needed something exciting to happen to me. Even walking down the road I found myself looking up at the sky and wishing that the planes above would come crashing down and into the streets below. Anything spectacular would do for me.

The morning that it happened began like any other. The sky was no more or less angry than it had been at the two preceding dawns. The gravestone-grey clouds were as moody as ever, with thick grey lumps which held like tumours to their bleak, static mass. My jaw was locked for some odd reason and a foul wake-up taste was clinging to the inside of my mouth.

Father always left the house early in the morning, leaving

me on my own. He did not care whether or not I left for school on time, in fact he had even bought a cat ('Derek') to keep me company during the daytime. That said, its purpose was more commonly to demand food from me, or urinate in the corner of my bedroom.

So this was just another morning in the life of Jim Barrett, aged ten-and-a-half. I would lie in bed for a while every day and ponder the infinite possibilities for the hours ahead. I could stay at home and watch the wallpaper or the sinful movies - else I could go out into that world outside. Maybe I could find a friend (if I still had any), perhaps somebody else had decided to skip school. Then again, maybe I could go out and do something else, something extraordinary. It seemed to me that while I lay in bed there was a universe of opportunity waiting outside, but as soon as I had risen and decided what to do I had narrowed down my options.

Light was billowing into the room from the bulb-lit hallway and the mournful and muddy morning sky. I always slept with the curtains open so that I could wake with my face pointed to the great outdoors.

Suddenly, with that image, I remembered what it was that I had dreamt of the night before: I had pictured myself in a dark room, asleep, with all the lights turned out save for the pallid bars of moonlight which crept through the curtains. The landing light had gone out and there, on my bedroom floor, lay a dark and still body. Alive. I could feel its heat and could hear its unsteady breaths. I was not scared of what I saw, and arched myself out of bed to peer over at the motionless face. It was the pungency of the cigarette stench which gave its identity away.

It was my mother. She lay there on the floor, serene and half-naked. I pulled the rest of my bare body from the bed and stood over the scantily-clad form, one leg on either side. Straddled her. I wanted her to look at me once more, to stare up at me... but all I saw were the whites of her eyes. She preferred to stare away from me, towards the door and into the carpet. Look at me, I urged her. I surveyed her beautiful white figure; her tattered exquisiteness, her imperfect grace. I bent my legs, lowered myself so that I was just touching her. I longed for her to respond, but she did not move... she simply wheezed away to herself.

It was one of those dreams that escapes the night and passes through to the waking moments. For several hazy seconds I remained stationary in bed, wondering whether I would land on my mother if I rolled out of bed. Was it real? Of course not.

Oh well, back to reality.

Remembering it all, there in the Recollection Room, nearly made me sick. Somehow, suddenly, Hell seemed to be the perfect place for me. I began to squirm uncomfortably in that stiff wooden seat. "I belonged here," I sighed aloud. Everything - every memory - was returning.

Another two hours passed before I made up my mind on what to do with the day. It came after the flavourless porridge, dressed only with a paltry dollop of sour crimson jam. It came after the burning black tea which stung my tongue and scorched my throat. It came after the chilly-grey morning walk and the stroll around the shop and twenty minutes on a roadside bench, looking up at the bent-backed streetlamps which stooped like giant scythes over everyone's head. Then I hatched my plan.

Instead of returning home I continued my walk on into the city centre. It was one of those mornings that could belong to either March or October; nothing about the weather disclosed its season. It lacked the common promise of spring; the sensation of summer making its charge on winter in sunny stutters and then, as it progressed, in gleaming brilliance. This was a dreary, anonymous morning; icy and unfeeling. You could feel the crisp frost underfoot as you cut corners on grassy garden patches. You could taste each caustic blast of cold which carried on the keen early wind.

The city was full of shallow puddles and unsmiling faces. I thought for a moment about abandoning my whole plan and buying myself a burger instead, or calling on somebody I knew and smoking their dad's cigarettes behind the garden gate for a while. It would be a lot easier than this... but it would not be spectacular.

I waited in the shopping arcade for a long time, enchanted by the deathless swarm of passers-by and secretly mocking them. I was on the lookout for the perfect face for my plot. For a time I leaned back on a second floor balcony rail and surveyed the place; gazing into each glass-paneled shop-face and then turning to search the ground floor below. Then I left the arcade and sat on a bench in the High Street, looking for my victim. Quickly I grew impatient and like a flustered clothes-shopper running short on time became desperate to take whatever I could. So there was nothing special about the face that I finally chose - he was just there when I needed him and close enough to a correct fit.

At the time I had no idea of his age, but he was short and sweet and smiled far too much for someone so small. His mother had nipped into a newsagents and left the little boy standing outside, aside his baby sister's pushchair. I moved towards him, and peered into the store where she was perusing fashion magazines. She looked thoroughly absorbed - almost as if she did not need the little thing she had deposited outside. Why had she left him there? Did she not want him anymore? Why not take him inside with her? I felt almost guiltless as I closed in on my prey and took his slim pink hand in mine. He smiled up at me; a grateful, trusting and pointless grin. Poor innocent creature, I told myself. He deserved this if only for his stupidity.

So I pulled him away while his mother read about lipstick or dresses or hair and bought her cigarettes and fumbled for the correct change. He came willingly. We were probably around the corner and two streets away by the time she came out of the shop to realise, at a second glance, that Little Thingy was not where she had left him.

We walked and we walked through Cambridge. The child grew tired, began to wonder where we were going, when we were going to meet up with his mother again.

"Mummy's gone home," I told him coolly. "I've got to take care of you today."

"Where are we going?" he asked, a tad breathless.

"To play."

146

From the moment I had his hand in mine I never thought twice. It was effortless from there on in; I simply suspended my emotions for an hour. Switched them off. It was almost comically mechanical.

Now I knew exactly what was going to happen. I remembered.

I jumped off the chair and ran to the door, then began hammering on it impetuously. "I want out! let me out! let me out!" I bellowed, scratching at the door's varnish in an effort to claw my way out of the Recollection Room. Within a second the door lurched open, hurling me to the ground in one movement. Above me was the dour, hopeless face of Humbert scowling down at me. "Get back in the chair," he snarled with thick cider breath, stooping uneasily to seize me by the hair and drag me up.

"I can't watch it!" I yelled, my face ribboned with tears of desperation, "you can't make me watch that!"

"They're the rules. You watch the film. They're the rules."

"No!" I insisted, shaking my head riotously.

Humbert barely had the time to emit a grunt before Flaxby came surging through the door with an uneven, purposeful wobble.

"Oh do we have waterworks?" he yelled, staring at me with wide angry eyes. "Well, I'm sorry but we're all out of tissues here."

"Do anything else!" I whimpered, "anything but that."

Humbert looked sadly at the floor, but Flaxby was beginning to smile. "I don't think so," he beamed. "Now you get your bloody backside on that there chair and you watch the film, okay?"

I remained silent for a few moments, trying to collect my breath but then, with a sorrowful inevitability, I returned to the chair.

"Thank you," said Flaxby in a slow ironical drawl. "Now shut up and watch the film. If you're a good boy and you watch it properly, then we'll call time in half hour - okay?"

I did not answer. Instead I gazed into the screen which had fallen blank before me, waiting for the corridor light behind me to disappear and signal the departures of Flaxby and Humbert. I wanted this over.

The film resumed in an instant. Once again I was walking with the child's hand in mine, marching wordlessly out of town, through the suburbs and towards the fields. I knew by then that somewhere in the throbbing heart of the city his mother would be looking for her lost one. I knew that there was no going back. I had come this far and now there was no halting me.

Finally we came to the dirt track. I clambered over the stile and was followed by my obliging customer, who still seemed wholly satisfied by the notion that we were going to 'play'.

"What are we going to play?"

"Err. I don't know. Whatever."

"Where are we going to play?"

"Down here. Just a bit further."

"Are we going to your house?"

"Maybe later."

I had already decided that we were unlikely to be disturbed by dog-walkers, cyclists or duffle-coated ramblers. Once we were away from the main road the path veered suddenly into a huddle of trees. Pleased with the location I stopped, gently picked the kid up and carried him through the trees. It began abruptly. I dropped the child and kicked him once, then paused just long enough to catch his last pathetic smile, to see the first sensation of horrified surprise sprawl across his scarless face.

So I booted him again - once, twice - again and again. He squealed, but a kick to the face hastily knocked the noise out of him. I saw the terror in his eyes for a second, but then it was all gone. The whole job became easier, became fun. I relaxed and found myself listening to the mellifluous whistle of wind through branches. I was at one with nature; throbbing against its bare naked mass, a partner to the tremulous breeze and quivering aside the soaring moans of all God's creatures. Every thud of boot into chest, every short release of air from the boy's dying mass seemed in time with the beat of the world around me. Then, in my frenzy, I reached down for hefty branches and sharp stones. At the time I did not notice that one of his ears was removed with the first strike of branch on temple. He was probably dead by then, or too far gone to feel that terrific pang of pain. At some point I seemed to break his backbone, his body seemed to turn limp and loose like water in a bag. I could hear his bones cracking against each other.

A hump was spawned in the crotch of my tracksuit bottoms as I drove the stone into that boy's young skull. With every chip of skull which splintered off and into the overgrowth I grew harder. I was loaded with the stench of purest impurity.

That day - for the first time - I went home and I masturbated. Then with every stroke I thought of the boy's fractured face and with every such image the sexual furnace grew hotter and the lust madder. I had wanted to do this there, then, over the body, over him - perhaps I should have buggered his lifeless form. I had wanted to empty the sexual tension all over his mangled remains. But it was impossible.

The burst eyeball, the glimpse of battered brain, the twisted bones did more to make my Y-fronts twitch than any porn magazine or video could have started to. I felt giddily high when I climaxed that afternoon, higher than I would ever, could ever, feel again, and sensed not the slightest remorse when I turned to see my father's startled face watching me from the landing. I simply turned away and continued to consummate my crime. Yet, oddly, no matter how much joy I stole from that child's shapeless corpse, I still could not clear any of my anger, any of my pain. It remained inside choking my soul.

I had made myself watch the film, if only to escape the Recollection Room without further delay. After that I prayed they would have no more to show me. I prayed I would never have to return to that dreadful place.

The room lights came on. The screen was blank. I could hear Humbert's jangle and Flaxby's uneven trot.

"Go on then you little bastard," said Flaxby, "tell me that you did it because your mother died or your dad didn't love you enough. Go on."

I looked back at him. "That wasn't me. It was another person."

He growled aggressively in return. "Well," he announced,

"that's all you're gonna get for today. And I've got to meet Mr. Anchors for dinner."

"For today? What do you mean?" I asked.

"Oh... there's more tomorrow," he replied, smiling again.

Chapter 17

The Aftermath

When Humbert woke me the next morning I wanted to plunge daggers into his green, rotten apple eyes. It meant another slow walk to the Recollection Room and another day of watching Jim Barrett's pitiable existence fold in on itself. After all that I had seen the day before it seemed unthinkable that I could have fallen into such a deep, undisturbed sleep that night, but somehow I had. Perhaps it was because I needed to escape from it all. Maybe my mind simply could not cope with dwelling on what had happened.

I managed to get into the seat without first being lambasted by Flaxby. Working on the principle that I had already seen the direst details of Jim's disturbed young life, I was almost pleased to see the action resume. I had cried for Jim's mistakes the day before, and now hopefully that was out of the way. By this point I was just eager to reach the end of my punishment and to cope with whatever came after. One thing that I could not understand, entirely, was my reason for being sent to the Recollection Room. Clearly they had no intention of trying to reform me, so why was I there? I decided that the only reason for the whole exercise was to torture me with the crimes that I had managed to leave behind me. In my mind the boy had become no more than an old passport photograph in a trouser pocket, bleached yellow and then, at last, bleached away by several trips to the washer. Even now, watching his face on the screen, he seemed to mean very little. Yet when I contemplated what I had actually done to him my mood began to change. When I thought of how the clumsy feet would have grown steady and strong. How his unmarked young body would have matured, gone through school, dated girls, lived a life and seen the world.
But for me. Then I began to feel monstrously dispirited. I considered for a second that I had also - through my crime -

spared him from the blight of adulthood, but the thought was dismissed hastily. Jim Barrett had, indeed, committed a dreadful crime... but then, *my* name was Joey Carlton.

I ceased to be the criminal when I ceased to be Jim Barrett but, just like when the mobs had chased me back in England, now I was not being allowed to move on either. I was not being allowed to be Joey Carlton. I had constructed myself a new life and developed a socially acceptable identity... but no matter how malleable I was, people could not be satisfied.

The film restarted about three days after the event. The boy, it turned out, had only just turned three-years-old. They found his body and exhumed with it one-hundred-and-one clichés. How could this happen here? He was such a beautiful boy... You got the idea that the murder had happened in Heaven and that the victim was Jesus Christ. At the time I found the whole business highly amusing.

On the news the reader announced that "he left his body in a small patch of woodland" which, I thought, made it sound as if the child had forgotten himself on a walk. I became almost hysterically enlivened by all of this language.

I noticed that most of the public had reacted to the murder in exactly the same way as they react to the death of a well-loved soap opera character. At times, I decided, it was more important for crowds of people to display their sorrow or their sympathy for that young boy's family than to actually feel it. There was no real interest in the human side - and that remained constant as details of the crime began to reveal themselves.

It could not have been especially hard to link me to the murder. When my father finally got the knock on the door, he greeted the officers with a preposterous pseudo-posh accent; pronouncing his words slowly, distinctly and with painfully precise definition. I think he may well have known what was coming already. I think it may even have been he who had phoned them in the first place.

The news hit the media instantly. After that I did not need a trial, people made up their minds in a moment. The country needed somebody to blame for this atrocity and I was there to satisfy their appetite. They needed to direct their hatred towards something - and a ten-year-old boy from a broken home seemed as good an object as anything else. There was a glimmer of intrigue in the nation's horror; it was as if they had needed the perpetrator of this terrible crime to be an abominable animal... and a psychologically muddled-up ten-year-old was fascinatingly apt. The fact that I felt no remorse did not help. When the social services asked how I was coping with what I had done, I told them that I did not need to cope with it which, at the time, was the absolute truth.

The people and I obviously shared the need for an item of interest to fill our insipid lives. I understood their obsession, but also felt strangely superior to them - as if I had achieved something quite magnificent by being the centre of their communal attention. I needed somebody to take notice of me for whatever reason and this had been the resolution.

I knew, of course, that what I had done was wrong but I was so accustomed to violence and hate that I did not understand how wrong.

Before I was taken to the courtroom I was addressed by what seemed like six million social workers. They asked me if I considered my mother's death to be a reason for what I had done. They asked how her suicide had affected me and whether I had felt 'anger' as a consequence of her demise. I told them that I could not have cared less about her dying; that I was glad she was gone. They asked me whether it was the violent or sexual movies that had caused me to kill, but I told them that I had only murdered the little boy because I had wanted to and that neither gore nor porn had exerted any bearing on the matter. Still they persisted, encouraging me to lie about the motives for my malice.

"Why, then, did you kill the boy?"

"Because he was there. Because I needed to do something."

In retrospect, looking back on such exchanges, I am not so certain. Perhaps it was Mother, or Father, or even the filth to which I was exposed that spawned the monster in me. Subconsciously.

One thing is certain, however, that the answers I gave

during those interviews were not enough to placate the tumultuous public. They did not understand my crime and so they hated me for it. I felt as though they detested me more, as a ten-year-old, for committing that murder than they would have if I had been a thirty-year-old - simply because the actions did not befit a person of my age. Ten-year-olds, they fancied, should be watching cartoons, playing computer games and sipping soda drinks. Murder is not what ten-year-olds do. Yet they failed to understand that life is not always so simple. At times the world conspires against us and we act in a way which is out of character; wrong; abhorrent. I was not a bad person: I was bright, I went to church, I read comic books and had never hit anyone in my life. Evidently, the tabloids delineated a different character: I was a smoker, a truant, a cold and heartless bastard who stood tearless at his own mother's funeral. Yes, they even used my mother against me.

I discovered that the public's perception of children is that on the whole they are sacred creatures - my victim for instance, was sacred - whereas I, as it happened, was quite the opposite. I did not entirely understand this anomaly, but decided that I must have been on the wrong side of some unspoken age barrier which left me exposed to the disdain of the public. I also struggled with the notion that all children should be indiscriminately held in such high esteem. At some point, then, Hitler and Stalin must have been cute and pure. That seemed wrong to me. Horrible people invariably start off as horrible little people and, for the sake of symmetry, end up as horrible old people. As such I failed to comprehend the colossal measures of respect designated to both the very young and the very old.

So the case went to court and I was clearly guilty. At the trial I did not cry or show remorse. Yet I *felt* no remorse - and it seemed to me that the world would have preferred me to have faked it, to have feigned compunction than to actually be honest to myself. I did not understand my crime - and the country did not want me to understand it - they merely wanted grief, devastation, distress. They never got what they wanted, though, and that yet again made me a cold heartless bastard.

While all of this was unfolding the mobs were in overdrive. They had uncovered my grandmother's old address and a group of wrathful parents hurled bricks through the windows. None of them knew that my grandmother had since sold up and that the only retribution caused by their vitriol was to a seven-year-old girl who caught half a blue brick on her left cheekbone. Nobody cared though. My cousin Jim spent a night in the local infirmary after being stabbed in the leg by an enraged fifty-year-old neighbour. To me it seemed far worse for middle-aged men to be mindlessly assaulting innocent youngsters than for troubled ten-year-old boys to be battering children.

The media adored it all. Mania sold newspapers. The way they spoke of me, you would have thought that I was born with fangs and horns. I was the embodiment of subhuman Satanism. The only letters of support that I received were from so-called Pagans saying that they were glad I had joined their fraternity of murderous freakiness. For everybody else, though, it was socially unacceptable to utter a line of sympathy for me. In fact it was perfectly permissible for one member of the public to express to another his desire to put a knife in my back. Even my father, suddenly upreared from his melancholy state, told me that as much as he loved me he would still be glad to see me dead.

After being sentenced I was ushered into the police van under the cover of a brown woolen blanket. While I was being pushed, prodded, jostled and jeered at in the darkness I heard a bang, then a soaring crackle somewhere in the void beyond. I later discovered that an ex-army man, stashed away in the midst of the vengeful bustling crowd, had surged to the front of the mass and tossed a fistful of explosives towards me. His aim failed him though. It had careered off the awaiting police van and into the air, causing no further damage than three shattered windows and a blanket of ash on the tall helmets of assembled officers. His intention, though, had been the same as mine - to take life. When, several months later, the same man was imprisoned for attempting to blow up a ten-year-old boy he was turned into a national martyr. For some reason his crime was justified. He was allowed to play God.

Then came the detention centre. Every youth in the building knew who Jim Barrett was and they also hated him, for one week at least. It was everything that I had expected; dark young faces against bright white hospital corridors and the penetrating taste of bleach thick through the air. The rooms were cosy and bare; I looked for hooks, window bars and dangling light sockets but there was nothing there to tie a noose on.

I was told that nobody would know who I was, but it took my roommate precisely one minute and eighteen seconds to ask me about the crime. I timed it. He asked whether I felt sorry for the young boy's family.

"No," I replied curtly, "I don't."

"Why?" he queried, a little meekly and somewhat taken aback.

"Because everybody is asking how a ten-year-old could kill a little boy, but nobody is asking why that little boy was on his own in the street in the first place."

He was so surprised by my articulate response and my sharp reasoning that he never again alluded to my crime. It was true, though. The country could have gained far more by highlighting that boy's mother as a negligent guardian or encouraging other parents to be watchful and vigilant, than it ever achieved through making a demon out of me.

Yet whatever the wrongs of the media frenzy were I could not help but feel sickened by my crime, on reflection. I had killed a beautiful young child, I had taken him from the world. I had erased his future and, most abhorrently of all, I could not have cared less about it.

At that moment the lights came on again. The screen went blank. I breathed a sigh of relief that the day's viewing had not been nearly as distressing as that of yesterday. I felt somewhat at ease.

Then Flaxby came into the room.

"Happy with that? See what an horrible little fiend you were?"

"Well..."

"Or does that seem okay to you? Blaming what you did on

156

the poor boy's mother? Is that right in your book?"

"Well..."

"You're an horrid bastard. Horrid educated bastard, there's no need for your likes on God's green planet."

"Actually..." I stopped for a second to consider Flaxby's latter insult - 'God's green planet'! "Flaxby, are you religious?"

He showed me the pendant hanging from his neck. "Yes I am sir, a born Christian," he answered proudly.

"You're a Christian?"

"Yes."

"Isn't that ironic?"

"What?"

"Isn't it ironic - that you are a Christian but you got sent to Hell. Didn't you think to question your faith?"

His face glowed redder than usual. His yellowish eye whites grew wider. "How dare you talk to me like that!"

"It seems a reasonable question."

"I ask the questions."

"You've said that before Flaxby."

"Mister Flaxby."

"Okay, Mister Flaxby. Whatever. How come you are a Christian? What did you do to end up here if you believe in God?"

All of a sudden the podgy little man glowering down at me from under the door frame was a little breathless. He paused for a second to assemble his fury, then spoke. "I have my faith and it's served me very well thank you. You'd do well yourself to take a few hints from the Good Book. I followed the good word of the Lord all my life and I'm still a believer. I know he exists. The reason I ended up here is.... well it's none of your bloody business!

"Fair enough Flaxby. It's just that you are obviously a criminal like me, so I don't understand why you feel you're permitted to patronise and abuse me so strongly."

"What? How dare you! I wasn't a bit like you - I'm not a vicious little infant killer! Back down on Earth I had a very successful career in industry. I was Area Manager for a major company and ran my own factory. I owned a lot of land as well, and provided for five kids."

"So how did you end up here?"

Flaxby glared at me once again; probably wanted to bellow at me even louder. This time, however, he did not. He exhaled, very slowly cleared his lungs of air, and then wiped the sweat from his wrinkly brow. He frowned, looked down at the floor. "As I said I ran a factory," he continued, this time in a much calmer, lower voice, "some of them that worked there thought that the machines we were operating weren't safe - they were sparking off and making odd noises. They used to come up to me and tell me they couldn't afford to feed their kids, that they needed more money and that the job was, like, too dangerous for the pittance they were getting. But I was the boss and I had a business to run. I told them to get on with it. So they did - they got on with their jobs and I got on with mine. I thought I did a very good job of it - and I gave that factory thirty years of my life. The factory put all of my kids through school and saw me through my retirement. I didn't realise, then, how badly off those people were, like... how scared they were of coming to work... how famished their families were..." Then Flaxby's voice rose once again, turned as proud and loud as before, "But I was a good manager. I was a successful businessman. I worked bloody hard and did my very best. That is where I am different to your likes."

"Don't you think the government were a bit hard on me considering I committed my crime when I was ten?"

"No I don't. It was the best thing for England when that lot got in - it's time they sorted out sods like you. Leave it to the people to bring your type to justice. Let them punish you - none of this comfy prison cell with three square meals a day nonsense."

"Come on, Flaxby, our main source of justice in the Middle Ages was vigilantism. I'd like to think we've progressed since then."

"You can come out with as much of this clever political talk as you like. The truth is that the only way to stop people doing what you did is to kill them. That's what you call a proper deterrent."

"And you really think I deserved to be killed?"

"Yes I do. In fact it's a damn shame they didn't torture you first as well."

"So everybody should be punished for what they did at ten years of age?"

"It's not just what you did when you were ten," Flaxby laughed with condescending falseness, "it's the way you ignored it afterwards."

"What do you mean?"

As I spoke Humbert came into the room with a rattle, and beckoned me out of the chair. I rose and walked towards the door.

"You'll see in time," replied Flaxby, after a delay, "I saw you cry when you were watching that little baby get beaten to death. But you cried because you got punished for it, not because you regret it. At the time you didn't cry, because you didn't care. And you didn't cry when your mother died, because you didn't care. And there's more as well. The problem is, though, that you're not actually sorry for what you did. You're sorry because you're getting nailed for it."

With that I was led out of the room.

Chapter 18

Detention

I did not sleep at all. The boy's shattered face and Flaxby's final words on the matter repeated on me throughout the night. You're sorry because you're getting nailed for it. Did he honestly believe that I could be so callous? I kept myself awake so not to allow the memories to slip from my mind again - this time I did not want to forget, I wanted to understand why.

Humbert came into the room after several hours and grunted at me politely. An unrefined grin flashed across his dopey face for a moment, which I took as a sign that he liked me. Perhaps, I imagined, because I had stood up against Flaxby. I walked to the Recollection Room with a little more obedient enthusiasm that morning, stopping to get a cup of black coffee and a sandwich from the machine on the way. I had not expected to find coffee and snack machines in Hell.

This time the film began in the prison. Repulsion gushed through me at first sight of the tall, blindingly white cells. This was a prison for young criminals; an institution charged with the task of flooding stubborn skulls with the ecstasy and blessedness that they had always been refused. Everywhere the desperate faces of guards and inmates sloped around against the incongruous, glittering backdrop of heavenly whitewashed walls and attractive yellow, red and green posters. I had read about these places in Sunday tabloid diatribes; I knew not to expect the bitter, cold, colourless hell-pit detention centres of the 1970s. This was a place built on ideals. A somewhat awkward, uncomfortable fit; there was too much hatred stored in there for the building to remain so superficially content. At times I wished that the walls were black and blood-stained, that the floors were gravelly with too many knocked-out teeth, that the air was foul with the stench of human waste. That would have seemed more appropriate.

From the moment I set foot in that place I craved heavy opiates.

Once again I saw the ice cube classrooms; river blue walls frozen by the cold sun's ferocious gaze. The room was tall and felt too empty, even when full. Gum-peppered desks stretched from one side to the other. Beneath our feet lay mock marble tiles, slippery with detergent.

Then in walked the teacher and, as I watched him there on the Recollection Room screen, he was familiar at once. A lot younger of course, but unmistakable all the same - still the same old idiot with the same old stupid stutter. Jackboot.

I had completely forgotten about knowing him *then*. Perhaps, in the back of my mind, that was the reason for my hating him in later life, when we worked together as teachers. Of course he would never - could never - have remembered me from those Maths lessons in the detention centre. Not one of the inmates ever made a big enough impression.

When he began to lose control of the class he would snap into a ludicrous rant: "Nnn-now look here you lot," he would start, wagging his finger at as many of us as he could. "I want to get through this work as quick as I can. I don't want to beat about the bush, I want to finish all of this all in one fell swoop. Sss-so let's just remember that when you're playing silly devils you're just shooting yourselves in the foot. You're wasting your own time. Now let's remember who's top dog. Do-don't forget I have the upper hand here, you'll only wind up in trouble if you carry on like this."

Then he would resume with a series of stammers, blithering on pointlessly about a seamless array of numbers and fractions of numbers. Then he would hear a clatter of loud whispers growing at the back of the room. "Hhh-hold on now. If you have something to say, then hang fire and sss-sss-stick your hand up. Now what were you going to say? Come on out with it! Well, if it wasn't worth whispering then it wasn't worth saying out loud was it?" Nobody spotted that he had got this last line the wrong way round. "I-if you have something to say, I don't mind. Put your hand in the air. Have nerves of steel, ss-ssay what you think. If I agree with you, you'll get a pat on the back.

'Absolutely, well done,' I'll say. If I don't agree with you, then I'll politely tell you that you're backing the wrong horse. 'No, young man, I'm afraid I don't agree with you.' Th-that's fine. I'm not going to tell you off. But don't whisper, okay chaps? Okay?"

Okay.

"Jolly good. Jolly good, we'll - er - press - er - onwards. Nnn-now... where were we? Ah yes! Isoceles triangles! Wonderful!"

So on he went while each of us patiently followed the hands of the clock and looked for something stimulating to stare at on the walls or out of the meshed windows. There were certainly a good few colourful pictures tacked to the flake-and-paint bricks of the classroom walls but none of them were worthy of anything more than a glance.

I never wrote anything in those lessons and I never looked at the blackboard, although I frequently gazed through it. I hated that room. I hated the bare pipes and the perpetually flickering white lights. I hated the wobbly tables and the tap-tap-screech of the chalk. Back at my old school we had been treated to whiteboards, computers - the latest in classroom technology. Here they had the last blackboard in England. In some ways, as I watched it on the screen, it reminded me of the classroom that I would teach in decades later.

Most of all, though, I detested the teacher. Sometimes I would stop searching through the room's inanimate objects and spend a while analysing Jackboot himself. Here, now, in the Recollection Room, I found myself doing the same again. I began to dissect his every move; the slow sway from side to side, the finger-tapping, the nose-rubbing. I examined the clothes he was wearing; immaculately ironed grey trousers, insanely shiny brown leather shoes and a well-ironed blue shirt which clung tightly to the shambling bare body beneath. I attained a sense of equality by looking deep into the fabric to where his nipples pressed against the shirt's inside. It reminded me that, although on the surface he was free and I a prisoner, we were still both naked underneath.

I did not make a great many friends in prison. I spent a lot of my time alone reading the gun magazines which my cellmate had managed to smuggle in. For a brief period I became engrossed in the different models and their potential for destruction, but then I grew bored with them. Eventually the warden found my magazines and they were all confiscated. Consequently my dedication was shifted to less sinister concerns. I began to write film scripts and cartoons, then learnt to play guitar on one of the battered plastic-stringed acoustics in the common room. I mastered the open chords from a teach-yourself book in the library, then picked up the barre and power chords from visual memory; imitating the rock 'n' roll shapes of Pete Townshend. I had seen him on an old video of my father's - one which Mother had bought him for his birthday but he never watched - and it was easy to recall his absurd posturing. For my first three years inside, until I had just turned fourteen, I spent hour upon hour ignoring my peers and pitching all of my energy into my writing and my music. That way nobody ever had cause to hate me, to beat me, to side with or against me. I observed such things with the others; I heard the wheeze of a man as his ribcage caved in on his lungs, I saw the gargle and froth of blood as it came up from his throat and into the wide open mouth. I detested these maulings - they were a loathsome distraction from my scripts, my songs, my cartoons. I looked in on them disapprovingly.

Everything changed at the start of my fourth year inside. For about three months my only visitor had been my grandmother. The visits of my father and my sister had ceased without warning. It did not bother me especially, because we never had much to say to one another and I was always a little embarrassed to have him seeing me in prison. He always asked the most stupid of questions, but I knew exactly what he truly wished to find out. 'Have you seen the error of your ways yet?' was what he was trying to say. Or even 'Have you seen the light?' Every time he saw me he must have prayed that some sudden miraculous transformation had taken place, that I had spontaneously become a 'decent man'. That was the only reason for persisting with me. He had no idea how to handle me, or deal with all that I was going through. It was impossible for him to relate my crime to anything that he had seen in the supermarket, or out fishing on the canal. He did not understand.

Yet it still seemed odd that he had not turned up. I did not dare ask grandmother where he was, in case the question was relayed to my father in the form of 'why haven't you been to see Jim? He's been missing you'. In the end, she told me herself.

My father had, it transpired, been into hospital for an operation to remove a cancerous growth from his neck. The procedure had failed and now he had only a couple of months left to live. Although he was still well enough to leave the house he had not felt the need to and seemed quite content to pass his final weeks back at home on the sofa with his television and teacups. When I was told of this I immediately expressed an urge to see him once more - in fact I surprised myself by how determined I was to look him in the eyes for one last time.

So Father came to prison - on his own this time - to see me for the very last time. It was a stark cold September afternoon with the sunlight burning mercilessly through the barred windows and full into my eyes. I sat scratching at the table until he came through and took up his seat without so much as a hobble. He pursed his lips, sighed - and the sadness ground into those world-weary eyes of his announced at once how appallingly dismayed he was.

"So son," he started, then stopped. He tried but failed to hold eye contact. I could see instantly that he wanted this, our final meeting, to also be our only ever profound discussion.

"Father," I replied, unsure at first whether to be unaccountably harmonious, but then reverting to my usual unwillingness, "this is a pleasant surprise."

"I want to talk to you," he replied uneasily, "...properly."

"Oh?"

"Yes, I want to talk to you - y'know - as a father should talk to a son. Like we've... in the way we've never been able to talk."

"Go on."

"It's... it's not easy for me, Jim. This is very hard... because..."

"Because it's the last time you're ever going to speak to me?"

"Well, yes..."

"And now you've decided it's time to start talking to me, after all these years?"

"Come on Jim," he squirmed, "don't make this hard. You asked for me to come here."

"Didn't you want to come?" Whereas Father fidgeted in his seat I was still, and my gaze pinned to his blinking eyes. For some reason I had decided to make this as hard for him as was possible. I wanted to make him feel like a coward.

"Of course!"

"So then, what do you have to say?"

"I want to speak to you, son..."

"There's no purpose," I hissed back, "in calling me son. You've never called me son before, so why start now?"

Suddenly Father looked straight into my eyes and stopped dead. Then, in that moment, he looked horrifically gaunt. I wanted to say sorry straight away, to tell him that I loved him, to somehow relay that I did not mean to push him away. Yet I could not - and he just sat there, looking pitiful and shocked.

"I never realised how much you hated me," he said finally.

Of course I did not hate him, but I could never say that. I wanted him to feel guilt for all of the neglect, for all of the banal breakfast discussions about Asians and supermarket dairy products.

"Do you hate me?" he asked directly.

I just looked back at the man; pathetic, ill, forlorn. I would not answer. He pursed his lips for one last time and then, quickly, rose to his feet and departed.

As soon as he was out of the room I understood the gravity of my rejection. I jumped up and ran for the door, but was stopped in my tracks. I babbled on to the warden about my father, his illness, what I had said, what I had not said. It did not matter, though. I would never see my father again and, worse, he would never know just how much I had wanted to say to him.

Ten days later, when he passed away, I was nothing more than the son who let him down. When I heard the news I imagined him lying there, gaunt, and thinking about me as the terminal surge of morphine gushed through his veins. Corrupt, evil, irredeemable.

Inevitably, when the lights flared up and the picture show folded into stuttering snow-screen it was Flaxby who came first into the room. He repeated monotonously what I had already seen; that I had been a cold, unaffected, soulless convict son. I tried to tell him that people could improve, that I made mistakes in my youth that I would never again repeat, that I was a totally different man to that represented on the mini cinema screen. I attempted to explain that my father himself was far from the model pater. Flaxby was not interested in any of this, and said that my excuses were the very reason for my being in Hell. I quickly became bored with the debate, finding myself increasingly able to ignore his banal diatribes. I asked Humbert to take me away from the Recollection Room and I was able to walk away without feeling the blight of Flaxby's pernicious rant.

Yet as I lay alone that night I found myself having to bear - for the first time ever - the weight of that prison visiting hour, and that heartless rejection of my own father. I spent the early hours alone with his ghost, longing to communicate my regret - but the chance was long gone. Father was dead. More dead even than I. Now I was suffocated by sadness, my withering spirits blasted and riddled with a blistering remorse. There were no tears that night, though, just silent grief. I sat looking into his lingering image perfectly aware for once that this was no dream. This was real.

The following morning, at the same time, I compliantly took my seat in the Recollection Room and, with a grim resignation, waited for my next dose of poison.

Chapter 19

Bob

Shortly after the death of my father a friend of his, Bob, came to see me. I had no idea that he had possessed any friends; I always thought that the supermarket and the fishing rod were his only mates yet, it seemed, there was indeed somebody who cared.

For some reason the Visiting Room was near-empty that afternoon. I sat at the back, on a table by myself and cut off from everybody else. Bob strode purposefully up to my table. I was astounded that he had recognised me so effortlessly, because I certainly had no recollection of him.

He was a short man, but he walked tall and with conviction. His head was held high and from the first moment he saw me I was fixed with an iron grey gaze. Bob sat himself down but with his spine pressed tight against the back of his chair, bolt upright. Instantly I could tell that he had been an army man in his younger years; before grey hair and arthritis had gripped him. Bob was the type of man who believed in good posture, in a stiff upper lip and in a short-back-'n'-sides. I decided that he was probably one of my father's pub domino or darts partners.

We exchanged a few awkward pleasantries before Bob turned to his chosen topic; my father.

"Your old man was a very decent fellow," he told me, as if I had never met my own father. In a sense, though, he was telling me something new, because all I could remember of Graham John Barrett was monotonous table talk and violent outbursts.

"You could have learned a lot from him," Bob continued. As he spoke, I could think only of my mother's head being thrown into cabinets and walls. I recalled the blood, the screams, the torture, the hatred. I wanted to stop remembering - to forget absolutely everything.

"Yes, a right champion, your dad. As good as gold he was.

I only hope, Jim, that one day you can become as good a man as he was."

There was something appallingly comical about Bob and what he had to say. He made me feel terribly unimportant; he made me want to forget everything I had ever seen, but he did not make me love my father and he certainly did not make me regretful.

Chapter 20

Jack Chambers

They told me that I could keep my initials, but nothing else. My grandmother and sister Lucy could remain in contact with me only through infrequent, clandestine reunions. I chose my new name from a list of fifty suggestions, lumping for the faintly familiar Jack Chambers. I liked the idea of being a Jack.

I was nearly seventeen and hopelessly institutionalised when they chose to cast me out into the great beyond. Since my father's death I had dropped the guitar and turned instead to education for my release, picking up seven A grade GCSEs which, I was assured, could be hastily transferred to the new Jack Chambers' academic record.

It was on a drizzly February evening that they led me undercover to the 'Halfway House' in Cheshire. I quickly made the acquaintance of the other semi-inmates and, before very long, we were being dispatched together on every rehabilitation day-trip imaginable. They were usually banal expeditions to identical cheerless seaside towns or dreary landscapes that happened to have a hill with a path situated among them. I think the objective behind such missions was to fill the convicts with a sense of rapture and shared delectation that we had never previously felt. It did not work, though. Partly because so many of us had experienced that blissful sensation before - through our crimes - and partly because, put simply, the day-trips were abjectly wearisome.

It was on one such journey that seven of us became lost on a ramble through some vast, tumbling sprawl of barren moorland. When the sun fell we followed the distant jumble of orange streetlights which indicated a town nearby. We reached a cricket field on the outskirts and decided to phone our group leader as soon as we came to a telephone box. Six of the group went on into the town and I decided to wait in the field, in case we had never left the right route and our guides were still close behind us.

Being alone, silent, in the purple light of evening comes with peculiar sensations. It falls short of total darkness's bleak finality and throws a comfortable glow on the world around. It almost feels as if everything everywhere is at ease; taking a breather and looking back on a day's hard work. Everything seems redundant, purposeless in the darkness. The brown and green trees, the red and grey rooftops and all on the Earth fades, then... at last, the boundless sky above adjusts itself to night. Grey at first, then clear purple, deep blue and eventually black.

After about two hours one of the others came back to join me. That other recovering convict, my company for the evening, was a young half-Asian thief called Kemel. Or Kemi to his friends.

So that was it! Suddenly I rocked back in my Recollection Room chair and remembered Kemi's parting words to me - how he said that he had known me... "From before"... And how he had called me Jack! It made perfect sense now - I suddenly understood exactly what he had meant. How could I have forgotten all about it? I asked myself whether Kemi had held that memory of me through all of our later years of friendship without letting on. Maybe he had. Perhaps, on the other hand, it was only in that terminal moment, the last time that he would ever see me, looking deep into my expression - that he could invoke the memory.

Kemi, in those days, was at his brilliant and mischievous pinnacle. He always had cigarettes and often had alcohol on his person - in many respects he was the best person I could have been left alone with. He was shockingly intelligent, cruelly witty and monstrously handsome. I knew him for only one day, but he was the kind of person who impacts easily on his peers; free and jovial enough for almost anyone to envy. As the night turned cold I was a pallid, unshapely, quivering child; lost and vulnerable in the chilly black air. Kemi, though, was delighted with his freedom and ripped off his t-shirt. Golden-skinned and broad-shouldered he jumped, leapt, bounded about with carefree ecstasy. In one moment he was playing football with a dog-chewed tennis ball, in the next he was recreating his own arrest to his one-man audience.

In those days Kemi had colour to his skin and a sparkle to his eyes. His dimples were deeper, his complexion browner than the vacant white countenance of twelve or thirteen years later. I envied his attractiveness and effortless joy. Normally, when seventeen years of age, it is common to look down on those a couple of years our junior, but Kemi was an exception in every way. In fact, it almost felt as if I was younger and less mature than this brilliant young creature of fifteen.

We talked to each other for most of the night. I became more comfortable with his presence and soon we were exchanging rude jokes and far-fetched boasts.

"Did you ever have a girlfriend?" he asked me, "before you were sent down, I mean."

I blushed secretly in the darkness.

"I have a girl," he went on proudly.

So we continued to talk; about everything from dirty magazines and drugs to rock music. We clambered up into a skip and lay back, side by side, on the container's sloping front wall, oblivious to the stench of gathered litter or the on-off spluttering rain. Being recovered and taken home was suddenly forgotten.

I decided that I liked Kemi that night. I liked him because he knew all sixteen main symptoms of manic depressive psychosis for no apparent reason. In fact, he had never even studied Psychology. He wanted to study Art but could not have cared less about the subject - he said that it was full of 'ponces, poofs and students with stupid hair'. He was more interested in women, drugs and rude jokes. And I liked him because he was clever. Every so often he would let slip a line that betrayed his immense underlying intelligence; perhaps something about Albert Camus or Egyptian burials or seratonin re-uptake, a casual comment that made clear his beclouded wisdom. Both his wit and his grasp of philosophy were sharper in those days as well - he had an effortless understanding of the universe; a simple, uncorrupted outlook on life. At times the conversation felt as if it was between two forty-year-old university lecturers, more often though it was truly the domain of libidinous teenagers. Occasionally, however, the discourse grew personal.

"Have you ever been home alone?" he asked me.

"Yes," I replied, "my dad used to go missing a lot."

"Missing?"

"Well, he..." I cut myself off and tried to avoid ruining the night by returning to Jim mode.

"What were you going to say?" asked Kemi, without being ostensibly fascinated in what I was about to say.

I remained quiet.

"Jack," he said with sudden earnestness, "what did you do?"

"What did I do?"

"To go to jail. Now you know I was a thief. That's me. I'm honest. But nobody knows what you did. None of the staff back at the house have ever referred to it. None of the others ever mention it..."

"I was a..." I wanted to lie, but I could not.

"What? Is it that bad?"

I stopped and sighed. "Yes," I confessed, "it is. I can't tell you, Kemi."

Kemi glanced up and around him; at the starry black sky, at the muddy green moonlit trees, at the grease and rubbish in the skip. "You can tell me," he insisted, softly. "I'm not going to grass..." and he spoke with such honesty that I could not possibly doubt his sincerity. So I told Kemi my story - from the death of my mother, through the murder, ending with the death of my father - and he listened silently, only interrupting me to crouch down and light a cigarette. Once I had finished I wholly expected him to respond; to psychoanalyse my story or to criticise me. Instead he simply stood up, put a hand on my shoulder and said "I'm sorry." None of this appeared to make him any more wary of me; in fact he made a somewhat distasteful joke out of the whole business and dismissed my crime as 'the kind of thing we do when we're too young to understand that what we're doing is wrong'.

"We all do things when we're ten that we wouldn't do at thirty, or even fourteen for that matter," he said. "If ten-year-olds knew the difference between right and wrong then there'd be no need for parents, would there? You've grown up and now you see the error of your ways. End of story."

I had wanted to tell him that I had known that what I (or Jim) was doing was wrong, but that I was too accustomed to hatred and violence to understand quite how wrong. For some reason, though, I decided not to continue the discussion. I did not want him to think that I was still, in any sense, a danger to society.

Nobody had ever spoken to *me* about me before - not as a friend, not without lecturing or chastising me. Kemi recovered quickly from the 'shock' of my revelation and we went for a slow walk in the rain. Then later, after it had stopped, we lit a bonfire and talked about football and school.

That night was the kind of night that I should have remembered forever as a distant, precious timepost of my youth and yet as the years progressed it slipped from my memory. It ceased to be important or relevant to me. As I watched Kemi and myself struggling to make each other out through the thick rain, or squinting into the bonfire's billowing white smoke, I felt a gaping sensation of loss open up within me.

I also realised, while slumping back into the seat and sighing sadly at those images of an extinct era, that my discussion with Kemi that night was to be the last - and first - time in my life that I would discuss my crime with anybody.

The next set of images were from later that year, when Jack was finally released into society. Several newspapers had reported that Jim Barrett was about to be 'unleashed' with a new identity. They made it sound as if I was Saint John the Prophet's Antichrist; anonymous, irredeemably vile, a mythical and amorphous monster who could be lurking anywhere at anytime. I was acutely aware that Jack was going to have to be very careful if he wished to avoid making headlines again.

Kemi, as the only person to know the truth, was also the

least of my concerns. Nearly nine months had passed at the 'Halfway House' since my revelation to him and he had been released about ten weeks before me, just in time for his sixteenth birthday. He had already had plenty of chances to sell his story, but appeared to have little interest in making money out of me. In fact I received a letter from him at the end of October telling me that he was already desperately bored with school and on the verge of permanent exclusion.

It was decided that I should be released a month before Christmas, so that I could enjoy the festive season with my new 'family'. Apparently the 'changeover' was relatively straightforward with me, because both of my parents were dead and my only contacts were my grandmother and sister. For Gran's part, she had been desperate to be my new 'guardian' and seemed keen to begin a new life herself, but the social services deemed her unsuitable for the role. I was, according to those in charge of my rehabilitation, an 'extremely delicate case'.

Consequently, it was decided that I should be taken into foster care and cared for by a series of people with no clue as to my original identity. I would be allowed to keep in touch with my grandmother only through hand-delivered letters and maximum security biannual meetings.

The first month was turbulent. I had begun studying for my A-Levels while in the 'Halfway House' but the transition from a small college in Cheshire to a large, bustling 11-18 school in Manchester was a difficult one. Within a week I had chosen to abandon courses in Politics, History and Music in favour of starting A-Levels afresh the following year.

Then I began the first of many pointless part-time jobs. I got a job in a city centre pub as a glass collector but was hastily dismissed for dropping too many glasses. Then I took to the till of a local supermarket, but found that my mind was too easily distracted by fantastic imaginary schemes and cutting observations on the customers. I would scribble down my thoughts and feelings onto the back of abandoned receipts, planning to piece them all together one day into a multi-million selling novel. Unfortunately, all of this meant that I was hopeless at keying the correct codes and scanning the correct items; while my mind buzzed with ideas the scanner would often skip bar-codes or even charge customers three or four times for the same item. My co-workers, the heroes and heroines of the shopping aisle, were infuriated by my lack of professionalism. I was sacked a day before the Christmas party, after charging the manager three times over the correct amount for a muesli bar.

In addition to this, life was not going very well at my new 'home'. My guardians were an overweight couple called Toni and Steve. Both of them smoked fifty cigarettes a day, liked gin and sported wispy moustaches. They wore matching beige jumpers, each with fag burns and thick yellow or flaky white food stains. Their breath was charged with the foul odour of coffee, their ever-bare feet with the stench of cheese. They had three children of their own, to which I was never introduced, and a crippled cocker spaniel by the name of Jeremy. All of the food was fried, all of the drinks alcoholic. I initially attempted to treat the family with gratitude and graciousness, but they did not approve and discarded me as 'dodgy' and 'suspicious'. All they knew about me was that I was an orphan who had been in a Young Offenders' Institution. Despite the fact that their eldest also had a criminal record, they must have taken this information as positive proof that I was a rotten, dishonest little crook. They tolerated me though; served my dinner, changed my bedclothes, offered me cigarettes and plied me with alcohol. They probably thought that they were being hospitable, but my perception could not have been more different.

All of which left me outcast and depressed; hopeless and wretched for the festive season. Then, on Christmas Eve, I decided that it was finally time to exploit my foster parents' loose grip on discipline.

I never told them where I was going, but simply exited without acknowledgment through the front door, next to which Toni and Steve were preoccupied with a petty row.

I went to a pub where I met a couple of acquaintances who had briefly been in the same Music class as me. They suggested that we went together to one of Manchester's more seedy clubs, but within several minutes of reaching the bar we had lost each other.

On that night it occurred to me that most dance music is twice as offensive as cancer and not nearly as engaging. Clearly the revelers felt the need to blot out the noise by drinking vast quantities of alcohol, screaming in one another's ears and exchanging punches to the face. I felt resentful; angry at society for treating so many young people in this way. They had placed us in a dark room fitted with a deep, repetitive thumping noise. Sold us legal depressants. Filled our mouths with smoke, our noses with the stench of a thousand mindless people all packed in and knocking one another from side to side. I was in a black hole with bright red lights dotting the dance floor like hypoestes or like fresh blood on black leather, mingling on and off with the broken glass and the shuddering, stinking clubbers. I hated the place and decided, at once, that it was almost exactly how I had imagined Hell to be.

Yet something exciting did come from that repulsive club. I met a young girl whose name I could not make out amid the relentless background noise. This was quite a novel experience for me; I was hopelessly inept with the opposite sex. Whenever I met a girl worth sleeping with I was always too scared to talk to her, and whenever I met a girl who was not worth sleeping with, I did not even *want* to talk to her. After a few clumsy passionate clinches we decided to make a hasty exit. I was still sober enough to know that she was truly beautiful; far too gorgeous for a misfit like me.

I knew that we were probably going to have sex and so I paid a tactical visit to the condom machine in the toilets. I waited in there for five minutes, pretending to wash my hands and hoping that everybody would disappear so that I could make my purchase in peace. That never happened, though, and I had to leave empty-handed.

We darted off arm in arm to a local park and jumped the padlocked gates. The paths, the swings, the slides and the grass were all ours.

I had no idea what to do in this situation and, besides, I did not have all of the necessary material to go 'all the way'. We sat side by side on the grass, staring into the cold bleak Manchester night ahead of us. I was nervous, uneasy, shriveled. Then, suddenly, she turned towards me and pulled a small, flat red package from her bag. So she had come prepared! Before even beginning to feel my relief there was a soft hand on the inside of my thigh - and my pulse quickened. For several seconds I felt embarrassingly inexpert, but the girl made everything as easy as possible. Gradually the unbuttoning, the nakedness, the contact ceased being awkward and started to become fun. She rolled onto me, under me, pushed me up above her. I felt the warmth of her flesh on mine, all over and all under mine. Then, with fingers firm on my behind, she pulled me down and tightly onto her. Throughout it all I followed her body's undulating rhythm and tried not to cause her any pain; tried to move in unison. Then, at the end, when it was all over, I looked up into the sky and then across at the naked trees, shaking in the freezing wind. Down here, though, we were warm. Even as chilly raindrops started to fall; even as my unclad back rolled over onto the frost-solid earth and my heart was only warmed by the icy ground.

We dressed quickly and then walked for a while in the rain. I felt as if this girl was the most precious thing to have ever entered my life and, perhaps as a consequence, I told her everything about me. She seemed fairly unstartled by the news of my crime; probably too drunk to make much sense of it. Besides, I only alluded to it in passing She listened politely to all of my stories, despite occasionally throwing a perturbed glance back in my direction. It was definitely stupid of me to tell her so much, but she did not really appear to be assimilating much of the information.

Finally we leapt back over the park gates and, after an exchange of numbers, went our separate ways.

As I returned home I could hardly contain my ecstasy.

I breathed out my body's warmth, shared it with the vast chilly universe and through the darkness blundered, stumbling on slabs and on kerbs that I assumed to be a little less steep than they really were. I smoked my last two cigarettes, ate my last three mints. The December mist was now so thick that streetlamps were like hazy suns in a featureless white sky and Christmas fairy-lights were like masses of shimmering, iridescent barbed wire tangled about invisible trees. People walking ahead were just dull inky splodges smeared unsteadily onto a murky, once-white canvas. They were distorted, distant and cut watery shapes into the dim night-light. At times, as they walked towards me, the people looked like ogres, goblins or vampires in the hazy darkness. Perhaps, I thought, they really were. Perhaps the land - invisible in the blackness - had turned to dust or buried itself for the night until it needed to be seen again in the morning. The truth, of course, is far less spectacular; everybody is as real in the blind night as they are in the stark yellow sunlight.

I cut through alleyways and over greens on my way home. As I reached the city outskirts some of the parkland was boggy and uneven. The fertile soil of the open land dipped into a viscous sludge as I stumbled into pits, trenches, puddles and nettled ditches. It had started to drizzle; drops of rain danced on streetlamp-lit puddles and looked like a clutter of gnat wings dipping in and out of glaring Tuscany sunshine. It did not matter to me how wet my feet or trouser-legs were. I was content.

A whole week passed before anything happened. I heard not a word from the girl; in fact the only phone calls I received were from bizarre mystery callers who hung up as soon as I answered.

The news came quite unexpectedly on New Year's Morning, in the form of a headline presented to me by an indignant Steve. It was my face on the front page; my old name on the headline and my new name in the photograph caption. My 'lover' had, it seemed, remembered every detail of our Christmas Eve conversation and recounted it perfectly for the tabloid press.

"I would kick you out," snorted Steve, "but I decided it'd be better to call the Police." He sounded proud of himself, as if he had in some way done society a favour.

"Why?"

"Because you're a bloody murderer," he snarled in response, with a wheezy rattle in the back of his throat. "I'd give you a good hiding if I was allowed."

I leapt up out of bed, grabbed my shirt, stepped into a pair of jeans and barged past Steve. I did not even have enough time to feel let down by anyone. Toni tried to block my route to the front door and Steve attempted to pull me back with a meek bear hug, but they were both easily knocked aside. I sprinted through the door and down the road, completely deaf to Steve's shrieking voice behind me.

I am not entirely sure of what Steve expected the police to do. I was a former young offender who had served my time; there was no genuine reason for them to come and arrest me. However, I did not consider any of this until long after nightfall. I just wanted to run; to escape from Steve and Toni and Jim and Jack and Cambridge and Manchester.

I never consciously chose to live on the streets. It simply transpired that I had nowhere to sleep after leaving Steve and Toni's. Then, the night after that, I again had nowhere to stay.

I shivered on brick walls and cowered in bus shelters. The wind-chill was bitter and the concrete icy underfoot. I chanced upon a half-empty fizzy drink can and feasted on an abandoned packet of crisps. There was more food and more company on the busy streets, but I preferred the tender serenity of the quieter lanes and alleyways. I could wander there without the fear of disapproving glances or cheap taunts. It must have been past midnight when I was joined by another wandering vagabond. We spoke very little initially and never exchanged first names, even after the conversation had warmed. We preferred merely to walk together for a time.

He was a pallid, raggedy fellow with yellow eyes, yellow teeth and although he spoke clearly I could smell the thick coating of whiskey on his tattered clothes. He told me that he had been homeless for a year; that he had left his wife because of mutual hatred and then lost his job because of drunkenness. He said that it was easy to find yourself on the streets and that he was not altogether dissatisfied with his lot. He explained how he now had the freedom to indulge his alcoholism; while the home comforts of squats and shop doorways were luxuriant in comparison to his erstwhile marital home.

179

We were joined later in the evening by another anonymous scrawny drifter. This man, on reflection, was somewhat like Baz - if only because of his unchained lust for substance abuse. He was one of those irritating characters who devotes their existence to the promotion of cannabis. Not content with merely enjoying the drug, he also felt the need to wear dope t-shirts, write dope songs, buy dope posters and give lengthy pro-dope acclamations to anyone polite enough to listen.

He sat himself next to us while we were propped up against a low and wobbly red-brick wall. He was well-acquainted with my companion; who in turn treated this newcomer with the same aloofness that had initially confronted me.

We were both invited round to his squat which, I was promised, was only two or three minutes walk away. "There's a few coming round," he assured me, "you can kip. We got bags." My companion shook his head immediately, but I was strongly tempted by the allure of the indoors.

"Are you sure? I don't even know you."

"That's alright. None of the others know me either. Come on, come round - it's pretty neat inside actually. Not what you'd expect."

I responded by saying that I was not bothered whether it was tidy or not. I told him that I was too tired to resist and wanted to lie down without scanning for excrement first.

The squatter smiled uncertainly. "Well," he said, "It'll save you walking round here all night."

So with that I bade farewell to my alcoholic companion and followed the squatter home.

The squat was dark; lit only by the dim red light of a solitary flickering bulb. The floorboards were bare and broken; decorated only by the occasional damp, dirty rug. As I watched from the Recollection Room I began to see everything once again through the eyes of a desolate teenager on the run from home. I was no longer poised on the bony chair looking into the room's giant screen; I was actually back in the squat slouching limply into the settee.

The ceilings were dripping and the walls a shade of

nicotine, except for the white patches where posters had been tacked onto them. The only picture was an old black and white painting. It was of a tall thin white light glowing over a pitch black backdrop - and it was indescribably eerie. A vacant, ghostly face was glaring through the thickest concentration of light and staring out emptily into the room beyond. There was no anger or despair or happiness in its expression; there was only emptiness and depletion. That picture was evidently the property of some previous owner and yet it indisputably belonged to the squat. It reflected everything that happened within the four walls of the front room - and that wild gaze fixed itself on anybody who entered. I wondered how such an image could ever have made anybody happy. Perhaps, I mused, it was the work of somebody else who had been rendered soulless and impotent by this building.

There were times that I just needed to escape from the picture's malevolent gaze. If I could break away from the broken settee's uneasy grip then I would leave for the bathroom, which was cold but also carpeted and therefore a softer bed than anywhere else.

The front room was thick with the scent of vanilla or aniseed joss-sticks; planted in an empty fireplace to hide the stench of mould gathered upon cluttered plates or damp excrement on the insides of junkies' jeans. The tabletop was clothed in cigarette papers, packed ashtrays, bong water and teacups. Everything and anything went here; whiskey, gin, lager, cider, cannabis, crack, methadone, MDMA pethidine, heroin, mescaline, acid or ecstasy. People came in; they drank tea, they smoked weed, they drank beer, they bought drugs, they sold drugs, they stayed, they left. It was an octopus ride of depravation.

I started smoking heroin because I wished to substitute being low and exhausted for being numb and exhausted. Then I started taking amphetamines because I was tired and bored with only taking heroin.

Heavy depressants made me blissfully sedate. I adored the sensation of lightly confounding abandon which came with being stoned on cannabis; so the next step had to be complete and utter oblivion. Not that cannabis was any sort of 'gateway' drug - quite the opposite in fact. From the moment I entered the squat I knew, unequivocally, that I would end up smoking heroin. I was desperate to escape myself and whether that came through suicide or heavy opiates, cannabis was always irrelevant. Of course that was not always the case. I saw other teenagers turn up at the squat to score pot and leave with a bag of brown powder. They would sit down, smoke too much and end up 'chasing the dragon' with the other lay-abouts. Then they became easy; nothing more than pawns in the trade.

More often than not I was glad simply to sink and sink and sink and sink into the bony threadbare settee or lie idle on the grubby floor. Heroin made me forget about my hunger and my hopelessness. I no longer loved or needed anything. I just lay back and bathed in my newfound insensibility where I occasionally grappled with confused thoughts or baffled emotions. Yet as soon as I made sense of a situation I began to lose it in the same moment; I could no longer deduce but rather found myself guessing without knowing. It became easier to sit back, to merely focus on the haze and watch that rotten old house falling down around me. I had stripped away all of my filthy complexity and now nothing more than the naked homosapien remained.

It was difficult to be clear about anything. Nobody seemed to live there - not even I could ever have called it home - but instead the place was occupied by a carousel of deadbeats; junkies, dealers and a brand of whore that was very different to the Whiplash Women I would come across in later life. Too many dead expressions and lost, floundering minds. During that time I became far too familiar with the black oblivion-eyes of helpless young drug users.

I am not sure where all of the time went; which moments were days and which were minutes. Who the people were. When I ate. Who I lived with. When I was awake. When I slept. Where I slept... For certain I was not always in the squat.

Of course I was not always lost. There were plenty of moments when I was alert, sober and ill. They were the most horrible times; having to confront reality once again. I could feel myself peering down at the bottomless precipice beneath my toe-tips. I kept looking in mirrors and I could see myself changing, slowly, for the worse. I was helpless and Godless, out on my own. It could have been any drug puppet that first introduced me to narcotics. Initially I was just one of their acquiescent subjects; experimenting without protest, yet I was soon comfortably submerged in this new way of life. During that time on the streets and in the squat I lost my fear of the great wild world. I suddenly had no problem with spending the night alone on doorsteps or draped over park benches in bad parts of the city. I became attuned to this new reality.

None of it lasted for very long. In fact I was only on heroin for a few weeks. When I ran out of the money to buy drugs I simply chose to stop using them. It was straightforward and even though I was surrounded by the hopelessly addicted I never felt the physical or psychological compulsion to continue abusing myself. In fact, in the week after I stopped using heroin I was seized only by the sudden, ravenous hunger for sexual intercourse. Apparently it usually takes a lot longer for the libido to return after heroin dependency, so I can only assume that my habit was so minor that I had never truly been addicted. In my opinion, the trick to my immediate recovery was a lack of respect for those around me; the horde of shifty, stinking, black-armed delinquents. It was easy for me to prise myself away from their odious company. This was certainly the exception rather than the rule. I saw too many people vanish into that place and fail to reappear because they were shackled by their friends; other junkies, other lay-abouts. I was lucky to find my way out so easy.

While recovering I turned back to the streets and stayed in either doorways or homeless shelters. After about two weeks I decided to return to the squat to check on my old acquaintances. I was shocked to find that I did not recognise a single person there and not one of them had a clue who I was. A couple of teenage lads were sprawled over the broken settee and they stared up at me under the rim of a baseball cap through half-shut, half-black eyes. There was an ugly woman darting about the room with a cigarette in her hand, picking up rubbish and re-lighting candles. It occurred to me that I could well have lived with these people for all of my time in the squat, but still would not have recognised them. I am not sure precisely what I had expected to find on my return to the squat but nothing remained for me whatsoever.

As soon as I had recovered I was quick to distance myself from what had happened and, as a consequence, never truly understood its significance. I never learned from what I had done.

It was a condition of my release from the institution that I remained in weekly, secret contact with my appointed rehabilitation officer. When Steve reported my departure to the social services and I failed to contact them I was suddenly in breach of my parole conditions and a warrant was issued for my arrest. I finally surrendered myself in early March, a couple of months after I had first hit the streets.

At the time most people were shocked by my ragged, rawboned appearance. My face was thickly bristled with soil-brown whiskers, my hair long and straggly. My fingers were nicotine orange and the rest of my skin tanned with dust and dirt. My two front teeth were framed by a dark green lining while the whites of my eyes were a network of raging red veins.

They never uncovered the true extent of my degradation, although I know they presumed some degree of illicit substance abuse. I decided that it was a story best buried along with Jack Chambers; a name which was quickly exterminated by those in charge of my rehabilitation. I had quite enjoyed being Jack - in many ways he had represented me for the most exciting period of my youth - so I was sad to leave him behind. Yet it was indisputably vital for Jack to die. If he was allowed to live, then I would be tracked down by the hysterical press and destroyed by the bloodthirsty pawns who followed them.

It was explained to me once more that I must never again breathe a word of my hideous past for as long as I lived. I was told, in no uncertain terms, that if I were to be discovered this time then there would be no new start.

The screen turned blank and Flaxby bellowed into my ear -
"That'll be all for today thank you!" - as if he was doing me a
favour by subjecting me to all of this.

"Can I go now, Flaxby?"

"Sit down. Humbert'll be here in a minute."

"Can't you take me back to my cell?"

Flaxby glared back at me incredulously, "I'm not your
bloody slave, you vile little urchin!" he yelled.

"I never said you were," I replied impatiently, "you
shouldn't get so defensive."

"Don't you dare speak to me like that!"

"Why not, Flaxby?"

"Mister Flaxby or Sir."

"What does it matter? I'm in Hell, locked up in a room,
being bombarded with images of my own downfall. Could it get
any worse? And you're not going to kill me, are you? Because
I'm already dead, you see!"

Flaxby, his face redder than ever, lurched forward and
struck me across the chin. After a moment's consideration I
thought better of hitting him back. "Finished now?" he snarled.

"I'm sorry, Flaxby."

"What for? Are you sorry for insulting me or are you sorry
for being a child murderer? Didn't it occur to you, while you
were watching yourself cavorting with that young tart in the
park or out of your mind in a grubby little squat, that perhaps
you have a lot to be sorry about?"

"Lots of kids take drugs. And nearly everyone has a one
night stand at some point."

"Haven't you ever read the Bible, Carlton?"

"Yes, in parts."

"Didn't think so," raged Flaxby, completely ignoring my
reply, "if you had then you might understand why, exactly, you
should feel sorry. Good Christian values. That's what bastards
like you need."

I chose not to respond to this.

"I've watched you while you're in here looking into that
screen. Now, you get very upset about it all and you cry and you
whinge and you blub like a little baby girl because you made

such a mess of your life, but you never actually feel sorry for what you've done. And that is why you're in Hell."

"How do you know that I don't feel sorry?"

"I've told you - I watch you while you're in here. I know sorrow when I see it. Maybe you feel a bit of sadness that your life was such a damn waste, but I don't believe you feel any remorse at all."

"So what is the purpose of me being in this room then? I still don't understand. Is it going to change me for the better?"

"No," blasted an exasperated Flaxby, "this isn't counselling or rehab or one of those modern bloody prison programmes where they pack a bunch of rapists off on holiday to make them feel better. This is Hell. This is your punishment - the punishment that we have chosen specifically for you. You are meant to be disgusted and miserable and it isn't supposed to get any better. You were a nasty little kid who didn't cry when his mum died and didn't give your dad the chance to say goodbye either. Then you were given a second chance and you blew it because you told your life story to a little slut who you bonked in the park. Then, after all that, you became a drug addict and then... well, there's more to come. And I'm sure you'll watch it and bleat about how terrible it all is, how your upbringing was to blame, how the world shafted you... but you won't for one moment feel any sorrow. And that's because you are a subhuman scumbag. Simple as that."

I gave this a moment's thought. "So if you're such an authority on right and wrong, how did you end up in Hell, Mr. Flaxby?"

His red face suddenly paled and his eyes quickly narrowed. His loud, pacy breaths fell silent and his pursed lips dropped open.

There was a pause.

"I've already told you my story," he answered finally, in a quiet and reflective tone. "But I've got myself a good little job here and I intend to do it to the best of my ability."

"You know," I said, sensing that I had a chance here to further challenge Flaxby, "I was killed because of a fascist regime which took over England. They encouraged the Press to hunt people like me down and eventually they murdered me. They encouraged mob rule and they were completely intolerant of anybody who stepped out of line. They didn't believe that people can change for the better, they didn't believe that people should be given a second chance. Their two main policies were war abroad and war at home. They exploited mass hysteria to keep control and they victimised the vulnerable in society. I remember hearing some of the bullshit rhetoric that they flashed about on the news but I still could never figure out what type of person would actually be ignorant enough to vote for them in the first place. But now, seeing you, I know exactly what type of person voted for them."

"Let's remember," returned Flaxby, with a self-satisfied smirk, "that you, Mr. Carlton, didn't vote against them either."

I reflected on the day's proceedings all through the night. It became clear to me that whoever I was - be it Joey the runaway, Jim the criminal or even Jack the junkie - I had always been an outsider. Yet when I lost Jack I had a terrible sense of leaving something beautiful behind; of missing an opportunity to genuinely make something of my life.

If the drugs had been an attempt to escape from reality then the death of Jack Chambers finally allowed me to abandon my past forever.

Chapter 21

Becoming Joey

During the night that followed I kept waking and then falling back into the same dream. Each time I felt drunk - immensely intoxicated - unsteady, giddy and afraid. The ground below was an expanse of shuddering brown water and above - set against a clear yellow universe - spun a perfect white globe. In each dream the sphere started off as being suspended ten metres above the ocean beneath. Then it would slowly, unsteadily, lower itself into the indistinct depths below. As, each time, it dipped into the beclouded sea so did I, and each time I watched its perfect white form become a freckled brown, then a filthy black. The water felt like cigarette smoke in my eyes and the dark globe hung closer, then closer again; swelling and quaking silently beneath the waterline. Each time I waited for its expanding form to explode before my reddened eyes. But it never did.

In some way I perceived this tumorous sphere's plight to be symbolic of my own shadowy planet's demise. There I was; eye to eye with the apocalypse, facing the end with a drunken swagger. I sensed the pending cataclysm - and yet it never occurred... at least not in this nightmare.

Back once more to the Recollection Room.

When I became Joey Carlton my first intention was to get through to university. I spent a year settling in with my new family and undertaking menial occupations before finally restarting my A-Levels. I was twenty before I made it to the university where Joey Carlton met Kemi for the first time. By that time I had formed a new disguise with long hair, sideburns and tinted glasses. I had already long forgotten that night in the container. Kemi was only at the university for a short time before disappearing and, of course, being convicted. Yet we formed a close friendship in those days and never lost contact.

University was one of the many places in my life that I have detested. At the time I abhorred the flat in which I lived with its rat-riddled back-room and inexplicable slug infestation. I despised the late nights of poker played around takeaway pizza, white powder lines and a million empty beer cans. I hated the computer game marathons in dark rooms which turned light as morning sun spilled out its tentative first rays. And yet looking back at it all, through the Recollection Room screen and the unwavering veil of cannabis smoke on the other side, I was unexpectedly charged with a bolt of nostalgia.

I had severed all links with my grandmother and Lucy as soon as I re-entered the world as Joey. I decided that I could no longer take any risks. The first I heard of them was through an urgent message which found its way to my campus address.

It was a brown-papered envelope from my social services contact which indicated, with minimal detail, the sudden deterioration in my grandmother's health.

> Dear Mr. Carlton,
> It has been brought to our attention by your sister that your grandmother has suffered a stroke. Your sister has requested that you visit her in hospital and wished us to emphasise the seriousness of your grandmother's condition. After making the appropriate consultations we have decided that this will be possible and, should you wish to visit your grandmother, this can be arranged by contacting me on 07970366846. Please do not attempt to arrange a visit yourself.

The letter itself had no impact on me. I was detached from my family both physically and emotionally - and yet I did make that phone call, if only out of a tormenting sense of duty. I called the social services and consented to the visit which took place just a couple of days later, shortly after my twentieth birthday, at four o'clock on a grey late-January afternoon. My grandmother, unbeknown to me, had been forced to leave Cambridge altogether because of the attention I had drawn to the family. She had moved to Truro, but the Press had caught wind of her illness so she had been taken against her will to a hospital in Plymouth.

I was driven to the hospital by a social worker who informed me, after an hour or so of building herself up to it, that my grandmother was not long for this world. She had suffered not just one stroke but five huge ones, all brought on by a lifetime of serial cigarette smoking.

I was greeted first of all by my sister Lucy, by now a beautiful fresh-faced teenager. I expected her to be the same demanding and exasperatingly fussy little animal that she had been at the age of three, but instead I found an attractive bright-eyed young adult. She neither hugged me nor smiled; but merely glared sadly into the depths of my eyes. She did not need to say anything because that stare carried more anguish and fury than words ever could. It told me at once that Jim Barrett had ruined her life when he should have been there for his orphaned little sister. She had been bullied in playgroups and infant school because of what he had done. She had dealt with the death of her father alone because of what he had done. She had nursed her dying grandmother with little assistance because of him and - worst of all - she had been raised without a brother because of his disgusting crime. All of my confidence fell away in an instant. I felt hollow.

My grandmother's life was coming to an ignoble end. She deserved better than liquid food and a colostomy bag. My grandmother could easily have died when her apoplectic body had first collapsed on the living room rug of her bungalow but, I was told, she seemed completely unwilling to pass away. Whenever her breathing became shallow she would suddenly shuffle about in bed and attempt to sit up. Occasionally her morphine-muddled mind would conjure up strange fascinations - she would ask for knitting patterns and needles, or eggs and cake mix - then she would lean forward in her bed, as if she was ready to go to work. At other times she would have moments of clarity, but according to the duty nurse they were becoming more and more infrequent.

From the moment I saw the distinctive wrinkles on my grandmother's face I was Jim Barrett once again. She looked up at me and offered a polite smile, but her eyes were baffled. She recognised the face and yet did not seem to understand where it had come from or why it was there.

"Hello?" she croaked, her blue eyes widening.

"It's..." It's Jim is what I wanted to say, but I could not bring myself to utter the words.

"Nan - it's Jim," interrupted Lucy from somewhere behind me. I could see the old lady trying to comprehend this new arrival; to put the face and the name together. "Jim?"

"Do you remember Jim, Nana?"

"Jim?"

"It's your grandson, Nana! Look - it's Jim!" Lucy pushed me closer to my grandmother, delicately picking up her hand and placing it in mine. I felt tragically awkward. "Hello Nan," I replied.

She smiled back.

There is nothing as terrible as realising that you can no longer relate to someone you love, knowing that whatever it was that once bound you together is gone and not coming back. I had the same sensation years later when I realised that my best friend, Kemi, was no longer the person that he once had been - but this was more terminal.

It is quite heart-rending to look at someone and realise that the person who once meant so much has departed for good.

However there was one short spell, during my hour-long visit, when my grandmother started to make perfect sense.

"Have you forgiven your father yet?" she asked with sudden clarity.

"My father?"

"Yes. You heard me. Have you forgiven him?"

I could not reply. There was a difficult silence.

"You weren't there when he died, Jim," she announced flatly. "Do you know how much that would have meant to him? I remember when he went to see you. He didn't hold out for much longer after that. He went out to seek your forgiveness, to

191

let you know that he loved you... and he got turned away. That killed off whatever fight he had left in him."

I decided that it would be inappropriate to defend myself. I was conscious of Lucy's presence just a few feet to my right.

"I was there," continued my grandmother. "He was 'with it' right to the end. Everybody said he was unconscious - they thought he didn't know who we were anymore - but he was conscious. When I placed my hand in his I felt his grip tighten... just a little, but I could feel it. Lucy and me stayed with him until the end, didn't we Lucy? He'd lie silent for hours on end. I remember I stroked his hair... but he didn't like that. 'I don't like that' he said to me, so I said 'okay' and I just sat back and I whispered to him. And you know just before he left us, when his breaths stopped rattling and got lighter, I kissed him on the head, like I used to when he was a babby. And when I kissed him he buried his head into the pillow and he smiled, just like a little kid who's off to sleep. Then he was gone. It was as if he'd just been sent off to bed by his mum and then... that was it."

And that was it. The next words to come out of my grandmother's mouth were a request for some wool and a cardigan pattern. A couple of minutes later the call came for me to leave.

"Say bye to Jim," insisted Lucy.

"Oh! Bye Jim!" responded my grandmother in bewildered compliance. After kissing the old lady and bidding my sister goodbye I felt an immediate urge to erase the whole encounter from my memory. I was looking for closure but it was going to be difficult. I would not be able to go to the funeral lest the Press were lurking outside so I opted instead for a visit to her old residence in suburban Cambridge. I had ascertained from what little Lucy said to me that Grandmother's old council bungalow had been left empty for nearly ten years. The young family who bought the property from my grandmother had sold up as soon as the media discovered that it had once belonged to my family. Since then it had remained derelict. Lucy told me that she had often contemplated a return to our old neighbourhood, but had not yet found the opportunity. She said that, to the best of her knowledge, a lot of Grandmother's old belongings still remained in the attic. Apparently a lot of the old estate had been demolished or redeveloped but the bungalow, she believed, was still standing. So two or three days later I caught the train to Cambridge then - needlessly disguised with bleached hair, sunglasses and a baseball cap - I began the journey from the train station, through the city centre and back towards my suburban home.

I looked down, as I walked, at the paving slabs below my feet - the same old slabs that Jim had once walked on. The same slabs over which he had once held a young boy's hand on one infamous walk to the suburbs. In the air above this concrete and clay Jim had lived his childhood; shaped his existence - but it meant nothing anymore. Not to me. Whatever had once happened here was now gone from this place. That great hunk of gas, rock and water that we call Earth had hurtled through millions of miles of space since those events. The place where Jim killed a young child was now nothing more than an empty expanse in the cosmos.

My old street had changed for the worse. The mysterious rolls of flat, unchartered, grassy wasteland were now stacked with identical, soulless red-bricked office blocks. Companies that meant nothing to anybody; computer-aided-designers that came and went without making the world any more or less interesting. Paintwork still flaked on the old council abodes but a great many of them had been demolished and replaced with flat blocks or town houses - all of which looked exactly the same as one another. In fact, the only eye-catching features of the whole neighbourhood were those few crumbling ex-council properties, eyesores made beautiful by blundering progress.

Then I came to my old house. I glanced quickly inside. I did not stop.

A little further up the road was my grandmother's bungalow. Her house still stood out thanks to its garish red windowsills and stark yellow door, but now it appeared that the whole row of properties had been deserted. The whole block was ready for demolition. Tentatively I walked up to the house and peered in through the windows. I was well aware that it was only ten years since I had left the area and, should any of the old neighbours be overlooking these nostalgic meanderings I was in severe danger. It had been risky enough walking through Cambridge city centre, let alone here. Too many people had seen my face before. I looked back at myself through one of my grandmother's windowpanes and my hurtling heartbeat slackened to its customary stroll. Here was a different man altogether. He bore virtually no resemblance to the vulnerable young thing who was dragged through the media's glare a decade ago.

Cautiously, I pushed the door to my grandmother's bungalow open. I half-expected a flicker of flashbacks to accompany me as I stepped inside, but there was nothing. The place was bare - and I was stripped of memories. After looking around the property for a couple of minutes I finally decided to go up into the roof, where Grandmother had left so many of her belongings.

The attic hatch opened easily and the place was predictably black; packed with stench of old rain in too many knitted jumpers. Everything was dark, cold and thick with a haze of new dust, pattering endlessly onto the sheets of old dust below. Shelves, shoe racks, chairs and tankards - all that was to show of her life was here in a thin, low and colourless attic. Often we register places by smell - and in that place it was the stench of shaved wood and pungent industrial solvents. It smelt like a carpenter's workshop. The air tasted like cardboard doused in red wine. I decided that it was wrong for me to be here and wrong for me to disturb these things. I left without delay - and that was the very last time I had cause to think of my family. Whenever it was that the letter finally came to confirm her passing it must have been lost among the clutters of junk mail.

I was sobbing shamelessly in the Recollection Room. I wept for what I had done - and it was me, not Jim or Jack or Joey but me. I had destroyed Lucy's life and then I had neglected her, just as I had neglected my grandmother - the only woman who had stood beside me through everything. I wept and I wept and I called for someone to spare me from this abhorrent picture show but there was no reply, nobody came. I was alone.

When I finished at university a couple of years later I moved into a flat in a nearby town. The rent proved a little steep and, finally, my old friend Kemi offered to help out. He had just returned to town and needed somewhere to stay We were both paying our way through a series of menial jobs; labouring, shelf-stacking, pizza delivery, canvassing and bar work. We promised each other that we would save up the money to travel the world, but we barely collected enough to get a Glastonbury ticket. Yet we both felt certain that we were not much longer for this little town. We would both move on and make our mark in the world.

There would be long spells of neither of us having a job. Kemi would occasionally complain about having nothing to do with his day, but I quite enjoyed the prostration.

Those days in the flat were very much an extension of my university life. Narcotics, booze and women (although, admittedly, the women tended to belong to Kemi).

I truly enjoyed living with Kemi. It was a friendship that meant so much to me - but never more than when we were young; with scrawny figures, cigarettes, label clothes and no transport. Strangely, something somewhere was forgotten with wisdom and maturity. With each mod con, with each healthy 'new leaf' life became less of a game and more of an arrangement. In the process we ceased to be people and we became citizens. At first there was still some Jim and Jack in me, but they both eventually died away. I began to follow the advice of my elders carefully. Drink a few, but not too many. Have a laugh occasionally, but not too often. Love a little, but not too much.

Finally I decided to apply for an English PGCE course back at the university, if only for the substantial bursary that accompanied it. I have to assume that there was a genuine oversight on my part when I denied - on two separate forms - having a criminal record and, similarly, I can only assume that there had been a colossal error on the part of the authorities when they failed to pick up on it. Of course, my mistake was probably more understandable- Joey Carlton had never hurt anybody, had he?

195

When I became a teacher I lost my urge to live. I found myself a job at the local 11-18 college and soon became downtrodden by the Kayleighs, Keelys, Kylies, Charlenes, Kierons and Kerrys. Pupils interested in little more than the inane gossip emanating from each others' big spotty mouths. With them my enthusiasm for English dwindled. They were not worthy of an energetic, exuberant teacher and, in turn, I ceased to be energetic and exuberant. I lost the love for my subject.

I watched my first ever morning of exam invigilation from the Recollection Room chair. The teachers stood in a line and directed the in-rushing youngsters to their seats like stewards on an airplane. The subject head's explanation of what and what not to fill in on the answer sheets was like the safety demonstration before a flight. The whirr of the boiler and the buzz of the drinks machines was vaguely reminiscent of an aircraft engine's piercing hum. Only the creaking gym floorboards were different. Here, patrolling through this surreal silence, I felt as if I was sneaking through the family home at midnight, into the kitchen for that secret shot of whiskey. As I tiptoed through the aisles I searched for minor things to keep my mind alive. First I tried to remedy the way my body swayed from side to side as I walked. I achieved this by walking with my feet less far apart, but then I had to eliminate the irritating rustle of trouser leg against trouser leg. My next occupation involved memorising as many pupils' names as possible. That way, by the time it came round to collecting papers I knew whose answer sheet was coming next without even reading the name. I made a point of standing over and breathing flu breath onto students I despised, knowing that I would almost certainly be putting them off. It occurred to me that the perfect silence and toil of those three or four hundred pupils could not have been replicated in any other arena. I started to wonder what would happen if, all at once, every pupil in the room decided to start talking to each other, lighting up cigarettes and flouting every other examination rule in the book. Would the staff, seeing their precious exam results fall to pieces, actually abandon the exam? I puzzled over this one for a minute, before becoming preoccupied by the array of colourful mascots and pencil sharpeners. I wondered briefly whether they were there for the benefit of the pupils, or the benefit of the bored invigilators. Occasionally the teachers on patrol would engage in a quiet, saunter-paced game of tag to pass the time, subtly jabbing one another as they strolled past "You're on" they would whisper. On other occasions I would stand near a pupil, keeping a safe distance, and attempt to mark their work as they wrote. It never got any more exciting than that.

People in my school - other teachers - took it upon themselves to crush and demoralise me. I never attained a truly penetrating insight into the cause for their hatred; the power issues and the insecurity. At first I hated them, but then I learned to live alongside them - and I absorbed their mediocrity. The searing conviction that had always toiled within me; the certainty that I was somehow vital and unique was depleted. I grew tired at school and grew increasingly blind to the inspiration and wonder which waltzed through the kids in my classroom everyday. As soon as I grew to hate the pupils I could no longer share their pulsating sense of open-minded wonderment. I stopped looking for the beauty and settled my eyes instead on the patchy ceiling paint, bent curtain rails and murky mock-marble floor tiles.

Eventually it became more important for me to be seen as competent by the old, dried-out Luddites who observed me occasionally, than to be perceived as vibrant and interesting by the adolescents in my class. The pupils became a byproduct of my job; a parasitic growth on the profession. Before long a good lesson enjoyed by all was less important than clear learning objectives and a comprehensive plenary.

The only misery that comes with age is that which tells a man he should have moved on in life when he had the chance. That cast-aside instinct that the time has come for a change. I promised myself that I would leave the school after two years and move abroad. I promised myself that I would leave teaching before I was thirty. I never did. So with each year that passed a greater sense of emptiness and loss would swarm upon me.

I met Agatha at the Red Lion on Quiz Evening. The pub had just been painted stark white and was unpleasant to breathe in. Harry, Kemi, Marc and Baz were all standing with me at the bar while Agatha – who Harry knew from school – was sitting between the cigarette machine and the payphone. She joined our quiz team, although she may as well not have bothered, and perversely amused me with her obliteratingly bland outlook on life. Within about fifteen minutes of sharing a table with her I was considering the comical merits of punching her; privately imagining her expression of utter perplexion. Of course, it never happened and within a week I was taking her out to dinner.

After a month with Agatha whatever it was that had once made me so special had scarpered. That was when I truly became Joey Carlton. I moved out of the flat and, within a year, I was getting a mortgage with my dreary new doll. Only once did she ask about my family and I promised her that she could meet my sister. As soon as I consented to this I began to regret what I had said, but thankfully Agatha lost interest in the idea after a few days and instead occupied her mind with a grudge match against a neighbour who was using her parking space.

By the time I was twenty-five, the memories meant nothing anymore. My life consisted of English lessons and pub quizzes, and I had no interest in anything that had gone before. The chaotic beauty of adolescence had cleared up. Faces from the past were just hollow patterns in my mind; they meant less to me than the colour of the sugar paper tacked to my classroom wall. The photographs all went as well; none of that seemed to matter when I had a job, a car, a mortgage and a pension. This was the new and better man. Jim and Jack were dead. Long live Joey.

I altered my personality to suit the figure of respectability that I had envisaged. I started drinking tea (which I despised) and watching rugby (which I also despised) because they fitted in with my idealized, sanitized Joey Carlton. I stopped smoking cigarettes, partly because I lived in the teaching catchment area and did not wish to set a bad example to my students. I wanted to be somebody who my students could look up to. Before long, however, I came to care so little about what they thought that I started smoking all over again.

My life had become a melee of shackles. Rising at six, school at eight, dinner at twelve, home at three, coursework folders, marking, lesson plans and revision classes. Dull sex, a loveless love-life, tea at five, soaps at seven, bed at twelve... and all in the same old rotten town. When we find ourselves a career and a motor and a mortgage and a wife all we achieve is the destruction of youth's precious randomness. That is the big 'WELCOME' sign on the doormat to the rest of your days. People spend every moment - till the end of their lives - in the same dependable surroundings. In the same square kilometre with the same square people. And for what purpose? It saves them having to cope with volatile change. It avoids unpredictability and the hazards of unchartered territory. People strive for continuity. Men become their fathers and marry women who look like their mothers to avoid breaking the cycle. Then the abused become the abusers; bound to the pattern.

We practically lived in the Red Lion pub, but life in that place was never especially exciting. Agatha would come out and flirt with Baz or Marc or Harry or Kemi. Then she would subtly insult me and, most probably, spit in my drink when nobody was looking. There was no mistaking the hatred between us, just as there was no mistaking the fear and the cowardice which kept us together. I went to the pub, though, because I could not stand a second alone with her. I was interested in nothing that she had to say, nothing that she wanted to do. I found her ugly and repulsive.

One of my most obvious problems was that I could never drink just one pint. I would try to match every two vodkas downed by Kemi with at least one pint of ale. After the thousand odd calories that came with a bitter binge I would inevitably talk myself into a portion of Singapore chow-mein noodles at the local takeaway and then, most mornings, I would wake up to the cruel sensation that my stomach had actually eaten itself. I felt permanently ill for years on end; chained to a pointless but unshakeable habit.

As time passed by I began to relive my youth vicariously through my pupils. I became obsessed with students like Aaron who were intelligent and young and enjoyed life and brought that youthful vigour with them into the classroom. They reminded me of how Kemi and I had once been. At other times I wanted to be like the thick, ordinary bottom set pupils; longing for their simplicity and the bland thrill of smoking behind bike sheds or stealing chocolate bars. I was perfectly conscious that most of my pupils enjoyed fuller sex lives than I did with Agatha - and I think that quite a few of them were of the same opinion.

Through all of this I had to watch my own friends grow older. My list of single friends grew thinner by the year and even Kemi was becoming oppressed by the banalities of an insular pub local's existence. He grew older. At some stages in the process he would be bloated and round, at others emaciated and gaunt. On nights out I would sometimes watch his greasy potato face wrinkle up into vile sleaziness, his expressions packed with cheap seductive clichés. At times like that I would wonder what had happened to the effervescent youth that I had once known; how he had managed to become so enmeshed in this mundane existence.

It came to all of us, though. I grew bored with life and, instead of learning from the lessons of my past, I opted to erase them from memory as soon as I could. With each new year I became a little less aware of Jim or Jack. I never had cause to either mention or contemplate them. Not until now, here in the Recollection Room, did I realize just how much I could have gained from them.

I tended to blame the school, or Agatha, or the town, or my friends for the numbness of my existence, preferring to overlook the inanity that lay within. I had become dull; as uninteresting as I was uninterested. Once upon a campus I had debated Benthamism and Marxism, but now I did not even bother to vote. I disregarded the revival of fascism in Britain and ignored the election of a right wing government which, ultimately, would destroy me.

In the midst of this wretchedness I was temporarily uplifted by the trip to Europe with Kemi and Harry. I felt at one with the hot, dusty and intricate charms of Florence or the sedate and cheery effortlessness of Zante. Then, later, I was again reinvigorated by that hallucinogenic evening with Kemi and Baz, but even then the sense of redemption was short-lived.

I sat in the Recollection Room and watched the man from

the government standing above Joey with his .38 revolver. I waited for it to unload; to see the back of my head upsurging in a flurry of deep red blood and splintering shards of skill... but the screen simply turned black.

It was then, in the moments before Flaxby returned to the room, that I began to understand that the real tragedy had not been Joey's persecution or death or even his crime. The real tragedy had been his disregard for the past and his refusal to face the present. When he abandoned his past he had also left his family, his memories and much of his character behind. The poignant lessons that could have made him – me – a better person had all been abandoned. The saddest thing on show in the Recollection Room was not the battered murder victim or the dying father or the dead mother or the heroin abuse... it was the fact that I forgotten them all and grown into a colourless, insular creature.

Once again I cried uncontrollably; but by now I was not weeping for Jim Barrett or Jack Chambers or Joey Charlton. I was not regretting what they had done. I was regretting what I had done – what had happened to me. I understood what I had done wrong and I wanted, desperately, to change it.

Eventually Flaxby came into the room. "Okay, okay," he snarled, "let's have less of it, Carlton. There's nothing worse than the sight of a grown man blubbing away like a little bloody baby. Dry your eyes out. Mr. Anchors is coming to see you."

"So?"

"So Mr. Anchors is coming to see you. And that means you show a little respect. Sit up straight and dry your bleeding eyes. Do as you're told."

There was something unusually restrained in Flaxby's tone of voice. His idiosyncratic blind aggression was replaced by a softer, slower vitriol. It was also more effective and I sat up without questioning him any further.

"May I ask why Mr. Anchors is coming to see me."

"You may well ask, but it doesn't mean you'll get a bloody answer."

"Okay."

"He's been watching you, Carlton. He's concerned about how you're shaping up. Thinks you're showing – what was it? - irregular remorse levels. I've told him, of course, that in my opinion you're just a horrid, self-piteous little scumbag, but it appears he's not so sure as me."

"I see. So what does this mean?"

At that precise moment Humbert came through the door, followed closely by the dapper figure of Mr. Anchors, smiling down at me through a pair of full-mooned spectacles.

"Carlton, isn't it?" he started, in his distinctive Queen's English.

"Yes sir," I responded. "Or Barrett. Or Chambers."

"That's right, that's right," he mumbled, stroking the dimple in his bearded chin and fumbling through a handful of papers he had plucked from an inside pocket. Flaxby stood, arms folded indignantly, in the corner of the room. "We've got a problem with you, Mr. Carlton. I want to have a few words with you about what you've just seen. Now, I assume you're aware that what you've just seen is a punishment, yes?"

"Yes I'm aware of that."

"And not a form of rehabilitation?"

"No."

"You're not actually meant to be learning from it. You're meant to be suffering from it. Do you see what I mean?"

"Yes, I think I do."

"Now," he continued, pacing around a little, "you're a man of reasonable intelligence. Maths teacher, isn't it?"

"English."

"Ah yes, of course, English, very boring. Never mind though. You are a man of reasonable intelligence, and you can probably see where I'm going with this line of questioning."

"I'm worried that you're suggesting that I've not been punished properly and that I need to undergo some other form of purgatory."

"Oh no, Mr. Carlton, not at all. I think both Flaxby and myself agree that you've been sufficiently punished by what you've seen. Don't we Mr. Flaxby?"

"Yes Mr. Anchors," nodded Flaxby humbly.

"Yes I think we do, and I think we've come to a point where we have to ask whether you're going to be of any great use to us. In Hell."

"What?"

"Well, the reason that people come here is usually because they are not especially pleasant. I'm well aware that it sounds tacky but it's also true. That's not to say they are all absolutely rotten to the core, it just means that they are not really nice pieces of work. Now, everybody makes mistakes – but the people who come here are generally those that don't feel a huge amount of sorrow for what they've done. It'd be no good having people here who are going to spend eternity wallowing in remorse. Do you understand?"

"What are you going to do with me? Kick me out?"

"Well that's a possibility, yes. You see, I have no doubt that you've done some terrible things and that you'd have plenty in common with a lot of the other residents, but the fact is that you do appear to show a great deal more sorrow for what you've done than we'd normally expect. Now, I'm perfectly used to seeing people burst into tears or express regret for the fact that they've messed up their lives, but my problem with you is that you appear to have learned quite a lot from sitting in the Recollection Room. You seem to be genuinely upset by what you have done. Do you agree with me?"

"Well... yes I do," I replied, uncertainly.

"Now, I'm only going to ask you one question and then I'm going to either recommend an occupation for you here in Hell or recommend a transfer. And I'd like to point out that the transfer quite often turns out to be the worst of the options. Okay?"

"Okay."

"Right, here we go then. What, Mr. Carlton, would you say was the greatest mistake you made in your life?"

"The greatest mistake," I responded without hesitation, "was forgetting what I'd done rather than learning from it."

Chapter 22

Heaven

Based on that response alone Mr. Anchors made the decision to send me for an interview in Heaven. His cheerfulness in discharging me contrasted with the reluctance of Flaxby, who was clearly keen to inflict more abuse on me. "Your kind don't fool me," he whispered as I left the Recollection Room.

For about twenty minutes I followed Humbert through a network of corridors and into an immensely tall and empty hallway, which looked as if it had once been some kind of canteen. He pointed to a door in the far right corner underneath a green 'exit' sign which looked as if it had once been bulb-lit. "Over there," he mumbled with a wag of his finger.

I wanted to say a fond farewell to Humbert but he was gone before I had the chance and I was certainly not going to run after him. I walked to the other end of the hall and found myself in a reception area.

"Can I help you sir?" queried a polite young lady who was busy grappling with a rubix cube behind her polished oak desk.

"Yes… I think… err…"

"Is it the transfer?" she asked with a raise of the eyebrows and a rummage through the papers on her desktop, "Mr. Carlton?"

"Yes, that's right."

"You can go straight through, Mr. Carlton. There aren't any more appointments today."

The interview seemed to go well. The interviewer remarked, somewhat dryly, that he considered me to be 'mostly harmless, if a little dreary and defeatist'. He asked me about Kemi who, it transpired, was also a resident. I nearly asked him whether Gwyn was also here in Heaven, but it seemed like a stupid question seeing as I still did not know whether or not she was even dead.

In the end my interviewer recommended an eighteen month induction programme made up of three days per week at work in Heaven and another four days roaming around paranormally back down on Earth. It all seemed both surreal and pointless at the same time.

"I'm not entirely convinced that you're quite ready to live here full time," remarked my interviewer. "So I think we're going to have to see how things go. I think you'll benefit from a few days a week back on the planet. It'll break you in gently."

I was told that I would have to work hard and behave myself if I was to secure a permanent residency in the place they called Heaven. The news of my provisional transfer from Hell to Paradise was a peculiarly anticlimatic experience, but I was nonetheless enthralled by the prospect of meeting up with family and friends – providing, of course, that there were more social opportunities here than there had been in the other place.

Heaven, like Hell, was predominantly a rabbit warren of identical corridors. It was a combination of meeting points, dining halls, dorms and offices, with the occasional convenience store thrown into the mix. At times Heaven seemed to be comically English and at other times it appeared to be paradoxically secular. It took me two days to find a church which, on discovery, was shut.

It took about a week for Kemi to find me, and another week passed before my father, mother and grandmother surfaced. I was assigned to a small hosiery just a few doors down from the carpet-makers where Kemi was working, so we met up on a couple of occasions.

I felt far more comfortable, however, on those days when I was allowed to return to Earth. It felt like no more than twelve minutes since I had been standing in that field with the gun poised against my face. Earth – and England – still felt a great deal more real than anywhere in Heaven or in Hell.

Chapter 23

All About Redemption

In life I never felt at home here but now, in death, I feel at one with the planet. I have been through Heaven and Hell and now I understand what makes this place so important. I wonder how many others, here in the cemetery, went through the same when they left these skins behind. Some of them died a hundred years before I was even born – and now, for the first time, I am close to them. As dead as they are.

I no longer feel uncomfortable aside death. And while I would never consider this to be a place of peace for those whose remains rot here in the earth I, at least, can feel a sense of repose. Death is everywhere. It is in your houses; in the spot where you sleep at night someone could once have screamed or whimpered their last. In the space between your sofa and your television a coffin may have lain open. Down the staircase a body might have been broken, or from the light fittings, hooks and beams a lost soul could once have swung.

During my days on earth I wander through the places that once were homes to me; Cambridge, Manchester and my own town with its school and its industrial estate and its park and its Red Lion pub. Sometimes I sit in the pub at night, adjusting my eyes to the darkness and attempting to absorb some of the features that had once made the place so significant to me. The barstools, the pool table, the dartboard and the jukebox. This is the place that Joey took himself to avoid becoming a success, to avoid trying to hit the big time... and he never did leave the town or move abroad or find a better life. No matter how sure he was that he was better than everybody else, in the end it counted for nothing. He had achieved nothing. My life, under whichever nametag, had seemed at the time to be largely wretched and hopeless. Of course Jack experienced a fleeting happiness in his days at the halfway house while Joey was briefly uplifted by university and his summer in Europe – and of course that hallucinogenic evening with Kemi and Baz, but life had otherwise been far less comfortable an experience than death is turning out to be.

On other occasions I sit in the packed bar and listen to the voluble and vulgar pub chatter. I hear that the government is planning to introduce a new identification system; a barcode implanted in each person's left palm. Apparently this would mean that people no longer need to pay for goods with cash, instead their accounts could instantly be accessed by the details at hand. Passports would, it seems, be cast into the past by this new instrument of indisputable authenticity. Underage drinking would become a thing of the past which, in the case of the Red Lion, would probably not make a huge impact on their intake.

Of course, I move further afield than the Red Lion these days. I am no longer chained to mile long triangle which links the school with the pub and the flat. I have passed through a thousand wildernesses in death; sheltered from a thousand storms and sprawled under a thousand blistering suns. I have wandered under amethyst and copper skies; forever alone; forever silent. And this is exactly how I had always longed for it to be.

Some days I go back to the places where Jack had once been young. I amble through the alleyways and red-bricked side streets adjacent to the 11-18 school where I went to the sixth form college in Manchester. I am not sure, but I think that they have re-paved the streets and taken away the bench by the chicken wire fence. We used to stumble along those pavements; our vision blurred at times by beer, at others by moonless dark. I wonder, sometimes, what it would be like if I was still alive and living there, back at Steve's, fighting free from 'be home by twelve' and having to pretend that I kipped at a friend's. The echoes never go away. I went back to the college for the dawn on my birthday. Winter had arrived and the landscape was paled by frost. That world has not changed at all and the kids still play there throughout the day and the night. Even then, set against the silent morning, there was a duffle-coated mother and two chattering infants. A little later the adolescents arrive. I often watch them and then I remember Jack through their bikes, burgers, bottles, skateboards and smokes… even their clothes look the same as his. And the girls. They never seem to change either.

I want to know these people. I feel like they are reliving my youth and that I know where they are going. I want to change it for them. I know that one day their teenage yelps will become tarred foghorn barks. I know that one day their slim, pallid figures will be pumped so full of fast food that they will struggle to pass through the factory doors. I know that one day they will grow their sideburns and grow their beards, and scar their faces with hair instead of acne. These gatherings, these snapshots of time are precious.

When I go there I can still see Jack and his 'friends' in the streets. The world never changes, although its shell is bruised, battered and warped. In my eyes, the kids are no different and although their bodies are different the soul has remained the same. Their births, their lives and – in many cases – their deaths are predefined by the equally narrow-minded youths that strutted these streets for generations before them, occasionally getting a little over-friendly in the park over the road. And that is how each generation is spawned. And that is how each generation dies.

In many ways things turned out differently for me. My life did not really follow the pattern and yet here and now I find that, finally, I feel quite ordinary. In fact, I feel just like everybody else – I am not a special case and I am not above anybody.

Being Joey was all about trying to become normal. Getting the nine to five job, the dull girlfriend, the social routines, the television fixation and the numbing insularity that comes with settling down. Here in the cemetery, it seems as if Joey won.

So for a few days every week I come here and walk among the memorials and the morbid onlookers. I feel as if I know all of the people who lie beneath my feet. Sometimes I have to stop myself looking forward to more people I know coming here. I want to see Baz again and I want to find out what happened to Gwyn and her Whiplash Women. I miss Gwyn. I assure myself that so long as there are people alive with the same spirit and resolve as her, there is still hope for this land.

I find myself indulging in a great deal of self-analysis when I am here in the cemetery, or in the deserted school where I once taught, or back at the college in Manchester, or in the house surveying the mess that Baz left when he could no longer afford the rates. At times like these I understand, at last, that Jim was not a good man. Jack was not a good man and neither was Joey. I am not a good man. I killed a child. I killed a child and I know that what I did was wrong. But it was equally wrong for the Press to destroy a ten-year-old's life for a mistake that he would never make again, just as it was wrong, later, for the government and their mobs to execute a thirty-something who had finally come to uneasy terms with his crime.

I have come to the conclusion that I spent all of my life attempting to redeem myself from that brutal crime. It did not matter that I had erased the murder from my memory, I would still have to atone for what I had done. Eventually there came a point, perhaps when I was in Zante with Harry, Kemi (and Robert) – or perhaps when I was on the run with Gwyn – when I decided that I did not wish to persist with the hollow tedium that had swarmed over my life. I atoned for my sins by turning Joey into an insipid, dreary and harmless character. By the end of my life, I did not want that anymore… and yet, I did not know how I could escape from it.

The dark globe is rising now from the waters – and whitening as it's lifted into a bluer sky. No more nightmares now. You can call me Jim, Jack or Joey - I do not care anymore. I have been released, at last, from the throttling shackles that I set for myself. I spent my entire life destroying what God had given me and now, finally, everything is in reverse. Now I am building, building, building.

Here and in Heaven, at last, I am free.